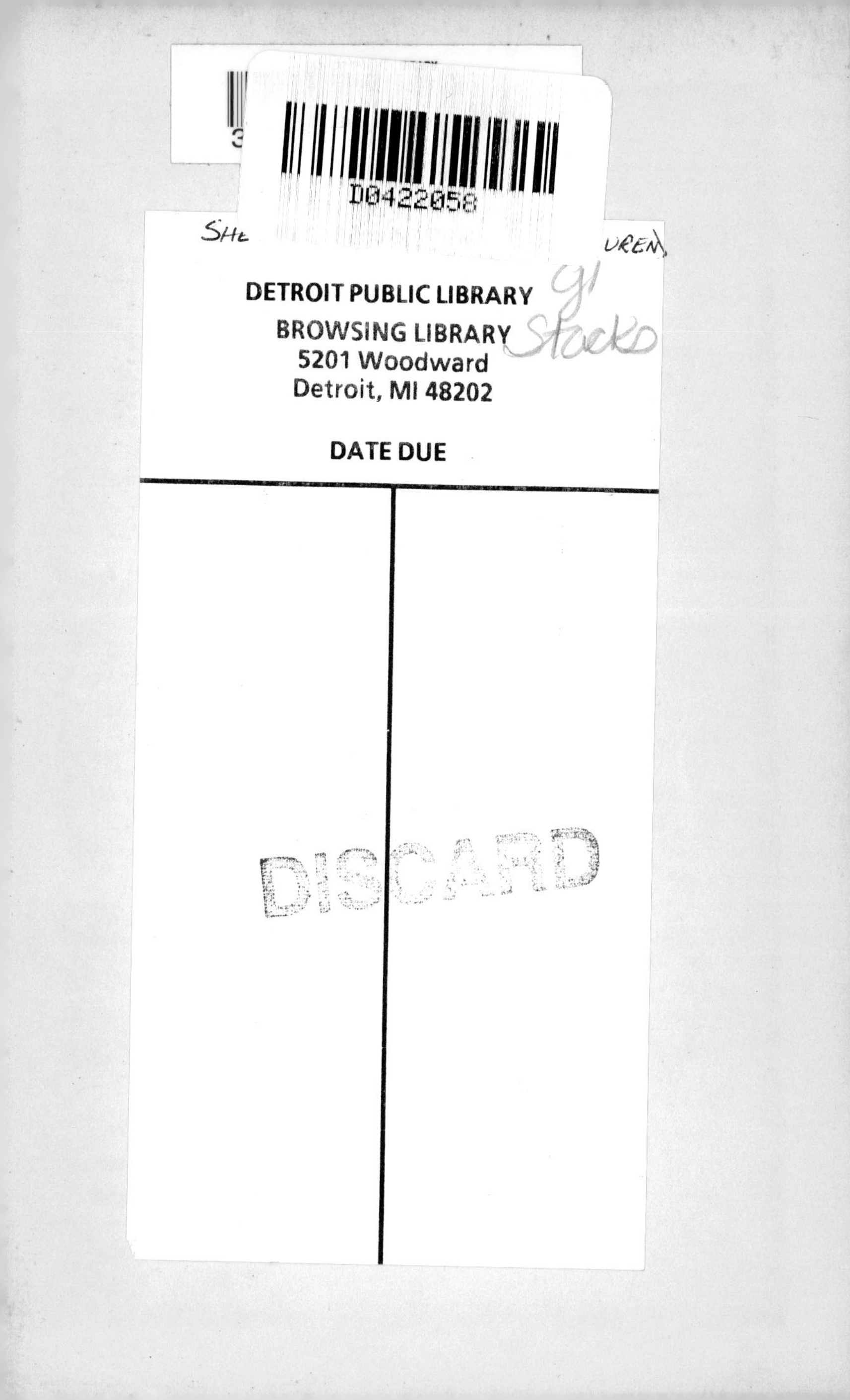

MOTHER IN MODERN STORY

MOTHER IN MODERN STORY

Edited by

MAUD VAN BUREN

and

KATHARINE ISABEL BEMIS

EDITORS OF "CHRISTMAS IN STORYLAND,"
& "CHRISTMAS IN MODERN STORY"

D. APPLETON-CENTURY COMPANY
INCORPORATED
NEW YORK LONDON

PRINTED IN U. S. A.

To the memory of our mothers

ROSINA BUHLMAN VAN BUREN

and

SOPHIA BEAUMONT BEMIS

FOREWORD

"Mother in Modern Story" is offered in response to the ever-increasing demand for a collection of "mother stories" for use in the home, the school, and the library. The stories included are realistic because *mothers* are the most *real* beings in the world.

About the word "Mother" cluster the tenderest sentiments of the human heart, and it is a happy privilege for sons and daughters upon a special occasion—a day set apart from all other days of the year—to pay honor and tribute to the love, solicitude, sacrifice, and faithfulness of these mothers.

"God could not be everywhere,
So he created mothers."

MAUD VAN BUREN
KATHARINE I. BEMIS

NOTE OF APPRECIATION

The editors desire to express their deep appreciation of the courtesy and kindness extended by both authors and publishers for permissions to include copyright stories in this anthology.

CONTENTS

PAGE

MOTHER AND THE GIRLS 3
Alice Booth

THE MOTHER OF GENNESARET 22
Agnes Sligh Turnbull

MRS. RIPLEY'S TRIP 46
Hamlin Garland

MOTHER MARTIN'S WING 66
Christine Whiting Parmenter

MOTHER GETS BACK ON THE JOB 85
Bess Streeter Aldrich

THE MOTHER 106
Ruth Sawyer

THE LITTLE GOLD KEY 121
Edith Barnard Delano

MOTHER'S BUSINESS 134
Juliet Wilbor Tompkins

A COOKY-JAR MOTHER 161
Florence Hartman Townsend

SO NOT TO BE ALONE 175
Carolyn Hosmer Rhone

THE LITTLE MOTHER 193
Ethel M. Colson

PAGE

THE MOTHER 213
Robert Haven Schauffler

MOTHER HARVEY'S STRATEGY 222
Olive Higgins Prouty

THE RASPBERRY DRESS 247
Ada Jack Carver

THE MOTHER IN PARADISE 270
Eugene Field

THE REVOLT OF "MOTHER" 275
Mary E. Wilkins Freeman

THE RETURN 303
Dorothy E. Norman-Smith

THE MISSION OF JANE 324
Edith Wharton

THE MOTHER 356
Alphonse Daudet

MOTHER

MOTHER AND THE GIRLS *

Alice Booth

It wasn't at all what the girls had expected. Somehow they had thought Mother would be—well, more of an object of charity, as it were. They had talked of it in that way. They had planned it in that way.

When they first took the little apartment at the beginning of fall term, they had no intention of using the second bedroom for Mother. One bedroom was for Helen and one for Isabel, and Mother would do very well back in Centerville—where she had always done well. Mother—well, Mother did not really come into the lives of Helen and Isabel at all as a person. She was just Mother, a frail, flying little woman whose sweet and tender smile never quite erased the nervous little wrinkle between her soft blue eyes.

There were always a few pins stuck into Mother's shirtwaist somewhere, and a basting thread floating down her back or dragging from

* Reprinted by special permission of the author and of "Good Housekeeping."

her skirt. And she never ate a meal completely through, in peace. Always there would be a ring at the door-bell, and Mother would jump up:

"That's Mrs. Hawley, I know, and her waist has to have the fastenings on yet!—Goodness, what shall I do? Well, she'll just have to wait until I sew them on.—The rice pudding's in the oven, chickies. Get it yourselves and be sure to get to school on time!"

And there would be just time for a hasty kiss for both of them, and a hug, and a "Mother's precious darlings!" before the bell would jingle in a long and determined wail, and Mother would hurry down the hall, sorting a needle and thread out of the pins in her waist as she went.

There never was time for anything at home. The girls were either going to school, or coming home from school, or studying at the library in the evening, and Mother was always covering the cycle of fall suits, winter woolens, spring serges, and summer ginghams and organdies. She was never quite caught up,—no system, the girls decided even as early as high school,—but somehow she managed to cook three attractive meals a day, and keep at least the parlor dusted, and dress the girls as daintily and as smartly as their natural figures and physiognomies allowed.

It hadn't been exactly easy to dress the girls. Even as children they were a little too angular, a little too long-faced and solemn-eyed, for the flippancies of childhood. And later it was evident that they were the type that runs to stiff collars, and flat heels, and straight-back coiffures from foreheads that had better been carefully draped with skilled marcelling.

The girls were not at all like Mother. Mother's blue eyes had a gleam in them that meant mischief. And her smile—why, even the iceman never forgot Mother's ice; that is what her smile could do. She must have been a lovely girl, but that time—to the girls—was far beyond imagination. They never even gave it a thought.

Mother had always done her best by the girls. She had done it with a smile and a kiss and a leaping of the heart that made joy pulse in her veins. But the girls—it looked as if they were going to grow up doing their duty by Mother.

You couldn't say they were not conscientious. After Freshman year they earned practically their whole way through college, and told Mother to keep for herself the money which she was proudly sending them. They were away all the summers, tutoring, and only took time for a brief visit home, during which they always took Mother to some good, improving lecture instead of a movie.

Sometimes Mother wondered just how she had ever got through her own three years and a half of college—the very same college the girls were attending, by the way. She felt so ignorant, and the girls seemed to know so much. Why, college, to Mother, meant a date every single evening, buggy-rides in the moonlight, flirtations in the library, and never a step taken on the campus without a man.

The girls were different. Books and studies were their life. And if they talked at all with men, it was certain to be something in the line of etymology, or subconscious stimuli, or the pre-Elizabethan drama. Books were all they knew, poor things, and that is why they had to send for Mother.

The little apartment hadn't gone just the way they expected. They rented it with a great deal of enthusiasm and a half-spoken desire of gathering about them a select little group of heavy thinkers who would come and discourse on deep subjects every Friday night. All the graduate students and unmarried professors were taking apartments, and altogether it seemed a delightful plan.

Only a few objections intervened. Meals would not cook themselves; dishes remained persistently dirty unless washed; dusting and bed-making also joined the conspiracy of inertia. The girls were distracted. For the first time their calm, uninterrupted course of study was broken by a round of harrying details.

Finally, one evening, Helen broke the tragic

silence that covered the whole subject of the apartment and all that in it abode.

"I wonder—if we could possibly—have Mother come and keep house for us!"

"Why—why—" stammered Isabel.

And then, when they had talked things over, "Why not?"

Of course she would have to stop that terrible dressmaking. And when that was done, there would be no more threaded needles and pins sticking in her shirtwaists. It might all be arranged. A tactful letter,—the girls prided themselves on their tact, working it out by logic,—an answer all bubbles of enthusiasm and appreciation and delight from Mother—and the thing was done! Renting the old house at home proved simple. It was so old and cheap that you could always rent it. And the girls went to meet Mother at the train.

Somehow it had never occurred to the girls how Mother might look. They had so seldom seen her out of doors. When she stepped off the train in her blue suit and her tiny blue hat, her hair waved and a vivid pink flush of excitement on her cheeks, the girls were stunned. Right down to her trim little patent leathers she was perfect. She looked like—like almost any wealthy and well-groomed woman; certainly not like the dressmaker she had been for twenty years.

The girls convoyed her out of the station like two solemn young sons, relieved that there was so little to correct, and yet faintly alarmed. They crossed the campus rather proudly—since Mother had no bastings about her anywhere—and the very first person they met was the High Serene Head of the English Department, of whom they both stood terribly in awe. He was striding along, hat in hand, his silver shock of hair gleaming in the sunlight. The girls spoke, deferentially; he bowed courteously but inattentively—and then—then—Mother stepped forward a pace, her face radiant.

"Why, Willie!" she said. "Willie! Aren't you going to speak to me after twenty-five years?"

And Doctor Randolph turned a deep, poignant mahogany and held out both his hands. "Mollie!" he said—and joined the party quite as if he belonged to it.

Isabel carried Mother's valise; Helen carried Mother's umbrella. Doctor Randolph strolled behind with Mother, and they talked and laughed disgracefully. The girls were bewildered, but they knew well enough that this behavior was unbecoming in people in their forties, and they mutually, without saying a word, decided to let them both know it by a decided coldness.

But they had no chance. Dr. Randolph invited them all to supper at the hotel, and Mother

—Mother accepted for them. The girls would have declined, but it was perfectly evident that Mother would go anyway, so they went along to chaperon her. And it went right on from there. Mother was a social success. Not a professor left from the old days when Mother had been the prettiest and most popular girl in college failed to come around and pay his respects. If he had a wife, she came, too, and they invited Mother and the girls to dinner. The college had a life the girls had never known, and it did not make it any more enjoyable for them to know that it had taken Mother to show it to them.

Yet Mother was tactful, too—without using logic. She never had company on the girls' study nights. Sunday evening suppers were her field. And for the girls' Friday evenings she made her most delicious chocolate and her crispest cookies, and served them at ten o'clock with determined hospitality, in spite of the girls' protests. There is no denying that the Friday evenings picked up in their attendance after the chocolate and cakes became an established custom. And the girls, unfortunately, couldn't help minding that, either. Also the debates were sadly broken up by guests who surreptitiously sneaked out to the kitchen to help Mother stir the chocolate and beg an advance cooky as pay. Some of them even stayed to help her wash the dishes afterward, and the classic beauty of the girls' intellectual—and slightly starved—evenings was gone forever.

The climax of Mother's misbehavior came in February. The spring term was just beginning, and Mother went about the dinner with a smile and a twinkle and a flush that told the girls before a word was spoken that she had been up to something. She was too flurried to eat. She sat looking at them—at their seriousness—and at herself in the mirror, and her twinkle threatened to spread all over her.

"Girls," she said at last, "what do you think I've done?"

The girls exchanged glances of doubt and fear.

"I guess you'd better tell us," said Isabel.

Mother took a long breath. "I've signed up," she said proudly.

"Signed up!" Helen's face went blank.

"I've registered for the spring term," said Mother. "I'm going to take English IV and XVII, and Psychology II," said Mother. "I guess you'll think I'm crazy at my age, but you know I quit just before my last term to marry your father, and I've never stopped regretting it."

The girls were speechless. They looked at each other again, seeking help and comfort.

"There's such a little to do here, in this little apartment," said Mother, "with my two little girls grown up, that I have more time than I know what to do with, and I thought—"

Something in the air stopped her. She looked uncomprehendingly from one to the other. What was going on behind those serious faces? Why didn't they speak? What were they thinking? She rose suddenly, leaning on the table.

"Why don't you say something?" she asked worriedly. "Have I done something very foolish?"

"Why, I hope not," said Helen, striving for tact and a broad comprehension. "But do you really think you can carry the work? That senior class in English is pretty stiff. *I* took it last year, and I had to give it everything I had."

"I'd hate for you to try it and fail," chimed in Isabel. "It would rather reflect on us, in a way. And then, too, it would make you rather—well, just a trifle ridiculous, wouldn't it?"

"It would certainly be undignified," qualified Helen.

A light flame rose in Mother's cheeks. Her eyes were very blue. "I'll try not to disgrace you," she said with lips that trembled, and she left the room without even carrying out the dishes.

The girls sat over their unfinished supper. Occasionally they looked at each other furtively, but neither put into words the thought that was in their hearts.

And as for Mother—Mother put on her hat and coat and walked straight out into the dark trees of the campus. At the turn she met a dark form progressing mildly toward her door, a bulky form that blocked her path.

"Here, what's the matter?" said Dr. Randolph in injured tones. "Isn't this Thursday night and haven't I got a date to have you make candy for me?"

"Go away!" said Mother snappily.

She continued on her way. Dr. Randolph turned and kept easy pace with her.

"Here, here," he said. "Where are you going?"

"Away from here," said Mother, tight-lipped still. Then she turned. "Willie, I've signed up for a full course next term. Do you think I'm an old fool?"

"Signed up," said Dr. Randolph. And he gave a shout of laughter. "You little devil! After all these years! Do you remember how we cheated on Freshman Algebra together?"

"Willie," said Mother in a voice that was blurred with tears, "have I been a fool? Tell me the truth. Do you think I can do it?"

"What are you taking?" said Willie, practical at once.

"The two regular senior courses under you, and Psychology II. I didn't dare try to get back my French or German after all these years. And

I used to write German, too. Do you remember?"

Dr. Randolph gave a sigh of exaggerated relief. "Well, you're sure of my two courses. I'll give you an A if you'll just come to class every day and sit where I can see you. But you'll have to work on the Psychology. Of course, Brander owes me money—but I don't want to use that as a threat unless I have to. Young woman, you'll have to let me coach you on that course three nights a week from now until June first. How about it?"

But Mother was not listening. Silently, without a sound, she was shaking all over with great sobs. Dr. Randolph saw her hands before her face, touched her arm, and felt her frail body quivering with her unshed tears. And in that moment his arms were about her, and her head was smoothed to his broad shoulder. Another moment, and he had led her to the class seat by the great maple, and Mother was having her cry on one of his big white handkerchiefs, spread clumsily but efficiently on his rough tweed coat. Dr. Randolph's hand was patting her shoulder, slowly, gently, carefully, and he was murmuring like a refrain,

"There, there, little girl! There, there, little girl! There, there, little girl!"

It was not long before Mother sat up, sniffed hard, and appropriated the handkerchief.

"What's the matter?" asked Dr. Randolph.

Mother shook her head.

"Told the girls?"

Mother nodded.

"What'd they say?"

Mother shivered and groped for the handkerchief.

Dr. Randolph swallowed a syllable or two and made a new beginning. "We'll show 'em," he said. "And while we're showing them, let's get something else straightened out, too. I've been lonesome for twenty-five years, Mollie, without you. And now, since you've come, I've been lonesomer than I ever was before. Will you come and keep house for me, Mollie, instead of those —those girls—forevermore?"

Mollie looked up at him, looked away. "Oh, Willie, I'd rather do it than anything in the world," she said, and rubbed her cheek against his coat.

Dr. Randolph looked down at her, and his voice shook just a little as he spoke. "You won't let me lose you—again—Mollie?"

And for answer Mother raised her face to his.

At home, the girls were still at the table.

"It makes me sick, just sick," said Helen at last. "We'll be the joke of the college. If there's anything the world has no place for, it's the middle-aged failure, the person who can't keep up."

"Do you suppose—" asked Isabel, and then stopped.

"What?" enquired Helen dully.

"—That she could possibly get through and make her grades?"

"If she ever had any brains, would she have sewed for twenty years?" countered Isabel.

The argument, to them, was unanswerable. Neither one knew—perhaps neither one ever would know—why Mother had sewed with three years and a half of college at her back. Neither one realized that if Mother had taught school they would have gone without a home—and, later, without an education. Making dresses, Mother was at home all day long. She kept her babies—one, three; one, four—near her. She earned money the year round to give them good food and good clothes and keep their house fit to entertain their guests.

Twenty years ago, with her babies in her arms, Mother had worked out her problem—alone. She had kept her home, paid the bills that were not hers—paid the doctor and the undertaker—and college had been forgotten.

Now, it all came back to her—college and the good old days of fun and laughter. Willie was near her, as he always had been. Recitations and the thrill of triumph! How she worked.

The English was easy. The poets were her favorites—Keats, Shelley, Wordsworth—she loved them all with a soaring purity of inspiration her girls would never know. But that Psychology! All her study and Dr. Randolph's devoted coaching were no more than enough to pull her through.

At home there was war. Not that anything was said, but hostility lurked in the atmosphere. And it was not altogether the girls' fault. Mother's twinkle could be a mean twinkle, and it worked overtime about the house.

First, there was the matter of Dr. Parrant. Dr. Parrant was a lean, intellectual young man of forty from the Department of Economics. Helen brought him home in triumph one night, from a departmental club meeting, and he became a fixture of the Friday evenings. It could not be said that Isabel was normally in love with him, but she did state that she thought his views on Economics more advanced than those of any other man in his profession.

But lately Dr. Parrant had been devoting himself to the chocolate and sandwich bringer. One night he even went out to the kitchen to help stir, and after that he joined the Sunday night supper consecrated to Mother's guests. He kept watching Mother, too, as she served the plates, in a manner that, Helen thought, was disgustingly transparent. But then Helen, behind her starched shirtwaist, was hurt. Proudly and secretly hurt.

Isabel, too, was unhappy. It was the Felton Scholarship. She had worked so hard, and a summer in Europe would do so much for her, and now—perhaps—

"You see, it's the fiendishly loose wording of the thing," she burst out finally to Helen. "If it only said 'high scholarship,' they would *have* to give it to me. I know I have the best marks. But 'the person who, in the judgment of the senior professor of English, seems best fitted to benefit by it!' Why, it leaves the whole thing simply at the whim of Dr. Randolph."

"He's liable to do anything," said Helen. "You heard what he said in class last week?"

"No," said Isabel faintly. "What?"

"He was reading the reports of the mid-terms, and the grades. I don't know what Mother got. She wasn't among the A's, for he read all those. But he said that out of the whole class special commendation was due to Mrs. Mollie Gray; that her understanding and appreciation of poetry were unequalled in his present classes."

"Do you suppose he was just leading up to giving her the scholarship?" asked Isabel miserably.

"I don't know," said Helen. "But I know one thing. This whole year has been a mistake."

She couldn't tell even Isabel about Dr. Parrant. Perhaps she did not understand it yet herself.

It was June before Mother and the girls really got together. All those frigid weeks, the ice never thawed. The girls' heavy-footed courtesy never changed. Mother's loving care never ceased, and if she was lonely and hurt and wistful, she never spoke of it. In fact, when the girls were around, she was almost conspicuously and defiantly gay. She redoubled her attentions to Dr. Parrant, while Dr. Randolph looked on in placid amusement, and she was coming along fine in her studies. Dr. Randolph did not have a chance to help her with Psychology any more. She worked it out for herself and worked it out well.

The girls' nerve broke first. They sidled out to the kitchen, where Mother was singing happily about her Sunday night supper preparations.

Isabel was hollow-voiced, but determined. "I'd just like to know," she said, "if you're going to get the Felton Scholarship. Of course, Dr. Randolph must have told you, and I'd like to find out so I can make my own plans for the summer." Her voice grew deeper and deeper as she went on.

Mother turned round and looked at them. Neither of the girls met her eyes.

"Why, no," she said, "of course I'm not

going to get the Felton Scholarship! I don't deserve it. And anyway, I'm—" She turned her back and began to stir something on the stove with singular irrelevancy. "I think I'm going to get married—" Her voice broke.

"To Dr. Parrant, I suppose—" Helen's voice was flat and dry and strained.

Mother faced round and sank into a chair. Her eyes were swimming. "Oh, my babies," she said, and she held out her arms to them. "Did you think Mother wanted to take things away from you—when I've worked my fingers to the bone for twenty years to give you more and more? Oh, my babies! My little girls!"

And somehow, before they knew it, Helen and Isabel were down on the floor with their heads in her lap, while Mother petted them and kissed them and cried on them just as she had been starving to do all these last weary months.

"Why, my little girl, you're going to have the scholarship. Willie told me about it weeks ago, but I promised not to tell. And I'm so proud of my big clever daughter. And Helen, you're going to have your professor. Why, my dear—did you think—could you think— Oh! my dear, didn't you know he was just being nice to me because I am your foolish old mother? He's told me all about it. He's even—" she began to laugh—"he's even asked me if I thought you could learn to keep house—"

Helen flushed, a slow, embarrassed flush, and Mother swept them both into her arms with an unrestraint she had not known since baby days.

"My little girls, my little girls," she crooned. "We're all going to be so happ—"

The doorbell rang, a loud, determined peal. Mother jumped.

"Here, Helen."

She held her off, whisked out a powder-puff, brushed her nose, and threw her own pale-blue apron over Helen's head.

"Wait a minute," commanded Mother. With a light hand she sprinkled a tiny trace of flour on Helen's sleek braids.

"Go answer that door," snapped Mother, and like a little girl Helen moved obediently to let in Dr. Randolph and Dr. Parrant.

"Supper's just ready," cooed Mother, trailing after her.

A great cake, a chocolate cake, formed the centerpiece. Mother had spent two hours in making it. It was a monumental achievement—and one that any man could be counted on to understand and appreciate. Dr. Parrant stood awed.

"What a wonderful cake!" he said, with as much enthusiasm as his scholastic manner permitted.

"Isn't it!" agreed Mother impersonally as they all sat down. *"Helen baked it!"*

Horrified, Helen looked up. Her astonishment

might well pass for embarrassment. Dr. Parrant looked at her, and under his admiring eye she crimsoned with a sense of guilt. But even through her flush she could see that something in his glance was different—more delighted, more admiring. Nevertheless she had opened her mouth for honest denial when Mother fixed her with an imperial gaze.

"This may be only 'beginner's luck,'" she said. "The next may not be so good. But *she's going to learn.* When I get through with her," there was a threat as well as a promise in Mother's tone, "she'll be a better cook than I am. I'm not going to have all her education wasted!"

And Helen was meekly, and serenely, silent.

THE MOTHER OF GENNESARET *

Agnes Sligh Turnbull

THE late sunset lay upon the Sea of Galilee. Already the steep bluffs along the eastern shore had lost their reflected colour and loomed, grey and bare, except where sharp, storm-cut gullies showed like black scars.

The last, golden rays of the day streamed across the sky to touch the immaculate, high-lifted snows of Mount Hermon in the north, and then settled softly upon the rounding, western hills behind the plain of Gennesaret. Within the enfolding of the warm, waning light, the towns of Bethsaida and Capernaum nestled like a pair of tired sea-gulls along the beach.

The sea was still. The clear, shining waters smiled back at the lighted hills; the fishing boats and the white-sailed shallops floated as though in a mirage; far down the lake, a showy barge from the city of Herod gave the only spot of colour. Peace had fallen gently, along with the first shadows of the evening.

* Reprinted from "Far above Rubies," by Agnes Sligh Turnbull; copyright, 1926, by Fleming H. Revell Company. By special permission of the publisher and of the author.

But in the heart of the woman who walked hurriedly past Bethsaida and Capernaum to the quiet vantage point where a jutting rock commanded the long view of the sea, there was no peace. For Miriam, wife of Jonas, the fisherman, was hopeless to the point of despair.

She was still a young woman, but her slender shoulders were bent as though from much lifting of heavy burdens, and the smooth hair that framed her thin face was streaked with grey, where once it had been black and glossy as the wing of a bird. Something of youth imperishable still occasionally shone in her dark eyes,—a quick, luminous flare as of a lamp suddenly lighted.

It was this bright upleaping in her eyes that had caused Jonas, the stolid fisherman, to set down his basket of fish, long ago, beside her gateway in Capernaum and wait until he had seen it again. It was the flame he suddenly desired to lighten the gloom of his poor hut on the edge of the sea.

Miriam threw herself down upon the rock. There was the weariness of physical exhaustion in the gesture of her body. In her face there was the greater weariness of her soul's discontent.

With a sad dispassionateness she was weighing the years of her life in the balance, and she began with the old days in Capernaum.

She and Lois had dwelt there from their orphaned childhood, with their mother's sister, Hannah, in the small stone house on the edge of the town. There had been peace and beauty there. Even as children they had sensed it. The tiny open court with its vine-covered walls; the garden, green with oleanders, and bright with flowers in their season; the clean, uncrowded rooms with shining brass lamps, and chairs of polished wood.

And then, everywhere about the walls, the adornments which Hannah's own fingers had wrought: the tapestries which rich men and women came to buy; the sale of which kept the little home in modest comfort.

As soon as they were old enough to sit before the large tapestry frames, Hannah had begun upon the education of the small maidens committed to her care. Very patiently, as a teacher who loves her subject, she guided the uncertain, awkward little fingers over simple patterns; she pointed out the beauty of the design; she blent soft colours under their gaze.

Perhaps it was due to the gentle enthusiasm of their teacher, perhaps to an inborn artistic sense, but slowly and surely the girls gained a fine ease with their needles. As time passed they began to try intricate patterns of their own, new blendings, fine, exquisite stitches.

Hannah was radiant. They would work together now. Her eyes, long overstrained, would have some rest. Her thin fingers which sometimes trembled as she sorted the threads, might now lie occasionally idle in her lap.

Happy, busy years followed. Lois and Miriam loved their work. It was pleasant to sit in the cool court with their sewing-frames before them and create beautiful things in purple and white, or rose and gold, while Hannah read to them from an old parchment of the Scriptures, or told them stories of Jerusalem where she had learned the art of needlework, long ago.

"They laugh at us Galilæans, those people of the South," she would say. "They call us barbarians. But never have I seen in Jerusalem, not even in the holy Temple itself, tapestries more beautiful than those my own hands have fashioned. And you, my children, will make others still more fair, for you will weave, along with the silken threads, the dreams of your youth. Age has no such bright magic! Only patient skill that has grown weary. Weave your light hearts into your patterns, my children!"

There was always a pleasant excitement when patrons knocked at the door, and Hannah ushered them courteously inside to see the glowing strips that hung for their inspection. Perhaps it was the nobleman who lived in the great house on the hill. He always bought when he came, and admired the pattern. If Lois and Miriam had shared in the work, they were allowed to come in to hear his praise with meek delight.

Sometimes Hannah came back, breathless and beaming, to the court to report that a rich buyer from Tiberias had just given an order which would mean a sum large enough that the girls might have new dresses, and still leave something to apply against the debt that they knew with a vague incuriosity hung over the house. There were always small, happy surprises to brighten the quiet, comfortable days.

It had been one morning in spring that Miriam, sitting alone in the court, singing as she matched her threads, had looked up to see a young man standing in the gateway. He was tall and strong with a face reddened and roughened from the wind. He wore a fisherman's cloak of coarse homespun and he carried the large reed basket that fish-peddlers bore.

Miriam's bright gaze rested upon him as she shook her head. "We do not wish to buy," she said.

The young man continued to gaze at her, not rudely but with an intense interest. Then he set his basket down and leaned awkwardly against the wall.

"I am Jonas of Bethsaida," he said slowly. "What is thy name?"

"Miriam," the girl answered a little proudly. "We make fine tapestries for sale."

Jonas was silent for a little while. Then, as he raised his basket, he said, "I have a house of my own down by the sea. And soon I shall buy a boat and catch only large fish." And then he had gone away.

Miriam's cheeks had burned, even while she laughed to herself. There was no mistaking the look in his eyes. A common fisherman! And he had looked in that way at her! She would tell Hannah and Lois when they came back from market and they would all laugh together.

But, somehow, when they returned she had said nothing.

After that, Jonas came every week to stand in the gateway, but always when he saw she was alone. Once he came over to look at the tapestry upon which her slender fingers were working. He made no comment upon its beauty. Only, at last, as he turned to go, he said slowly: "I fear thou wouldst find my house too small and dark for thee."

Miriam pondered the speech that night while Lois slept soundly beside her. Strange, little, trembling fires sprang up in her heart. Life stretched before her like a far, unknown country wherein one might walk in many paths. Some would open, no doubt, into fair enchanted valleys, and others lead to dark, stony mountains that would shut one in like dungeon bars. One must be very careful in choosing.

Meanwhile a new skill with her needle seemed to come to Miriam. Perhaps it was because her mind had suddenly wakened from its childhood sleep into the sweet, startled questionings of maidenhood. But, in any case, Miriam's fingers began to be moved by the creative power of the artist.

Old Hannah watched with eager pride. The change was subtle, but it was there. A little more vividness of outline, a daring dash of colour, a new but inevitable shading—and Miriam's tapestries took on life.

And with her growing power there came, too, with a rush of deep wonder, her knowledge of it and joy in it. She began to study the sunsets, to watch people and animals, to see flowers and trees with new eyes. For now nothing but perfection would satisfy.

Lois laughed at her earnestness and envied a little, too. After all, though, her own finished work looked well enough. Why take such foolish pains!

And so life had gone its busy, happy way until Miriam was sixteen. Then the stroke fell. Old Hannah, whose fingers had been trembling more than usual of late, did not answer one morning when they called her. The girls found her quite still. The mysterious door which men called Death, must have closed upon her suddenly in the night-time, shutting her away from all the bright gladness of life!

Like a heavy dream of pain the next hours passed. Wailing women filled the house. Miriam shrank from them. All that remained of the kind-hearted, beauty-loving little woman who had formed the centre of their lives was at last carried to the tombs on the hillside.

When the sisters returned to the empty house, a man awaited them. It was Philus, the rich merchant. He stated his business with cruel brevity. He owned the house, now. Hannah had borrowed money from him years ago. He must take the property and its furnishings to pay the remainder of the debt. He was obdurate, for he knew the helplessness of his victims.

When he had gone Lois flashed upon her sister a look so eagerly resolute that it was almost joy.

"I know what we shall do!" she cried. "Have I not dreamed of it? Longed for it? There is a city where beauty abounds like the sunlight; where there is luxury and romance! where there is a palace and a castle that seem to touch the sky; where soldiers in shining uniforms keep marching through the streets; where courtiers in magnificent silks go out upon the sea in barges trimmed with gold! Where . . ."

Miriam's face was white with amazement.

"*Tiberias!*" she gasped. "The city of Herod! Thou canst not mean the *city of sin!*"

Lois went on undaunted.

"I know all thou wouldst say," she replied. "Have we not been taught that no Jew enters that city undefiled? But it calls me! I will see its beauty, if I die for it! Hearken! Dost thou remember, months ago, when the Tiberian woman whose name was Annis, bought the piece of rose and gold? I overheard her from the hallway. She told Hannah she was herself a needleworker. She had heard of us. She came to ask if Hannah would allow one of us to go to be her helper. Ever since I have kept it close in my heart. I should still have gone if Hannah had lived. But now! What have we here? What can we do, alone and homeless? The sight of Capernaum sickens me. It reeks of fish and ugliness. I want to see the Towers of Herod against the sunset! I want to embroider garments for courtiers and princesses! I want to be a part of all that rich beauty and movement and excitement . . . I want . . ."

She stopped in triumph, for her sister's eyes were shining with a light that dazzled her.

"Yes, *yes,*" Miriam cried. "I, too, can see it! I can feel myself there, with the wonder of it all about me! I can feel myself making such patterns that Herod himself would marvel and say, 'Who hath wrought this?' We might become rich . . ." She stopped. The light went out of her eyes. She clutched her sister in horror.

"I am *mad* to speak so. Thou art beside thyself to urge it. We would stain our souls to enter those wicked gates. It must never be spoken of again!"

Lois flung her head. There was strength in her tone, as she spoke.

"We are homeless. We have no close friends to whom we may turn for help. My mind is made up. I shall go to Tiberias. It is the golden dream of my heart. I shall seek the woman who made the offer to Hannah."

Suddenly they clung to each other, each wildly beseeching, each unmoved in her own resolve.

"But what wilt thou do, if thou comest not with me?" Lois cried wildly.

A vision of Jonas in the gateway rose before Miriam's racked brain.

"I can marry," she half whispered.

When Lois understood she began again with new arguments that seemed invincible. A common fisherman! A dark hut by the seaside! She had seen them. She knew their poverty. It was unthinkable for Miriam.

Through the long night they wept, arms intertwined, each pleading desperately, as she saw it, for the very life of the other. When morning brought the sleep of exhaustion there had been no victory. Lois, fixed and fearless, exalted with a fervid, reckless hope, would go to seek her fortune in Tiberias; Miriam, agonized between the same longing and the clear call of her faith, would remain behind, would become a fisherman's wife, if need be.

On the second morning, after a long embrace, Lois took the path that led south over the Plain of Gennesaret to the City of Herod.

"If I find it as beautiful as my dreams, I shall never come back. By that, thou shalt know," she said.

Jonas came to the court that afternoon, as he did each week. There were only a few broken words spoken. But at sundown Miriam walked beside him up the beach to Bethsaida, her bundle of possessions in his empty fish-basket, her precious tapestry frames under her arm. She was to be his wife.

The house which he owned stood outside the green circle of village verdure. It was rudely built and had but two small rooms, each lighted only by a narrow window. The battered clay lamp with its rag wick, the mill at the doorway, a table and pallet and stool,—these were the furnishings. The bare sands stretched down to the sea. Opposite rose the grey eastern bluffs.

But, at sixteen, every sunrise brings a song. Miriam's desolate distress lifted as she bent all her energies toward adapting herself to her new life. She rendered the little home spotless;

she disposed about the few good articles she had brought with her. She listened sympathetically to the great ambition of Jonas, toward which he was feverishly saving every penny; the buying of a boat of his own.

Every day when she had done all she could to help him, she sat down before the frames and wrought at the old beloved task and thought of Hannah and Lois, and the great Power that had so separated them. Hope usually took the place of sadness. Jonas was kind, though he did expect her to do her full share of the work. The years might somehow yet bring joy.

But they had brought hardship instead. They had fallen upon her bright soul like a crushing avalanche. Her slender strength did not prove equal to the burdens: the water to be carried a long distance, the heavy clothes to be washed in the sea, the bags of barley to be lifted, to be ground, and made into endless loaves, the fish to be cleaned for market—and more and more fish!

Then in the close, sultry summer days, when the hills shut away all the air—days when there was now no cool and shaded court in which to sit, there came the dreaded fever and ague.

As time passed, intolerable pain came again and again to rack her, and to haunt her with its memory or its fear. And the dull burden of every day grew heavier. There was no time now to

work at the tapestry frames, and besides, the delicate fingers that had once blended the threads were now so rough and stiffened that they could not safely touch the soft strands.

Before Jonas could buy his boat there were new, hungry little mouths to be fed, and so he compromised upon a rented one, the money for which ate relentlessly into his small earnings. Grim, biting poverty came to make his permanent abode with them.

The children were sound and strong. Jonas looked upon them with pride. Miriam loved them, but with a weary, passive affection. She ministered all day to their needs; she followed the grinding round of each day's toil without complaint. But at sunset, when sometimes a sail, far down the sea, flashed a pale glory against the sky, she gazed toward Tiberias with a strange, set look upon her face. Lois had never come back. It had all been as beautiful, then, as they had dreamed!

As soon as little Mark, the eldest child, was old enough, Jonas took him with him in the boat. And when he was twelve years old he was allowed to make the trip alone to Capernaum with the baskets of fish.

One evening he came back running along the beach. He was breathless when he reached the doorway. He started impetuously upon his story. There was a man visiting in Capernaum

at Simon Peter's house,—a rabbi. He was a friend of Simon's and His name was Jesus and everybody was going to hear Him teach.

"I could hardly sell my fish," the boy rushed on. "Nobody was at home. And then all at once I saw the crowd before Simon's house. They were standing away out in the street. I tried to get in but no one else could get near the door. *And just then,*" the boy's shrill voice rose impressively, "I saw four men carrying a pallet. They went close by me and I could see the sick man on the bed. He could not walk. He had the palsy. And they tried to get in to the rabbi, but the people were so crowded they could not move them, so the bearers went up on the outside stairs to the roof and lifted some tiles and let the sick man right down. And in a few minutes he came out, *walking!* The rabbi had healed him! And he was saying, 'Glory to God! Glory to God!' over and over!" The boy paused again, breathless, his eyes shining.

"Come and eat thy supper, Mark," Miriam said wearily. It had been a hard day.

Jonas was faintly curious. "I have heard some of the men talk about this rabbi. What did He look like?" he asked.

"I do not know," Mark said regretfully. "I could not see him."

Some time later, he had another strange story to tell.

"Dost thou know the nobleman who lives in the great house on the hill above Capernaum?" he asked his mother eagerly.

How well Miriam remembered the days when he came to Hannah's door!

"Yes," she answered quickly. "What hast thou heard of him?"

Mark spoke earnestly. The nobleman's son had been very sick. He was dying. The nobleman had gone to Cana to ask the rabbi to come and heal him. And the rabbi had but spoken a word and told the nobleman to go back home and his son would be well. And truly he was! The servants had gone out to meet their master with the news and everybody in Capernaum was talking about it.

Mark's face grew wistful. "I should like to see the rabbi," he said.

But it was another happening more strange and full of portent to Miriam than either of these, that had driven her out from her home on this spring evening to seek refuge where she might face a great temptation and meet a sharp struggle alone.

Yesterday, for the first time since her departure to Tiberias, she had received a message from Lois. As a voice from the dead it had come. A youth travelling north had brought it. Lois had sent word many times before, but the messenger had always failed to find her. Lois

feared her sister dead, but sent tidings once more. She was well and happy and prosperous. She had not married and still worked with Annis. The prices paid for tapestries in Tiberias were marvellous. They received large orders yearly from the court. She begged Miriam to leave everything to come, even now, and work with her. She had longed for her all these years. And it was not yet too late!

So in the waning sunset Miriam reviewed her life slowly and bitterly and trembled under the desire that tore at her heart in this crisis. To be free from the drudgery that was wearing out her body, and crushing her spirit; to have a chance to use again the great gift that was hers! A few weeks' care of her poor rough hands, a few weeks' practice again with the needle, and she *knew*, with the old sense of power surging back within her, that she could do finer work than either Lois or Annis, for she could make her patterns *live*.

And then to know comfort again: a dress of soft linen instead of this coarse, unlovely homespun; food, nourishing and palatable, instead of the barley bread and fish that made up their only fare! Rest, refreshment, bright rooms, cool courts, strength once again, laughter—life! Her very soul cried out for it.

But to desert Jonas and the children! She shuddered at the blackness of the thought.

And yet her mind presented the temptation in a new and logical form. If she had died last summer with the fever, as they all thought she would; if she should die *this* summer, would it not be the same? Had not Jehovah smitten the wife of Jabed who lived just up the beach, and whose children were small and sickly?

Nay, had He not taken her own parents and then taken away Hannah, and left her and Lois alone? Why should she not take her own life into her own keeping? Why must she be bound here, forever, as to a millstone?

So she wrestled while the shadows lengthened. Over and over again she forced herself to see the thing she contemplated in all its cruel selfishness and its defilement of the faith to which she had been born. But only to have sweep over her once more the waves of hot rebellion, the deep hatred of her lot, the passionate craving for freedom and comfort and beauty which urged her on.

It was time to go back, and still her mind seethed in indecision. To-morrow she could perhaps think more clearly. She dragged her weary feet back along the shore.

The next morning Miriam opened her heavy eyes curiously upon the new day. Would something rise from the dead level of its untried hours to lift this pain of suspense? To persuade, reassure her, set her free? Ah, something *must*

Jonas left early for the boat. Mark was to make a quick trip to Capernaum with a small basket of fish. Miriam watched them go. The other children swarmed about, playing, quarreling, shouting.

Miriam began mechanically to put her house in order. If she *should* leave. . . . She swept and scrubbed, and baked fresh barley loaves, many more than usual. She worked hard, drugging the questionings of her mind with action, postponing the final decision even as she made her vague preparations.

Just at noon Mark came running in, and tossed down his empty basket.

"Mother," he cried, his dark eyes burning with excitement, "the rabbi I told thee of—the one that healed the palsied man and the nobleman's son—is over there, across the sea on the mountain and every one from Capernaum and Bethsaida is going over to see Him and hear Him teach! Mother, wilt thou let me go? I *must* see Him!" His voice broke with eagerness.

"Thou must first eat," said Miriam.

"But I am not hungry. Mother, I dare not wait! I must overtake the crowds now. If I tarry I may miss Him!"

"Still, thou must eat," Miriam returned firmly. "Here," catching up a handful of barley cakes she had just baked, and two of the small fish on the table, "take these with thee. Thou canst eat them on the way. And be not later than sundown in thy returning!"

She put the food in a small, lidless basket that lay near her hand. The boy grasped it and sped like an arrow across the sands.

The afternoon hours passed. Miriam washed clothes at the edge of the sea—still strainingly busy, still preparing, still warding off the last surrender.

Jonas came in for a hasty supper and hurried back again for a late night's fishing. Miriam watched the slanting sun. Mark should be home. Why had she allowed him to go at all? Something might have befallen him. An unusual restlessness took possession of her. She bore it until the sun lay red upon the top of the hill, then she, too, hurried along the sands to where the boats for crossing lay. Jonas knew one of the owners and had often served him. She was sure of his help.

In a few minutes they had reached the eastern bank.

"The crowds went on up that way," the boatman told her, indicating the steep hill. "Never have I seen so many people together! Thousands, there seemed to be!"

Miriam took the path he pointed out. It led to the opening at the upper end of the hills. Her heart beat quickly. Now that she was nearing the spot where the boy must be, fear for his safety gave way to a strange curiosity and anticipation.

At last she had reached the crest of the final low hill and started to go down. As her eye swept the wide, grassy hollow below, she stopped with an involuntary cry. The scene before her was so close, so real with a grand and vivid beauty, and yet so far from anything her artist's brain could have imagined.

There on the broad, green slopes, their brightly coloured turbans showing like a mass of blooming flowers, was seated a multitude; a great, dense, ingathering of living souls, which might so easily have been a confused, clamorous throng, but which instead sat motionless, listening, intent upon the figure of the man who stood before them. The sunset light streamed across the narrow sea and rested upon His face, as He spoke.

Miriam, creeping closer, watched it with the eyes of a creator who sees the chiseling of the soul. Suffering was there, and longing; and the lonely sorrow that does not speak. Ah, Miriam could recognize those lines. There was love and sympathy in the tender mouth; there was infinite strength in the high forehead as if of a will that knew the royal power of overcoming.

But stronger than all, there shone upon the features a light that the sunset did not bring.

It was the light of a rare and holy joy, of the peace that passes understanding.

He stopped speaking. Several men came close to Him as if to confer. Miriam could not hear their words. Suddenly one of them turned and pointed behind him. It was then that she saw Mark. He sat in the front row of people, his slender young body leaning forward, his dark eyes fixed on the rabbi's face. In one hand he absently clutched the open basket. Miriam could see that the food she had placed there was still in it. The eager, foolish child! He had taken no time to eat.

But all at once Miriam's eyes grew large with wonder. The young men who seemed to be the rabbi's disciples, were going about among the people, separating them into groups, making paths among them. It was all done with a singular quiet and order.

Then when all was finished one of the men went up to Mark and, after a word, took the basket from the boy's willing hands, and turning, gave it to the rabbi. The disciples fell back to the sides. The rabbi stood alone with the little basket extended in His hands, His eyes raised to heaven. Before Him in utter stillness sat the watching multitude.

Miriam put her hands wildly to her head. Was she mad? Was she dreaming? The coarse loaves her own hands had baked that morning; the wretched little fish her own fingers had prepared —now, the centre of this scene, held up in blessing by this strange, God-like man, watched by the waiting thousands with expectancy, and by the disciples, *and Mark,* with eyes of shining faith?

The hush deepened. Not a breath, nor a movement! The rabbi gazed steadfastly toward heaven, then beckoned to the men who stood near. They came, bringing their large, empty traveller's baskets, and waited beside him.

There was a sudden straining forward on the part of the multitude, a sharp sound as of the quick intaking of many breaths. For out of Mark's tiny basket, held directly in their view, *the rabbi was filling the others!* Heaping them with the loaves and the fishes!

Unquestioningly, apparently without surprise, the disciples passed them to the waiting people and returned to the rabbi. Their baskets Were refilled again and again. The hungry thousands were fed.

Miriam was upon her knees, trembling. This common air she breathed must be athrill with God. This man, this rabbi, had taken her poor food from the hands of her own little lad, and with it *had wrought a miracle!* Here, under the evening sky, her own eyes had witnessed it! It was as if God had reached down from His heavenly place to touch her humble hand!

At last she raised her head. The rabbi was watching her, with clear, searching eyes. They read her heart and then seemed waiting for her answer. With a cry she stretched forth her hands. She had forgotten the multitude. To her there were but herself and the Master upon the hillside with the celestial throbbing of the air about them.

"Master," she whispered, "Thou hast opened mine eyes! I will be faithful!"

He smiled and turned to look upon Mark, who still sat rapt, his eyes upraised to the Master's face in worship. Miriam watched him, too, as if for the first time. Her little lad! And she had never seen the beauty of his soul.

There was a stir among the thousands. Miriam turned and ran quickly back over the path by which she had come.

It was dark when she reached home and the children were frightened and crying. They clung to her. How suddenly sweet was the realization that these little bodies were of more value to her than all the gold of Herod's palace.

Mark came and she heard his tale of wonder. She listened lovingly and the child, warmed by her new interest, showed her the adoration in his heart.

At last they were all asleep. Miriam walked out upon the pebbled sands and looked far down the sea.

Tiberias? The old temptation was broken. It could never meet her again. Against the living mystery on yonder hillside, the glories of Herod's city must be tawdry and dead.

Freedom? Never had she felt so free, with a sudden kinship for the wide spaces of the sea and sky and mountains. But greater still, there was the freedom of a mind lifted up into high reaches of vision; of a soul drawn upward to meet the reality of God.

Tapestries? Oh, blind, blind that she had been! To her had been given tapestries of tender flesh and blood upon which to embroider the fair patterns of the soul.

She raised her head in the darkness. The old glad light had returned again to her eyes. For she knew now that the common daily elements which her heart had so despised, had been transfigured. She knew that through each day's patient, wearing toil, she would see again the Master's face.

MRS. RIPLEY'S TRIP *

Hamlin Garland

THE night was in windy November, and the blast, threatening rain, roared around the poor little shanty of Uncle Ripley, set like a chicken-trap on the vast Iowa prairie. Uncle Ethan was mending his old violin, with many York State "dums!" and "I gol darns!" totally oblivious of his tireless old wife, who, having "finished the supper-dishes," sat knitting a stocking, evidently for the little grandson who lay before the stove like a cat.

Neither of the old people wore glasses, and their light was a tallow candle; they couldn't afford "none o' them new-fangled lamps." The room was small, the chairs were wooden, and the walls bare—a home where poverty was a never absent guest. The old lady looked pathetically little, weazened, and hopeless in her ill-fitting garments (whose original color had long since vanished), intent as she was on the

* Reprinted from "Main-Travelled Roads." Harper and Brothers, Publishers. By special permission of Hamlin Garland.

stocking in her knotted, stiffened fingers, and there was a peculiar sparkle in her little black eyes, and an unusual resolution in the straight line of her withered and shapeless lips.

Suddenly she paused, stuck a needle in the spare knob of her hair at the back of her head, and looking at Ripley, said decisively: "Ethan Ripley, you'll haff to do your own cooking from now on to New Year's. I'm goin' back to Yaark State."

The old man's leather-brown face stiffened into a look of quizzical surprise for a moment; then he cackled, incredulously: "Ho! Ho! har! Sho! be y', now? I want to know if y' be."

"Well, you'll find out."

"Goin' to start to-morrow, mother?"

"No, sir, I ain't; but I am on Thursday. I want to get to Sally's by Sunday, sure, an' to Silas's on Thanksgivin'."

There was a note in the old woman's voice that brought genuine stupefaction into the face of Uncle Ripley. Of course in this case, as in all others, the money consideration was uppermost.

"Howgy 'xpect to get the money, mother? Anybody died an' left yeh a pile?"

"Never you mind where I get the money, so 's 't *you* don't haff to bear it. The land knows if I'd 'a 'waited for *you* to pay my way—"

"You needn't twit me of bein' poor, old

woman,'' said Ripley, flaming up after the manner of many old people. ''I've done *my* part t' get along. I've worked day in and day out—''

''Oh! I ain't done no work, have I?'' snapped she, laying down the stocking and levelling a needle at him, and putting a frightful emphasis on ''I.''

''I didn't say you hadn't done no work.''

''Yes, you did!''

''I didn't neither. I said—''

''I *know* what you said.''

''I said I'd done *my part!*'' roared the husband, dominating her as usual by superior lung power. ''I didn't *say* you hadn't done your part,'' he added with an unfortunate touch of emphasis.

''I know y' didn't *say* it, but y' meant it. I don't know what y' call doin' my part, Ethan Ripley; but if cookin' for a drove of harvest hands and thrashin' hands, takin' care o' the eggs and butter, 'n' diggin' taters an' milkin' ain't *my* part, I don't never expect to do my part, 'n' you might as well know it fust 's last.

''I'm sixty years old,'' she went on, with a little break in her harsh voice, dominating him now by woman's logic, ''an' I've never had a day to myself, not even Fourth o' July. If I've went a-visitin' 'r to a picnic, I've had to come home an' milk 'n' get supper for you men-folks. I ain't been away t' stay overnight for thirteen years in this house, 'n' it was just so in Davis County for ten more. For twenty-three years, Ethan Ripley, I've stuck right to the stove an' churn without a day or a night off."

Her voice choked again, but she rallied, and continued impressively, "And now I'm a-goin' back to Yaark State."

Ethan was vanquished. He stared at her in speechless surprise, his jaw hanging. It was incredible.

"For twenty-three years," she went on, musingly, "I've just about promised myself every year I'd go back an' see my folks." She was distinctly talking to herself now, and her voice had a touching, wistful cadence. "I've wanted to go back an' see the old folks, an' the hills where we played, an' eat apples off the old tree down by the well. I've had them trees an' hills in my mind days and days—nights, too—an' the girls I used to know, an' my own folks—"

She fell into a silent muse, which lasted so long that the ticking of the clock grew loud as a gong in the man's ears, and the wind outside seemed to sound drearier than usual. He returned to the money problem; kindly, though.

"But how y' goin' t' raise the money? I ain't got no extra cash this time. Agin Roach is paid, an' the interest paid, we ain't got no hundred dollars to spare, Jane, not by a jugful."

"Wal, don't you lay awake nights studyin' on

where I'm a-goin' to get that money,'' said the old woman, taking delight in mystifying him. She had him now, and he couldn't escape. He strove to show his indifference, however, by playing a tune or two on the violin.

''Come, Tukey, you better climb the wooden hill,'' Mrs. Ripley said, a half-hour later, to the little chap on the floor, who was beginning to get drowsy under the influence of his grandpa's fiddling. ''Pa, you had orta 'a' put that string in the clock to-day—on the 'larm side the string is broke,'' she said, upon returning from the boy's bedroom. ''I orta git up early to-morrow, to git some sewin' done. Land knows, I can't fix up much, but they is a little I c'n do. I want to look decent.''

They were alone now, and they both sat expectantly.

''You 'pear to think, mother, that I'm agin yer goin'.''

''Wal, it would kinder seem as if y' hadn't hustled yerself any t' help me git off.''

He was smarting under the sense of being wronged. ''Wal, I'm just as willin' you should go as I am for myself, but if I ain't got no money I don't see how I'm going to send—''

''I don't want ye to send; nobody ast ye to, Ethan Ripley. I guess if I had what I've earnt since we came on this farm I'd have enough to go to Jericho with.''

"You've got as much out of it as I have," he replied gently. "You talk about your goin' back. Ain't I been wantin' to go back myself? And ain't I kep' still 'cause I see it wa'n't no use? I guess I've worked jest as long and as hard as you, an' in storms an' in mud an' heat, ef it comes t' that."

The woman was staggered, but she wouldn't give up; she must get in one more thrust.

"Wal, if you'd 'a' managed as well as I have, you'd have some money to go with." And she rose and went to mix her bread and set it "raisin'."

He sat by the fire twanging his fiddle softly. He was plainly thrown into gloomy retrospection, something quite unusual for him. But his fingers picking out the bars of a familiar tune set him to smiling, and whipping his bow across the strings, he forgot all about his wife's resolutions and his own hardships. "Trouble always slid off his back like punkins off a haystack, anyway," his wife said.

The old man still sat fiddling softly after his wife disappeared in the hot and stuffy little bedroom off the kitchen. His shaggy head bent lower over his violin. He heard her shoes drop —*one, two*. Pretty soon she called:

"Come, put up that squeakin' old fiddle, and go to bed. Seems as if you orta have sense enough not to set there keepin' everybody in the house awake.''

''You hush up,'' retorted he. ''I'll come when I git ready, and not till. I'll be glad when you're gone—''

''Yes, I warrant *that.''*

With which amiable good-night they went off to sleep, or at least she did, while he lay awake pondering on ''where under the sun she was goin' t' raise that money.''

The next day she was up bright and early, working away on her own affairs, ignoring Ripley entirely, the fixed look of resolution still on her little old wrinkled face. She killed a hen and dressed and baked it. She fried up a pan of doughnuts and made a cake. She was engaged in the doughnuts when a neighbor came in, one of these women who take it as a personal affront when any one in the neighborhood does anything without asking their advice. She was fat, and could talk a man blind in three minutes by the watch. Her neighbor said:

''What's this I hear, Mis' Ripley?''

''I dun know. I expect you hear about all they is goin' on in this neighborhood,'' replied Mrs. Ripley, with crushing bluntness; but the gossip did not flinch.

''Well, Sett Turner told *me* that her husband told *her* that Ripley told *him* this mornin' that you was goin' back East on a visit.

"Wal, what of it?"

"Well, air yeh?"

"The Lord willin' an' the weather permittin', I expect I be."

"Good land, I want to know! Well, well! I never was so astonished in my whole life. I said, says I, 'It can't be.' 'Well,' ses 'e, 'tha's what *she* told me,' ses 'e. 'But,' says I, 'she is the last woman in the world to go gallavantin' off East,' ses I. 'An',' ses he, 'but it comes from good authority,' ses he. 'Well, then, it must be so,' ses I. But, land sakes! do tell me all about it. How come you to make up y'r mind? All these years you've been kind a' talkin' it over, an' now y'r actshelly goin'—well, I *never!* 'I s'pose Ripley furnishes the money,' ses I to him. 'Well, no,' ses 'e. 'Ripley says he'll be blowed if he sees where the money's coming from,' ses 'e; and ses I, 'But maybe she's jest jokin',' ses I. 'Not much,' he says. S' 'e: 'Ripley believes she's goin' fast enough. He's jest as anxious to find out as we be—"

Here Mrs. Doudney paused for breath; she had walked so fast and rested so little that her interminable flow of "ses I's" and "ses he's" ceased necessarily. She had reached, moreover, the point of most vital interest—the money.

"An' you'll find out jest 'bout as soon as he does," was the dry response from the figure hovering over the stove; and with all her manœuvring that was all she got.

All day Ripley went about his work exceedingly thoughtful for him. It was cold blustering weather. The wind rustled among the cornstalks with a wild and mournful sound, the geese and ducks went sprawling down the wind, and the horses' coats were ruffled and backs raised.

The old man was husking all alone in the field, his spare form rigged out in two or three ragged coats, his hands inserted in a pair of gloves minus nearly all the fingers, his thumbs done up in "stalls," and his feet thrust into huge coarse boots. The "down ears" wet and chapped his hands, already worn to the quick. Toward night it grew colder and threatened snow. In spite of all these attacks he kept his cheerfulness, and though he was very tired, he was softened in temper.

Having plenty of time to think matters over, he had come to the conclusion that the old woman needed a play-spell. "I ain't likely to be no richer next year than I am this one; if I wait till I'm able to send her she won't never go. I calc'late I c'n git enough out o' them shoats to send her. I'd kind a' lotted on eat'n' them pigs done up in sassengers, but if the ol' woman goes East, Tukey an' me'll kind a' haff to pull through without 'em. We'll have a turkey f'r Thanksgivin', an' a chicken once 'n a while.

Lord! but we'll miss the gravy on the flap-jacks." (He smacked his lips over the thought of the lost dainty.) "But let 'er rip! We can stand it. Then there is my buffalo overcoat. I'd kind a' calc'lated on havin' a buffalo—but that's gone up the spout along with them sassengers."

These heroic sacrifices having been determined upon, he put them into effect at once.

This he was able to do, for his corn-rows ran alongside the road leading to Cedarville, and his neighbors were passing almost all hours of the day.

It would have softened Jane Ripley's heart could she have seen his bent and stiffened form among the corn-rows, the cold wind piercing to the bone through his threadbare and insufficient clothing. The rising wind sent the snow rattling among the moaning stalks at intervals. The cold made his poor dim eyes water, and he had to stop now and then to swing his arms about his chest to warm them. His voice was hoarse with shouting at the shivering team.

That night as Mrs. Ripley was clearing the dishes away she got to thinking about the departure of the next day, and she began to soften. She gave way to a few tears when little Tewksbury Gilchrist, her grandson, came up and stood beside her.

"Gran'ma, you ain't goin' to stay away always, are yeh?"

"Why, course not, Tukey. What made y' think that?"

"Well, y' ain't told us nawthin' 't all about it. An' yeh kind o' look's if yeh was mad."

"Well, I ain't mad; I'm jest a-thinkin', Tukey. Y' see, I come away from them hills when I was a little girl a 'most; before I married y'r grandad. And I ain't never been back. 'Most all my folks is there, sonny, an' we've been s' poor all these years I couldn't seem t' never git started. Now, when I'm most ready t' go, I feel kind a queer—'s if I'd cry."

And cry she did, while little Tewksbury stood patting her trembling hands. Hearing Ripley's step on the porch, she rose hastily and, drying her eyes, plunged at the work again.

Ripley came in with a big armful of wood, which he rolled into the wood-box with a thundering crash. Then he pulled off his mittens, slapped them together to knock off the ice and snow, and laid them side by side under the stove. He then removed cap, coat, blouse, and finally his boots, which he laid upon the wood-box, the soles turned toward the stove-pipe.

As he sat down without speaking, he opened the front doors of the stove, and held the palms of his stiffened hands to the blaze. The light brought out a thoughtful look on his large, uncouth, yet kindly, visage. Life had laid hard lines on his brown skin, but it had not entirely soured a naturally kind and simple nature. It had made him penurious and dull and iron-muscled; had stifled all the slender flowers of his nature; yet there was warm soil somewhere hid in his heart.

"It's snowin' like all p'ssessed," he remarked finally. "I guess we'll have a sleigh-ride to-morrow. I calc'late t' drive y' daown in scrumptious style. If you must leave, why, we'll give yeh a whoopin' old send-off—won't we, Tukey?"

Nobody replying, he waited a moment. "I've ben a-thinkin' things over kind o' t'-day, mother, an' I've come t' the conclusion that we *have* been kind o' hard on yeh, without knowin' it, y' see. Y' see I'm kind o' easy-goin', an' little Tuke he's only a child, an' we ain't c'nsidered how you felt."

She didn't appear to be listening, but she was, and he didn't appear, on his part, to be talking to her, and he kept his voice as hard and dry as he could.

"An' I was tellin' Tukey t'-day that it was a dum shame our crops hadn't turned out better. An' when I saw ol' Hatfield go by I hailed him, an' asked him what he'd gimme for two o' m' shoats. Wal, the upshot is, I sent t' town for some things I calc'late you'd need. An' here's a ticket to Georgetown, and ten dollars. Why, ma, what's up?"

Mrs. Ripley broke down, and with her hands

all wet with dish-water, as they were, covered her face, and sobbed. She felt like kissing him, but she didn't. Tewksbury began to whimper too; but the old man was astonished. His wife had not wept for years (before him). He rose and walking clumsily up to her timidly touched her hair—

"Why, mother! What's the matter? What've I done now? I was calc'latin' to sell them pigs anyway. Hatfield jest advanced the money on 'em."

She hopped up and dashed into the bedroom, and in a few minutes returned with a yarn mitten, tied around the wrist, which she laid on the table with a thump, saying: "I don't want yer money. There's money enough to take me where I want to go."

"Whee—ew! Thunder and gimpsum root! Where'd ye get that? Didn't dig it out of a hole?"

"No, I jest saved it—a dime at a time—see!" Here she turned it out on the table—some bills, but mostly silver dimes and quarters.

"Thunder and scissors! Must be two er three hundred dollars there," he exclaimed.

"They's jest seventy-five dollars and thirty cents; jest about enough to go back on. Tickets is fifty-five dollars, goin' and comin'. That leaves twenty dollars for other expenses, not countin' what I've already spent, which is six-fifty," said she, recovering her self-possession. "It's plenty."

"But y' ain't calc'lated on no sleepers nor hotel bills."

"I ain't goin' on no sleeper. Mis' Doudney says it's jest scandalous the way things is managed on them cars. I'm goin' on the old-fashioned cars, where they ain't no half-dressed men runnin' around."

"But *you* needn't be afraid of them, mother; at your age—"

"There! you needn't throw my age an' homeliness into my face, Ethan Ripley. If I hadn't waited an' tended on you so long, I'd look a little more's I did when I married yeh."

Ripley gave it up in despair. He didn't realize fully enough how the proposed trip had unsettled his wife's nerves. She didn't realize it herself.

"As for the hotel bills, they won't be none. I ain't agoin' to pay them pirates as much for a day's board as we'd charge for a week's, and have nawthin' to eat but dishes. I'm goin' to take a chicken an' some hard-boiled eggs, an' I'm goin' right through to Georgetown."

"Wal, all right, mother; but here's the ticket I got."

"I don't want yer ticket."

"But you've got to take it."

"Well, I haint."

"Why, yes, ye have. It's bought, an' they won't take it back."

"Won't they?" She was perplexed again.

"Not much they won't. I ast 'em. A ticket sold is sold."

"Wal, if they won't—"

"You bet they won't."

"I s'pose I'll haff to use it." And that ended it.

They were a familiar sight as they rode down the road toward town next day. As usual, Mrs. Ripley sat up straight and stiff as "a half-drove wedge in a white-oak log." The day was cold and raw. There was some snow on the ground, but not enough to warrant the use of sleighs. It was "neither sleddin' nor wheelin'." The old people sat on a board laid across the box, and had an old quilt or two drawn up over their knees. Tewksbury lay in the back part of the box (which was filled with hay), where he jounced up and down, in company with a queer old trunk and a brand-new imitation-leather hand-bag.

There is no ride quite so desolate and uncomfortable as a ride in a lumber-wagon on a cold day in autumn, when the ground is frozen, and the wind is strong and raw with threatening snow. The wagon-wheels grind along in the snow, the cold gets in under the seat at the calves of one's legs, and the ceaseless bumping of the bottom of the box on the feet is almost intolerable.

There was not much talk on the way down, and what little there was related mainly to certain domestic regulations, to be strictly followed, regarding churning, pickles, pancakes, etc. Mrs. Ripley wore a shawl over her head, and carried her queer little black bonnet in her hand. Tewksbury was also wrapped in a shawl. The boy's teeth were pounding together like castanets by the time they reached Cedarville, and every muscle ached with the fatigue of shaking.

After a few purchases they drove down to the station, a frightful little den (common in the West), which was always too hot or too cold. It happened to be hot just now—a fact which rejoiced little Tewksbury.

"Now git my trunk *stamped,* 'r *fixed,* 'r whatever they call it," she said to Ripley, in a commanding tone, which gave great delight to the inevitable crowd of loafers beginning to assemble. "Now remember, Tukey, have grandad kill that biggest turkey night before Thanksgiving, an' then you run right over to Mis' Doudney's—she's got a nawful tongue, but she can bake a turkey first-rate—an' she'll fix up some squash-pies for yeh. You can warm up one o' them mince-pies. I wish ye could be with me, but ye can't; so do the best ye can."

Ripley returning now, she said: "Wal, now, I've fixed things up the best I could. I've baked bread enough to last a week, an' Mis' Doudney has promised to bake for yeh—"

"I don't like her bakin'."

"Wal, you'll haff to stand it till I get back, 'n' you'll find a jar o' sweet pickles an' some crab-apple sauce down suller, 'n' you'd better melt up brown sugar for 'lasses, 'n' for goodness' sake don't eat all them mince-pies up the fust week, 'n' see that Tukey ain't froze goin' to school. An' now you'd better get out for home. Good-by! an' remember them pies."

As they were riding home, Ripley roused up after a long silence.

"Did she—a—kiss you good-by, Tukey?"

"No, sir," piped Tewksbury.

"Thunder! didn't she?" After a silence: "She didn't me, neither. I guess she kind a' sort a' forgot it, bein' so flustrated, y' know."

One cold, windy, intensely bright day, Mrs. Stacey, who lives about two miles from Cedarville, looking out of the window, saw a queer little figure struggling along the road, which was blocked here and there with drifts. It was an old woman laden with a good half-dozen parcels, which the wind seemed determined to wrench from her.

She was dressed in black, with a full skirt, and her cloak being short, the wind had excellent opportunity to inflate her garments and sail her off occasionally into the deep snow outside the track, but she held out bravely till she reached the gate. As she turned in, Mrs. Stacey cried:

"Why! it's Gran'ma Ripley, just getting back from her trip. Why! how do you do? Come in. Why! you must be nearly frozen. Let me take off your hat and veil."

"No, thank ye kindly, but I can't stop," was the given reply. "I must be gittin' back to Ripley. I expec' that man has jest let ev'rything go six ways f'r Sunday."

"Oh, you *must* sit down just a minute and warm."

"Wal, I will; but I've got to git home by sundown sure. I don't s'pose they's a thing in the house to eat," she said solemnly.

"Oh, dear! I wish Stacey was here, so he could take you home. An' the boys at school—"

"Don't need any help, if 't wa'nt for these bundles an' things. I guess I'll just leave some of 'em here, an'— Here! take one of these apples. I brought 'em from Lizy Jane's suller, back to Yaark State."

"Oh! they're delicious! You must have had a lovely time."

"Pretty good. But I kep' thinkin' of Ripley

an' Tukey all the time. I s'pose they have had a gay time of it'' (she meant the opposite of gay). ''Wal, as I told Lizy Jane, I've had my spree, an' now I've got to git back to work. They ain't no rest for such as we are. As I told Lizy Jane, them folks in the big houses have Thanksgivin' dinners every day of their lives, and men an' women in splendid clo's to wait on 'em, so 't Thanksgivin' don't mean anything to 'em; but we poor critters, we make a great to-do if we have a good dinner onct a year. I've saw a pile o' this world, Mrs. Stacey—a pile of it! I didn't think they was so many big houses in the world as I saw b'tween here an' Chicago. Wal, I can't set here gabbin'.'' She rose resolutely. ''I must get home to Ripley. Jest kind o' stow them bags away. I'll take two an' leave them three others. Good-by! I must be gittin' home to Ripley. He'll want his supper on time.''

And off up the road the indomitable little figure trudged, head held down to the cutting blast—little snow-fly, a speck on a measureless expanse, crawling along with painful breathing, and slipping, sliding steps— ''Gittin' home to Ripley an' the boy.''

Ripley was out to the barn when she entered, but Tewksbury was building a fire in the old cook-stove. He sprang up with a cry of joy, and ran to her. She seized him and kissed him, and it did her so much good she hugged him close, and kissed him again and again, crying hysterically.

"Oh, gran'ma, I'm so glad to see you! We've had an awful time since you've been gone."

She released him, and looked around. A lot of dirty dishes were on the table, the table-cloth was a "sight to behold" (as she afterward said), and so was the stove—kettle-marks all over the table-cloth, splotches of pancake batter all over the stove.

"Wal, I sh'd say as much," she dryly assented, untying her bonnet-strings.

When Ripley came in she had her regimentals on, the stove was brushed, the room swept, and she was elbow-deep in the dish-pan. "Hullo, mother! Got back, hev yeh?"

"I sh'd say it was about *time,*" she replied curtly, without looking up or ceasing work. "Has ol' 'Crumpy' dried up yit?" This was her greeting.

Her trip was a fact now; no chance could rob her of it. She had looked forward twenty-three years toward it, and now she could look back at it accomplished. She took up her burden again, never more thinking to lay it down.

MOTHER MARTIN'S WING *

Christine Whiting Parmenter

MOTHER MARTIN stood at her window and smiled as she looked across the campus to the big assembly hall. Through its wide doorway groups of men were passing whose voices rang out in jovial greetings. It was a reunion of the class of '93—her own boys, they seemed, who had come under her wing as freshmen—little boys then, too young, she thought, to be sent away from home; but they had found a mother in the matron at Durban Hall.

It seemed incredible that so many years had passed since she saw them graduate, no longer the homesick laddies she had mothered, but fine, big, strapping fellows, ready for college—and for life. Some of them had forgotten her, perhaps; but there were very few who ever passed through Holden without dropping in for a chat about old times. They would not forget her today. Mother Martin smoothed the folds of her best black silk, and turned, as the door opened without the courtesy of a knock. Could it be—

* Reprinted by special permission of the author.

No, it was only the new matron, her successor. Miss Gibbs fairly bristled with efficiency.

"Shall you be here this morning, Mrs. Martin?" she asked crisply.

"Yes; some of—"

She was about to explain that some of "the boys" would be dropping in; but Miss Gibbs interrupted hurriedly: "Will you look out for Brigham? He promised to clean up that fudge immediately after class. If he doesn't come, I shall report him. He's the most careless— Well, of course, you can't take any stock in their promises, but—"

"Harry's a good boy," broke in Mother Martin. Two bright red spots burned on her wrinkled cheeks. "He's never been taught to be careful, having so many servants in his home to pick up after him."

"Well, he'll learn to be careful here," snapped Miss Gibbs. "You tell him he'll be expelled if he doesn't mind. Now I must run along. You won't forget?"

"I'm not apt to forget," said Mother Martin.

The door closed, and she sank down wearily, oppressed by a sense of things gone wrong. For more than a quarter of a century this had been her home. Now she must leave it. The old president, who had understood, was dead; and the new one was so terribly efficient—like Miss Gibbs. They didn't know that homesick little boys needed mothering. They didn't understand that one must love a boy if one is to reach his heart. There was Harry Brigham, who had spilt the fudge and walked in it. He came from a home where love was absent. He was a little hard for a boy, a little boastful, perhaps; but he had good qualities. When Mother Martin was sick he had spent his allowance for a plant, a wonderful climbing rose in a gilt basket! He was generous, and could be made a man of; but if one did not *trust* him—

Mother Martin looked with dim eyes across the campus. She loved its maples towering against the sky. Some of them she had watched grow from saplings into big, sheltering trees. She loved the ivy-covered buildings. She had rejoiced as heartily as any boy in the wonderful new gymnasium. This was home—the only home she had known since that black week when she had buried her own two boys and was left alone. There had followed terrible days for the lonely little widow; and then the old president, who understood, had brought her here.

And she had never been lonely since—she had not had time! There were so many boys who needed her. How could she leave them? She was an old woman, yet inwardly she felt as young as ever. It would be terrible to go away, even with the generous pension they had given her.

A slamming door, and, "Harry!" called Mother Martin.

"Yes'm?"

A boy appeared, his hair tumbled, eyes shining.

"Those old reunion guys are going to play the seniors! It'll be bully fun. I—"

"Have you cleaned up that fudge?" asked Mother Martin.

His face clouded, rebelliously.

"There's not time. I wouldn't miss that game for anything."

"But Miss Gibbs said—"

"Oh, *her!"* His voice was bitter, not like a little boy's. Then his eyes brightened. "I'll tell Carrie. She'll do it for fifty cents."

"And get into trouble when Miss Gibbs finds out?"

"She'll never know."

"But that would be deceiving her, my boy."

"Who cares? She—she's an old *pill!* You know it, Mother Martin."

Yes, she knew it; but she managed to say sternly, "You mustn't speak that way about the matron. How soon's the game?"

"In twenty minutes. I gotter go. I—"

"You promised, didn't you?"

Under her serene gaze the boy flushed.

"Yep—but—"

"A gentleman keeps his word, Harry; but of

course you must see that game." She was pinning up the skirt of her best black silk. "Skip up, sonny. I'll help, and we'll be through in no time."

Fifteen minutes later, back in her own domain, Mother Martin hastily unpinned her skirt and pushed a tell-tale scrubbing cloth behind a drapery, just as Miss Gibbs came in. She felt as guilty as any criminal as the matron said, "Did Brigham come?"

"Yes. He's at the game now; but he cleaned the rug."

"Well, I *am* surprised! But I dare say it's not half done. If I find— Oh! there's the telephone!"

Mother Martin drew a breath of relief and, stepping out onto the porch, watched the men and boys hurrying toward the ball field. In the distance she could not see their faces, but when one of them waved a greeting to her she responded joyously.

"That's Milton Treavor," she mused thoughtfully, as he disappeared around a corner of the gym. "I know him by the limp. The doctor said he'd outgrow it, but he never did. Poor little lad! I remember how it discouraged him; but he wouldn't give in to it! There was good stuff in Milton. And now he's president of a railroad! Dear me! It seems like yesterday. . . ."

For a time she was lost in dreams, while from the distance was wafted the sound of voices, cheers, laughter, familiar sounds to one who lives in a boys' school. They were a part of life itself to Mother Martin. She waved to a senior who passed on a bicycle, bound for the ball field. She watched two freshmen hurrying across the campus in the same direction. A big boy paused at the gate to greet her. "Going to the game?" he questioned. "Oh, come on, Mother Martin! Be a sport!"

She chuckled as he continued on his way. That was Lester Grant. His father was one of her boys, too. Good boys both of them. They'd never given her any trouble, though they were ring-leaders in every shindig that occurred, especially Lester the elder. Let's see—what year was it that he graduated? Oh, yes, of course! It was the year that Skinny Edridge filled all the ink wells with coffee on April Fool's Day. Skinny was Lester's room-mate, and a team they were! The class of '93—that was it—Leonard's class.

Leonard Van Ander! Mother Martin closed her eyes a moment, the better to visualize the past. She saw him clearly: the dark-eyed, black-haired, handsome little boy. Quick to anger, was Leonard, but quick, also, to forgive. Hot-headed, impulsive, generous to a fault, and so sensitive that an unjust reproof cut him to the heart. . . .

A wild cheer arose from the ball field, but

Mother Martin heard it only subconsciously. She had slipped back more than twenty years. The campus was no longer sunny, but wet and rain-washed. The big maple by the house of the old president was no longer big—not big enough to hide the slim young figure that skulked behind it as Mother Martin raised her umbrella and started home. At the gate she paused when a flash of lightning brightened the whole scene. The thunder drowned her involuntary cry, a cry not at fear of the storm, but fear of what she read in the passionate young face that the lightning had revealed.

Well, *that* was over! She opened her eyes again and breathed deeply of the soft air. "All's well that ends well," she thought happily; and Leonard Van Ander had just received the appointment of professor of history at Holden. Only yesterday she had listened proudly to the words of the new president. He was glad, he said, to introduce to the students "one who had lived as he hoped they all would live—a Holden man himself, whose record held nothing to regret—the sort of man that should be typical of Holden and its fine traditions: Professor Leonard Van Ander of the class of '93."

Mother Martin had thrilled at the words! During the applause that followed she had rapped the floor so vigorously with her umbrella that Miss Gibbs had turned to throw her a reproving glance. But Mother Martin did not see it. She was leaning forward tensely, the offending umbrella already quiet, listening to the few modest words that fell from the lips of the new professor—*her boy!*

Mother Martin slowly turned and went back to her own room. It had been built for a reception-room, and stood at the right of the front door. Years before she had taken it for hers, in order more easily to keep track of the boys who came and went. Her door was rarely closed. Her work basket stood beside her chair, ever ready for the fastening of a suddenly loose button, or a torn shirt. It was a room fragrant with memories for many an important man today. Its owner stooped to remove the evidence of a scrubbing cloth largely smeared with chocolate, and started nervously at a step. Then, "Oh, Leonard, it's only you!"

The new professor laughed; yet his eyes were troubled.

"What you been up to, Mother Martin? You act like a boy caught stealing jam." Then he saw the cloth, and grinned. "Been doing somebody's dirty work again?"

She put a silencing finger on her lips. "No; I only helped. Harry had promised; but that game came up, and it wasn't human nature for a boy to do housecleaning just then."

"I see," said Professor Van Ander.

He walked to the window uneasily; then turned.

"Mother Martin—I've just heard."

"Heard what, sonny?"

"That you're leaving us. The place won't be the same without you. Do—do you *want* to go?"

She sank down into her big chair, and he saw her lips tremble.

"*Want* to?" was all she said.

"Then why—"

She smiled, a smile that seemed to the man more pitiful than tears. "It's only the tragedy of old age, sonny. It comes to most of us. I suppose I've outgrown my . . . usefulness."

"Bosh!"

The professor tramped angrily across the room. His face was grim. It reminded Mother Martin of that rain-swept night so long ago . . . in this very room. . . . What a struggle she had had! And now— But Van Ander stopped before her.

"I'll *do* something about it, Mother Martin."

"No! No!" She sprang up, her hand upon his arm. "You mustn't, Leonard. You're new here. The president would resent your interference; the trustees would think you a sentimentalist. They may be right. I guess I'm not very—efficient."

"Efficient!"

Again that scowl, reminding her so forcibly of

the boy. Then his face softened. "Now don't you worry. Perhaps—"

They were interrupted by shouts from without. The whole school, it seemed, was thronging from the ball field. Mother Martin, as excited as any boy, hurried out to the porch, and as she was surrounded by a crowd of youngsters Professor Van Ander slipped away.

"But you see, Van Ander, we must consider the good of the school." It was the new president who spoke. "She's an old woman. She has no discipline—"

Van Ander raised his head. "If by discipline, you mean harshness, tale-bearing, reporting a boy for some thoughtless carelessness, I grant you're right; but ask any one, from the freshmen of to-day to the men in that class of '93, who were her first boys, if one of them ever told a lie to Mother Martin. There is something better, more character-building, than discipline, Doctor McCallum."

There came a silence; then the president said, a bit uncomfortably, "We are giving her a generous pension."

Van Ander shrugged, and a gleam of anger shot through the president's gray eyes.

"As it happens, Van Ander," he explained, "her room is needed. The freshmen have no suitable assembly hall. Elaborate plans are made to include that room in a new wing, which will give the younger boys a place to get together. This will be built as soon as we can finance it, and no other part of the building can be added to so advantageously. If Mrs. Martin has implied that we are harsh—"

The president stopped suddenly, because his new professor seemed not to be listening. He had walked to the window and was examining a crack in the left-hand corner of the glass. When he faced about his eyes were alight and eager. He glanced at his watch.

"It is almost lunch-time," he said thoughtfully. "Doctor McCallum, if I agree to raise funds for an addition, a larger, better one than you have planned, opening out of Mrs. Martin's room but not disturbing it, will you consider leaving the old lady where she is?"

The president looked his surprise. "Where could you raise anything?" he temporized. "The alumni have already been bled for the new gymnasium."

Van Ander's handsome lips curved in a smile. "There is one thing," he answered, "that never bleeds quite dry, and that's love for one's mother; and I'll wager, Doctor McCallum, that to many a Holden graduate Mother Martin has filled that place. All I ask is your promise that if I raise the money for that wing, she shall not be disturbed."

"Well," hesitated the president, "if the trustees agree."

It was as the luncheon of the class of '93 was drawing to a close that Professor Van Ander arose from his seat at the faculty table. As he did so, an instant hush fell on the big room, for the professor's reputation as an after-dinner speaker was an enviable thing.

"I have been asked," he began, "to say a few words on the future of Holden; but I have decided to speak about the past. I am going to tell you a story."

Van Ander paused a moment—then he squared his shoulders and went on:

"Some of you were here yesterday, and heard the words with which Doctor McCallum introduced me to the students. For the benefit of those who were absent, I must say (if you are to understand the incentive of this story) that he referred most kindly to my record as a student at Holden. This was correct. There was nothing in that record of which I am ashamed; yet as I arose to speak and looked down into the audience, I saw only one face, a face lined, now, and old, and I knew that it was to Mother Martin I owed that record."

There was a stir of applause, which subsided as Van Ander went on:

"It was in my sophomore year. Perhaps some

of you remember me as a hot-headed youngster. I had a temper which, until I came to Holden, no one had taught me to control. I resented going to boarding-school because I knew, with the uncanny instincts of a child, that my father, who was an invalid, was sending me away in order to get rid of me. I had no mother.

"I was abnormally sensitive. A fancied slight would hurt for weeks. An unmerited reproof was not forgotten; and on this special day I had been reproved severely—held up to ridicule, indeed, for something I had not done.

"I must say, in defense of our old president, that it was, I think, his first mistake of the sort, and I know it to be his last. But to me it was—tragedy! I burned to 'get even,' to do something that would hurt *him*. Boy-like I lived through imaginary scenes in which I was the victor; but, boy-like to the end, I resorted to quite primitive methods of revenge."

Van Ander smiled, and a ripple of merriment swept his audience as they too remembered old experiences.

"It was at this time," he continued, "that plate-glass windows were considered the last touch in elegance. In the president's house the old front windows had been removed, and were replaced by large sheets of clear plate glass. When the job was finished it was discovered that one of the windows in the president's study had been damaged, and that a crack marred the left-hand corner of the glass. It is still there! I saw it only this morning. The president was much disturbed about it. I heard him say so, which gave me the idea for my revenge. If he cared so much about that crack, what would he do if every shining pane were smashed!''

Van Ander paused for a sip of water, and some one called impatiently, ''Go on, Van. We didn't know you had it in you!''

The professor smiled as he continued: ''Everything favored my plans. It was an easy matter to collect the suitable ammunition and leave it in a convenient spot. My idea was to wait till lights were out, descend via the trellis that adjoined my window, do my deadly work, and escape before any one could get down-stairs. To aid me, a thunderstorm was brewing, and my room-mate had been called home. In my eagerness to begin, however, I arrived too soon; and as I reached the big maple the door of the president's house opened, and out came—Mother Martin!

''She came,'' continued Van Ander, ''simultaneously with the loudest crack of thunder I have ever heard. It would have been an ideal time for smashing windows! As it was, the lightning brightened the whole campus, and she saw me. I was furiously angry; but you remember how it was with Mother Martin. If I'd run she'd have followed; and there was no use lying. There was nothing to do but surrender, which I did, very ungracefully, I fear.

"She took me to her room, that same room where I saw her putting iodine on a boy's bruised knee last evening. She closed the door and lowered the shades before she turned on a light. She wasn't going to give me away, anyhow. I can see her now, as she said quietly, 'Suppose you tell me about it, sonny.'

"And I didn't answer. I wasn't, even then, angry with Mother Martin, but angry at the fate that had frustrated my plans. So I refused to speak. I must have looked more like a thunder cloud than did those that were rumbling overhead! I sat in her big chair, a prisoner, my lips closed tight; and at last she went to her cupboard and got the cookie jar (you all remember it!), set it conveniently within my reach, and sat down to read."

Van Ander smiled in reminiscence. "She read," he continued, "or pretended to, for eighteen minutes. I watched the clock. By that time the cookies had done their salutary work. But it took her an hour to get the story out of me, and another to show me that revenge is not so sweet as it is painted. It was, I think, the turning point in my life. She gave me the finest sermon on character that was ever preached. She showed me what the letting-go of one's temper may lead to; and that reproof, if unmerited, is no shame to him who receives it. She made me promise to go to the president in the morning and tell him everything; and then, though it was past midnight, she went out into the storm again and waited at the foot of the trellis till I had safely climbed back to my room. She was a sport to the last minute, as she always was!"

There came a murmur, a smothered cheer from the listening men; but Van Ander silenced them with an upraised hand.

"You are wondering, perhaps, why I have told this story. If you will give me a moment more. . . ."

In a few well-chosen words he told them of Mother Martin's impending fate. Briefly he sketched the need of a new assembly hall, told of the promise the president had made him, and his own idea of having the new wing open into Mother Martin's room, so that she might sit there and watch her boys. "And if there is one of you here," he ended, "who has no tender memory of her, who is not, perhaps, a better man because of her, we shall not ask his help. . . . We shall not *need* it."

There followed a silence, so long that the president stirred uneasily. He did not know that the men before him were no longer lawyers, doctors, professors, ministers, and business men. One and all, they were, for the moment, little boys again. Memories long dormant were flooding back. Then one of them, a fat man who had looked bored through the whole proceeding, sprang up, and emptying the contents of a silver cake basket upon the table, threw into it a roll of bills.

"There goes friend wife's anniversary present," he grinned good-naturedly. "Come on, boys! Not while we live shall Mother Martin be turned out!"

He was moving slowly down the room, cake basket in hand. There was an emptying of bill-folders, a scratching of fountain pens.

"There goes my new automobile!" laughed a Boston banker.

"Here! Take my trip to Bermuda with you," said another.

"I guess I can give up my new motor boat," declared a third; while in a far corner, lost to the world, a famous railroad president was remembering a gentle hand that had, on many a long-gone night, rubbed the pain from a leg that had never been quite right, rubbed till the tired eyes of a discouraged boy had closed in sleep.

As the basket, bulging with bills, and checks, and I O U's, was laid down before Van Ander, the railroad president arose. Slowly, limping decidedly, because he was very tired, he moved forward and laid a check on the top of that overflowing pile. Van Ander, glancing down, started visibly at the figures that met his eyes. They meant, those figures, that Mother Martin would live out her days among the boys she loved. He started to speak, then stopped, for the railroad magnate had raised his voice.

"I think," he said, "that we owe a vote of thanks to Van Ander for giving us this opportunity to pay, ever so slightly, a debt that we all owe. And if I may make a suggestion, it would be that the new addition be called 'Mother Martin's Wing.' What name could be more appropriate, since it is a gift from the men who were welcomed beneath that wing as homesick little boys? Indeed, I doubt if we have ever left its shelter."

For a moment the room was very still, so still that the song of a bird drifted in through the open windows; and in that moment understanding came to the new president in a blinding flash. Van Ander was right. There was "something better, more character-building, than discipline." These men had proved it. He started to rise. He would tell them. . . .

But the president was never to make that speech. The rising tide of cheers could be suppressed no longer. It rose, and rose again, carrying across the campus to where a little old lady sat rocking gently on the porch of Durban Hall. She smiled at the sound and, as is the way of those who have lived for others, her own troubles were forgotten.

"What a good time the boys are having!" she said happily. "I wonder whom they're cheering now."

MOTHER GETS BACK ON THE JOB*

Bess Streeter Aldrich

NUMBER FOUR (the ten-o'clock passenger) wheezed tardily, like an asthmatic old man, up to the Meadows station, and pulled out as soon as three people had alighted in the dark and the rain.

From this statement you will no doubt deduct that Meadows, the abode of the Cutters, was not a city. And you will be quite right. It was a small town in one of the Mid-West States, where there are almost as many hogs as automobiles. It had some pleasant homes, a good school, five churches, and a few blocks of stores.

The street on which the stores faced was called by an extremely common name. No one was ashamed of this, for everyone knew that a few thousand famous folks had come out of similar towns. And Nazareth was not metropolitan. It is quite possible that the street which runs on

* Reprinted from "The Cutters," by Bess Streeter Aldrich. Copyright, 1926, by D. Appleton & Company, New York. By special permission of the publisher.

either side of the tree of life whose leaves are for the healing of the nations is called Main.

One third of the incoming passengers this drizzling night was Nell Cutter. The Meadows "Mirror" in its next issue would say that Mrs. Ed Cutter spent Friday shopping in Dale City. It sounds like a small, uninteresting item. But if you were the mother of four, if you had not been shopping in Dale City for seven months, if in that time your wildest orgies had been two or three kensingtons ("kensington" being the Meadows equivalent of "sewing circle"), the day would have taken on the nature of an event.

Ed Cutter, big and solid and substantial-looking, stood under the eaves of the dripping station holding an umbrella and a flashlight, like a masculine version of the Goddess of Liberty. He grinned a whole-hearted, cheerful welcome at the sight of his trim-looking wife. Many a woman has been met at the pier after a trans-atlantic voyage with less sincere gratitude for her return.

Simultaneously the two said, "Well?" The conversation of long-married people is often carried on in shorthand. By that one lone syllable Ed Cutter meant, "What kind of a day did you have?" and Nell was inquiring, "What has happened at home?" For of course in fourteen hours anything might have happened: broken bones, company, mad dogs—anything.

Ed could think of nothing except that the Ball administrator had come to have him start probating the old man's will, and they had had new peas for dinner.

But Nell had more than that to tell. In fact, she was full to the bursting point of news and ideas. So as they walked up the street under the soggy elms she did most of the talking. She had been to the Dale City Woman's Club in the afternoon. She had nearly gone to a matinée instead, but very luckily she chose the club. She had heard a Mrs. Johnson Peabody-Mills from the East give an address. It had been wonderful, a perfect inspiration.

Mrs. Peabody-Mills was lecturing under the auspices of some organization, The Order of Perfect Parenthood or Trained Motherhood, or something—Nell wasn't sure of the title. Ed ought to have heard her. She was so pretty and bright and animated . . . the mother of three charming children, too.

Ed made his first masculine inquiry: "Who said they were?"

"Well, *she* did," Nell admitted grudgingly, but added confidently, "I can believe it, though, for their mother was so lovely. And she's brought them up herself . . . no nurse for *her* . . . by what she calls the *reasoning* method. She reasons with them about everything, you know, treats them as though they were mature."

Ed threw his second little dipper of cold water. "Who's got 'em now?" There was a suggestion of ice in the water.

"Well, of course, a nurse, a *trained* nurse, has them just now—" Nell was a little provoked at Ed—"while their mother makes this Western trip. But she's only out this way because it seemed her *duty* to help other mothers."

Nell sensed that Ed's logical mind was noting a fragile plank in the lady's platform, so she hurried on: "She was *very* much opposed to corporeal punishment. She made it so clear. It just made me *sick* to think I'd ever spanked the children. She gave illustrations of the workings of the child mind, and they sounded so reasonable. She said we seem to children just like monstrous animals when we punish them, and of course it must be true. I'd really known most of the things she said, for I had child-study in college. But one gets slack, and she certainly brought it all back to me. Ed, I know that with patience and reasoning I won't need ever to touch the children again. I'm going to start right to-morrow and be more patient, and treat them as though they were *reasoning* beings."

Ed was quite willing. He was one of those good, substantial American fathers who look very thoroughly after the ways of their business but who are rather like guests in their own home. Josephine adored him, the baby cried after him, and he was his boys' boon companion. But it was their mother who really made them toe the mark.

"And here's something I forgot to tell you." Nell was all animation. "That new Mrs. Ramsey attended the meeting, too, and she and I together succeeded in getting Mrs. Peabody-Mills's promise to come out here next Thursday and speak to our own club. It will be such a treat and such help to these small-town mothers."

They were on the last block now and the light shone in the windows of home. Nell hastened her steps unconsciously. That low, rambling house set well back in the big yard was her world.

There are people who say the lives of such women are narrow. They are not narrow. They are as wide as sympathy and as broad as love. They reach from the depths of little graves to the end of the stars. A person may encircle the globe with mind open only to bodily comfort. Another may live his life on a sixty-foot lot and listen to the voices of the universe. As a man thinketh in his heart, so is he!

In the house Nell went immediately, without removing her hat, to the room where the baby slept. She bent over him, listened to his breathing, dropped a kiss on his fat hand and removed a little quilt. Gramma in her anxiety over his welfare had covered him too warmly.

Then she stepped into Josephine's room. By

the light of the living-room she could see her daughter sleeping, a pair of ten-cent earrings, large, turkey-red, flamboyant, screwed on her ears, a mirror fallen from her relaxed hand. The eternal feminine, sympathized the mother.

From there she went to the boys' room. There they both were, apparently with the required number of arms and legs. It was further noticeable that the pair resembled a white boy and a mulatto. Craig was obviously a well-scrubbed Anglo-Saxon. Nick she recognized from his general size and appearance but not through any definite sight of his features.

The casual onlooker would have been satisfied: one boy had simply gone to bed dirty and one had not. But the sleuthlike instincts of motherhood told her that something was suspiciously wrong in Craig's absolute and unusual cleanliness. She turned the bedclothes down.

"I thought so," she nodded. He had gone to bed in his underclothes, a proceeding he had long threatened, "to save time." Just why he had scrubbed to the point of nearly skinning himself, in the hope of detracting from his misdemeanor, is one of the peculiar and devious twists of the child mind which the mere adult may not follow.

Nell Cutter stood looking down at the sturdy bodies of her little sons. Well, she would be more kind, more just, give them the very best that was in her. Never again would she touch them to punish. Flesh of her flesh, they should have all the chance in the world to grow into reasoning and reasonable creatures, their initiative developed, their originality directed.

For two or three days the Cutter household ran along fairly well. Even a thrown wagon wheel stays precisely upright from sheer velocity for the distance of a few yards. Then things began to go wrong.

Now, it becomes necessary to insert here that the Cutter family, due to the various and ardent interests of its offspring, lived in a state of perpetual enthusiasms. Whether other children were as changeable as her own, Nell Cutter did not know. What she did know was that the members of her tribe would live for a period with the most impassioned eagerness for some cause, think of nothing, talk of nothing but its immediate interest only to have that interest quite suddenly die down and flicker out like the last feeble sizzle of a piece of punk.

They rode on waves of excitement, as it were, with each wave a different interest. Their lives were one constant crescendo and diminuendo. A diagram of their enthusiasms would have looked like a government chart of temperatures, or an erratic grain market.

It worried their mother. "What shall we do about it, Ed?" she would complain. "They remind me of an old Mr. Hensley who used to live near us when I was a girl. I *know* he changed occupations oftener than he did his shirt."

"Oh, boys are like that," was the head-of-the-family's complacent rejoinder. "I guess a boy's will is going to be the wind's will as long as there are boys."

Just that spring there had been a prolonged enthusiasm for maple sap on the part of the sons of Cutter. The boys had tapped their own trees, borrowed the use of others from the more generous of the neighbors, and rented a few from one youthful Shylock. They had taken every kind of receptacle from the house which a long-suffering mother would allow, and a few which escaped her eagle eye. In the midst of this inundation of maple liquid they heard about a boy who made a vast fortune (or was about to make a vast fortune) by selling bluing. And, presto! the unemptied sap pails dripped clammily on passers-by while the erstwhile maple-sugar merchants pored over enticing literature about the bluing market.

This indigo-hued adventure had been succeeded by one mighty enthusiasm for keeping chickens. The boys had worked diligently on the chicken fence, and gone through the hazardous feat of purchasing four old hens and setting them. They fairly camped by them through the incubation period and for a few weeks watched over the lively results with rapt attention. Then, lo! the boys of the neighborhood started a baseball team, and the daily conversation dropped with a dull thud from eggs and grit and chick feed to bats and base hits and home runs. Once more had a Cutter enthusiasm died an unnatural death.

So in the days that followed Nell Cutter's return from Dale City she found her greatest task consisted in getting the boys to attend dutifully to the discarded chickens. "Cut your grass now for the chickens," she would tell them a dozen times a day, to be met with a volley of excuses.

On Monday following her trip she reminded them patiently of their duty. For several quarter-hour stretches she reasoned with them collectively and individually. With alacrity each always assured her that it was the other one's turn. By night, when the grass had been finally amputated from its roots, she was worn out.

On Tuesday, after more philosophical reasoning, gentle persuasion, and patient inducements, the boys put forth feeble efforts to cast some grass into the chicken yard. There were fifty chickens, but the total clover and blue-grass crop that day consisted of a handful that would have fitted comfortably into Nell's best cut-glass vase.

On Wednesday there was no grass cut at all, approximately one third of the day being given over to heated discussions concerning whose turn it was to perform the stupendous task.

Thursday was club day. It turned out to be unusually hot, one of those humid days known in the Mid-West as "cracking good corn weather." Opal Peterson had gone to her church picnic. Concurrent with this state of affairs, Josephine developed a tragedy-air aversion to assisting with the work. Instead, she spent half the morning ransacking every isolated nook and corner in the vain endeavor to find a pocket-book containing real and personal property to the extent of fourteen cents, which she frankly and unhesitatingly accused the boys of taking. They, in turn, dragged from their hiding places various and sundry recollections of evil things Josephine had done to them in the past. Altogether pandemonium reigned in the usual semi-peaceful, if noisy, household.

The time between dinner and club consisted of one hundred and fifty of the most strenuous minutes Nell Cutter had ever put in. Added to her other duties she had to assist Gramma to get into her new white dress, as Gramma was going to the club meeting, too. After a display of temper Josephine grudgingly wiped dishes and promised to take care of the baby while they were gone. Then Nell began again on the question of cutting grass. "It's too hot now," the boys wailed, but they would do it soon; in fact, they would do it while she was at the club. It would be in the chicken yard, honest it would, a scad of it, when she got back.

As they talked fluently, volubly, their mother surveyed them as with the eye of a stranger. They were dirty. They had on soiled waists and overalls. They wore disgusting red handkerchiefs around their necks and tin revolvers protruded from sagging hip pockets. When she insisted on a rigorous cleaning before she departed, they refused peremptorily to change their blissful state of hobodom. She felt too tired to combat their robust wills.

When Nell and Gramma arrived at the club meeting, Mrs. Johnson Peabody-Mills was already there under the ponderous escort of the new Mrs. Ramsey. Yes, indeed, Mrs. Mills remembered Mrs. Cutter and the interest which she had taken in child psychology. Nell thought a little wearily that much water had flowed under the bridge since she had last listened to Mrs. Mills. Also much grass had grown . . . and was *still growing.*

She sat down wearily in one corner and looked over the room. Others besides herself looked tired. Mrs. Horner and Minnie Raymond. She wondered how they managed their children. Little Mrs. Marks was there with Jimmie, Junior. She looked fagged, too. Jimmie kept whining and mauling his mother's hair and nose. Mrs.

Ramsey looked fresh. Well, *she* didn't have any children. . . . And Mrs. Parkham and Charlotte Gray-Cooper, . . . they were merry and vivacious. Yes, it was children and the attendant responsibility that took the pep out of one.

Mrs. Ramsey introduced Mrs. Johnson Peabody-Mills and the lecture was on. But to Nell Cutter, sitting there and listening to it for a second time, it seemed to have lost its flavor. It was no longer a sparkling, humorous, decisive thing. The words seemed far off and meaningless.

The speaker made the same sprightly references to the older generation and its haphazard methods. She spoke of the dignity of labor, and ridiculed people who failed to give their children a few light tasks to perform. She wittily traced the thoughts of a small child when attacked by a giant parent with a switch. She spoke pathetically of keeping down a child's originality and initiative by constant watchfulness over him. She referred often and glibly to the theory of making the punishment fit the crime. Wearily Nell Cutter wondered just what punishment fit that uncut grass.

At the conclusion the speaker asked lightly, pleasantly, whether any one had anything to add. Her words welcomed further remarks, but her tone expressed finality. It was as though it conveyed the idea that there *was* nothing more to say.

Nell glanced around the room at the impassive faces and it was then that she noticed Gramma. Gramma was pale, and she was getting up. She must be sick from the heat. Nell started to rise, too. Then she sat down suddenly, weakly. Gramma was addressing the speaker; Gramma, who had never belonged to any organization but her church, who had said apologetically just before they started to the club, "Nell, just what *is* psychology?"

And now she was speaking: "Will you let an old woman who has never done anything for the advancement of the world, who has just kept house and had eight babies, say a word or two?"

Mrs. Johnson Peabody-Mills was most gracious. She raised her aristocratic-looking eyebrows questioningly and smiled. If her smile was rather too saccharine in quality, simple-hearted Gramma was unmindful of it.

"Not for the world would I want you to feel I'm being discourteous to you about your views," Gramma was saying. "But somehow, sitting here, I felt like I must explain a little to you about us older mothers. If it was just for myself I'd let it pass. But the others who ain't here, someway they seemed to be whispering to me to talk for them, urging me to get up and sort of take their parts before you younger women, who have had so many more advantages.'' She was still pale and her lips were trembling a little from the embarrassment of the unusual thing she was doing. But she went bravely on:

''Now, I don't want to stand here and find fault with the times. I've seen a boy of mine, who was fast losing blood from an accidental gunshot wound, put into a lumber wagon to be hauled to town because there were no autos. I've suffered the pains of childbirth all alone in the house with three other babies, while my husband was racing through the storm for help because there were no telephones. I've buried two little girls in one grave—dead with diphtheria—because the doctors had never heard of antitoxin. So I'd be ashamed to say anything against progress.''

Gramma paused a moment and, perhaps sensing a sympathy among her listeners, went on more easily. ''I've been a pioneer twice. When I was ten we left our old home and journeyed West with oxen and teams. There are events in that trip that stand out clearer than recent happenings. I have only to smell the pungent odor of burning spruce and hemlock, and it calls up the vision of all of us children playing around the wagons, the teams munching the grass in an open space near by, the supper cooking over the open fire against the dark pines of the woods and the sun going down in a glimmer of gold."

Every one was listening attentively. There was something majestic about the picture Gramma was drawing.

"Then, when I was in my twenties," she went on, "and the mother of two babies, we moved on again to the West. I've gathered my babies up to me and prayed that we'd get through the night without the Indians coming. I've lived in a sod house and shared the last of our family supplies with rough strangers. I've seen the grasshoppers take all our crops and a tornado lay every building low. I've seen the raw prairie with its long wild grass turn to mellow farm land and towns and cities. I've seen saplings grow to giant trees, and little boys to manhood."

"How could Gramma do it?" thought Nell. Why, it sounded dignified, regal—like the Psalms. Nell had a swift vision of Ed's mother going quietly to her room every day to read a Book. Gramma had, indeed, associated with good literature.

"With all this for the setting of our home life," the elderly woman continued, "we bore and brought up our children. We had our children work, not because we had theories that a little work is good for them, but because we had to eat to live, and it was absolute and sometimes cruel necessity that made every child have tasks to perform. For punishment, we couldn't keep their spending money from them; for, you see, none of us had any. We couldn't deny them much in the way of candy and sweets, for Christmas and Fourth of July were about the only times we had those things. The children worked hard and studied hard and played hard when there was time left over. And when they disobeyed they were punished. Someway, I never looked upon punishment as breaking the self-reliance of a child. I never dreamed that it was contrary to the best interest of the child mind. I thought of it as their first lesson in law and order and justice."

Gramma looked appealingly at the speaker . . . humbly . . . as though seeking forgiveness for the things she had done, as though asking mercy for the things she had left undone.

The speaker filled the gap graciously, as one who was trained in the ways of diplomacy. "And your children?" She might have been sincere and she might have been merely covering the slight embarrassment of the moment with a perfunctory question. "Your children . . . have they . . . have they turned out well?"

Color had come back now to Gramma's face. The loose skin was covered with a flush that concentrated itself in two vivid pink spots on her wrinkled old cheeks.

"That's a natural question," she answered

quickly, "and a fair one. Yes." Into her brown eyes, windows of a temple in which the altar fires would soon die down to embers, there came a humorous ripple, the same slow drollness, thought Nell, which was so characteristic of Ed. "Yes," she nodded. "I can say honestly that they're real good boys. Eddie, now, he's a lawyer." Unconsciously she was using the old childish names as she began the roll. "Sammie's on the old home-place, and has the best equipped farm for miles around. Joey's pastor of one of the largest churches in Minneapolis. Johnnie's on the faculty of the state university. He's studied at Oxford and written some text-books. Davy's on the staff of one of the Chicago hospitals. He specializes in abdominal surgery. And Bobbie, the rascaliest one of all, Bobbie's the new governor of the state where he was paddled."

Involuntarily every one broke into applause, quick, staccato applause, and high bubbling laughter. It seemed to frighten Gramma. She looked around like a scared child and slipped into her seat behind fat Mrs. Farnham.

There were a few more perfunctory remarks, and the meeting adjourned. Nell edged her way to Gramma to whisper, "Good for you!" And immediately, in the vague fear that Mrs. Peabody-Mills would notice a change in her own manner, she went to her and urged her to come and see her before leaving town. Then, without waiting for the punch and wafers, she slipped out and walked hurriedly home.

Head high and mind clear, she walked determinedly. In fact, she went as one called to the foreign field. As she went up the walk toward the house she saw the boys lolling under an apple-tree. They were still dirty, tangled of hair, and engaged in that most pernicious, mischief-engendering occupation of boyhood—doing nothing. As she went to her bedroom and got out of her pretty foulard dress into a gingham, she could still hear their aimless pushings and slappings and arguments.

Out again to the yard she walked. "Get your cobs in and your grass cut, boys," she said cheerfully, emphatically.

"No," Craig said. "I don't wantta. Nick's gotta. 'Tain't my business!"

"Well, I guess, you crazy-Ike—"

"Boys," said their mother firmly. "Will you start this minute for your cobs and grass?"

"No. I don't wantta . . . Nick's the one."

"No sir-ee, I ain't. Craig's—"

With the same hands that had rocked their cradle and ruled their baby world, Nell Cutter took her two boys by the hindmost seams of their collars. They tried to shake away, but by a strategic move as carefully planned as one of General Foch's, she clutched them tightly.

Straight to the cob house she marched them. There are people who dislike to hear ghastly details. There are censors who cut out grewsome particulars. These people of delicate sensibilities this account is going to offend.

By the simple process of slipping down the civilized garments which covered nature in her primitive garb, this mother began the lurid proceedings. Mrs. Peabody-Mills would have contended that it humiliated the boy's embryonic manhood. Maybe so. Nell Cutter did not stop to debate the psychological effect on futurity. For, friction being the resistance to motion caused by the clashing of two bodies one against the other, this educated, well-read, club-woman mother, with the flat of her good right hand, made friction.

Mrs. Peabody-Mills had said spankings only made children mad. It merely roused their anger. Right she was. The boys were mad. They were madder than hatters and wet hens combined. They ran around and bumped their heads and fought and kicked and said saucy things. And ever and anon as they did so, their mother casually manufactured a little more friction. Physically she was hot. Mentally she was cool as a cucumber. And as she worked she soliloquized: "I'm not a cruel monster. I'm a sensible mother. I'm not angry. But I'm in earnest. And I'm not lazy. I'm the spirit of Eve and Sarah and Rebecca. I'm Columbus' mother and John Wesley's. I'm a Pilgrim mother and Nancy Hanks and Gramma Cutter. I'm Law and Order and Justice."

At the conclusion of the program Nick had his arms around his mother, was clinging tightly to her and crying humble tears. Craig was off in one corner sobbing quietly. Almost the mother was sobbing, too. But not all the brave mothers lived in Sparta.

"Now," she said, "get in your cobs, then cut your grass, and then clean up good and thoroughly."

They ran for the cob basket. They gathered cobs as though a flood were coming to cut off the entire supply. They fed and watered the chickens. They cut grass, great heaping basketsful. Nay, more, they painstakingly swept the walks where they had spilled a few blades.

"Anything more you want, Mama?" they inquired solicitously. *Uriah Heep* was not more humble. They entered the bathroom dirty and unkempt. They came out scrubbed and combed, with clean waists and trousers.

While they had been performing their ablutions, Nell announced to her daughter, "Josephine, set your table. And I might as well tell you that if you argue about it, as big as you are, I'll paddle you, too."

Supper was a pleasant meal. The children

were unargumentative and they were carefully polite.

After supper the entire family gathered on the porch. It was here that Mrs. Ramsey and Mrs. Peabody-Mills found them. Mrs. Mills talked pleasantly and animatedly. She referred to the darling grandmother and her quaint little speech.

"And your own lovely family," she indicated. "Your children are charming. What methods are you employing?"

Nell looked at the boys, playing catch now in the side yard, playing noisily but without dissension. In her mind's eye she could see dull red patches on their posteriors, anatomically speaking. She knew that by means of the Bertillon system a detective would be able to match those spots with the contour of her own right hand.

Then, carefully avoiding Ed's eye, which she sensed would be twinkling, she answered blithely, "I make it a point to choose the best from various systems, so I rather expect it would be called an eclectic method."

THE MOTHER *

Ruth Sawyer

SHE lay in her bed and tried to piece together the things that were happening to her into a pattern that would show something familiar. Not that she was eager to plumb the depths of her experience; it was more a casual wondering, as you wonder about the people and the places you pass in a journey, conscious that you will never really find out about them.

As the wife of a plain, plodding man and the mother of six children, life had doled her an abundance of love, responsibility, and work. She had never learned to live on twenty-four hours a day. She had always been forced to borrow from the day after and had gone about her housework with a rare good cheer, firm in her belief that one day, when the children were older, she would pay back her debt to time and start even. Then there would be a chance of better adjustment. She would have time to think, to read and prepare her mind to keep pace with

* By special permission of the author and of "Good Housekeeping."

the children's; she knew she was doing little more now than feed, clothe, and keep them well. And in the midst of her inveterate borrowing had come this sudden call to the hospital.

For those few hours before her operation she had lain aghast as she went over in her mind the endless list of things left undone. The dishes had been left draining in the pantry—the beds unmade. The mending for the week and the week before lay untouched. Little Bob had no change of underwear; Johnnie was down to his last pair of mended stockings; the three pairs of bloomers Dot needed for school were only cut out, and she hadn't touched Jean's Sunday dress. And the knitting! Skating stockings for the two oldest and mittens all round. The kitchen sink had stopped up the night before, and she had not had time to send for the plumber— And so it went. She worried and gave a hundred futile directions to big Bob, who heard none of them. He was watching her with a white, strained face, thinking of nothing but what was before her. Concerning the operation she had worried not at all, and as they carried her away, she called back more directions to the dazed man still sitting beside her bed:

"The baby's formula is under the clock in the kitchen. Do you hear, dear? And don't forget—if the mending doesn't get done, there are the children's new stockings in the second drawer in the clothes-press, and Jeanie will have to wear her plaid dress to Sunday-school until I—"

The swinging door cut off the last of it, and she turned her head away with a deep rebellion in her heart. Why did Providence let mothers go to pieces inside like an old quilt—just when they were needed most? And the last thing she said to the surgeon was:

"Please don't leave me unfinished like my little girl's new dress. Cut me out, and baste me and sew me, and turn me out all ready for wear as quick as you can."

Very clearly she could recall taking the ether. She could follow herself step by step into oblivion. She could tell almost to the instant when she had reached that wall of blackness through which she had struggled somehow back to a torturing consciousness. But she had been glad to struggle. It was borne in upon her that according to the measure of her will would be meted her chance of returning to the children, and those dishes draining in the pantry, and the stockings with a hole in every knee. So she fought, the face of her husband bending over her, his eyes a silent, steady challenge to a superhuman effort of will and soul. And somewhere, in the dim background of the room, were doctors and nurses doing their bit to help her win the battle that was so absolutely hers.

Suddenly she realized that the struggle was

over. Evidently she had won. She could no longer see her husband, and the nurses and doctors bothered her no more. She closed her eyes, and then had come the wish to piece together all the happenings into something that might seem familiar—something that might prove to her her own reality. She felt strangely free of anxiety for the children and their crying need of her. Dishes and mending and unfinished dresses and stopped-up sinks somehow became trivial and inconsequential. She smiled when she thought of them, and wondered whimsically who had discovered the dust she had left under the rugs downstairs. She had been too sick, the last day she had swept, to take them up—or even fold them back. Did a little dust really matter in the big scheme of things?

Again she felt that sudden dropping away that she had felt with the first whiffs of ether. Was she going to have another operation? Was not the first successful? Would she have to struggle up out of the blackness again, and again fight for her right to go back to her children? She wanted to beg the surgeon to leave her alone, to make big Bob understand, but somehow she could not open her eyes, and their voices came from so many miles away that they would not hear her.

Then came that quick, exhilarating plunge into space. It was like a plunge in the ocean, electrifying and vitalizing. In a strange way she thought of it as a baptism and smiled at the thought. Not for years had she been in the salt water—not since she was a girl—but the memory and the feeling now were the same. She emerged as from a deep sea dive and came up to look upon old, familiar places. Only this was space, not water. She knew that. There were three places that she saw, and they held all the beauty and intimacy that memory had given them.

First came the clump of white birches beside the cascade brook where she had played house when she was a very little girl. There were the three seed cookies, cut star-shape, on the flat rock, and beside them the red astrakhan and lump of sugar that served for daily provisioning. Under the juniper sat her two dolls—Kitty in the lavender silk and Cynthia Jean in the flowered muslin. And across the brook, sitting tailor-fashion, was her playmate washing the dishes left over from yesterday's play. Years had not laid a disturbing finger here, and she found herself waiting for the magic words that always put the spell upon them, "Let's pretend!"

Suddenly she passed beyond the brook and found herself scrambling up the cliffs that overtopped the sea. She was much older, turned seventeen, and having gained the top she threw herself down on the rocks where she could feel the spray on her face and hear the gulls as they screamed above the salmon nets. The sea was hers. Not a schooner or a pleasure yacht to claim it as far as eyes could span the horizon. Her heart was full of a strange, deep longing—a longing for life, the fulness of it. She knew she couldn't understand what life was, only sense it in a dim, far-off way, but she yearned for it, the good and the bad, the sweet and the bitter.

This same yearning was with her now for something beyond her knowledge and experience. It grew like an exquisite pain in her breast, and again she felt spindrift on her cheek and knew she was alone, as she had been alone with the sea.

She passed on to the mountains. It was the morning after her marriage, and she and big Bob were climbing the highest peak. They climbed hand in hand, without speaking. The trail led first through woods that were flecked with sunshine and the golds and reds of fall. The trees were full of birds, but only the jay and chickadee were heard, and every once in a while a rabbit scuttled out of the brush ahead of them. Then the woods gave place to scrub growth, oaks, and spruce. Their feet knocked the dew from the moss and lichen, and at last they came to bare rocks with cairns to mark the trail. They reached the summit, and the wind blew flecks of clouds about them. When the clouds broke, down below them they could see valleys and rivers, houses and people—the whole world below them. She drew in great breaths of the clear air. All sense of tiredness had gone. She was young again, and she turned to her husband for the look that she knew would be waiting her—the look she had found that first morning.

She wanted to tell him how well the years had kept the promise of that day. She wanted him to know, as she knew, that love—the giving and the taking of it—was the only thing in life that counted. It was the only thing you took with you through sickness into space and oblivion. And even as she had it in her mind to tell him, she was swept out and downward, once more, into the all-engulfing blackness of that oblivion.

She felt a hand drawing her slowly back to consciousness. She knew it was not the surgeon's this time, or big Bob's. It felt more like the hand of a mother. When she opened her eyes, it was not the place she saw, but the person whose hand had brought her there. There was a mixture of strangeness and familiarity about the face.

"Were you frightened, Jeanie?"

The words sounded funny. That was what she called little Jean; it was what her mother had called her when she was little.

"Frightened at what?"

"Death."

Then she understood. She looked closer into the face beside her and marveled that she had not known at once it was her mother's.

"How stupid! I thought it was part of the delirium. I was waiting for the struggle to begin again—the struggle— You know?"

"Yes, I know."

"If this is death, then there is no need to fight back?"

"No need."

She was conscious of a sense of freedom—a freedom from habit and restraint, from the needs of others. She had felt this way as a child. "It seems almost absurd, the naturalness of it all. Why does this seem more real than the struggle for life was? That was suffocating. That frightened me."

She bowed her head and covered her face. She wanted to think. She seemed to be losing that sense of freedom almost on the instant of gaining it. She felt herself still in the inevitable grip of life; the realization of her debt to time sickened her. She uncovered her face to see if her mother was still with her, and finding her there, she questioned her.

"How long do we remember? Why do we keep going back to the things that are beyond our reach?"

"You are taking your inventory of life—everybody does. It is like any other journey. When we first start, there is so much that seems necessary to our comfort and peace of mind, but the longer we travel, the less we find that we need."

"But I don't want to bring things with me. All that I want is to set right the things I have left behind."

"So do all mothers."

"Do all mothers leave much undone?"

"Always."

"Then what do dead mothers do?"

"What you are doing—some of them. But there are others who always want to go straight back before they have had time to think. They want to go on directing and advising and caring in the old way. They want to see who is doing what they have left undone, and if they are doing it right. It is always very hard and disappointing for those mothers. I call them the sorrowful ones."

"But can't they help? I should think—"

"There is only one way to help; there is only one bond between the world of the living and the world of the dead."

"Love?"

"Love."

The mother smiled. She had known this long before—she had plunged into the oblivion that divided these two worlds. The only thing that really mattered was leaving love behind. But had she? She wanted to make sure, and with that desire came another. She laid an urgent hand on the figure beside her.

"I want to go back. All my life, since I was married, I have wanted time to play with the children, to sit and listen to them, having nothing in the whole world waiting to be done. Life never gave this to me. Can death? Is it too late?"

"No. Come!"

And so it happened that once again she passed through oblivion and found herself on the road leading home. The things that had been troubling her had dropped from her like an outgrown garment, and her heart was singing like a child's. She knew she need not hurry. For the first time she was climbing the hill with no household duty urging her steps a trifle fast. What was bringing her now would wait for her coming. And as she climbed slowly, she found herself hugging close to her heart the eager happiness that seemed to grow with each step she took.

It was mid-winter, but she felt no cold. The wind blew past her without her feeling it. She saw it flash at the snow-covered boughs of the evergreens, she heard it crack the bare branches of the elms, so she knew it was there. It was delightful to keep about one an abiding calm and peace in the midst of a winter's gale—to pass through it and be unshaken. She smiled again as she remembered the past tiredness that had always climbed with her up the hill when she had to breast such a wind.

She reached her home and entered before she realized she had passed over the threshold. It was late afternoon, and the children were gathered indoors. A fire blazed on the hearth in the living-room—she could catch its reflection in the mirror in the hall—and the first thing she heard was a shout from Johnnie above as he let go the upper stair-railing for a slide down the banisters. He came with a whoop. What a joy it was to stand at the bottom, exulting with him, and not feel that she must forbid it!

Little Jean's voice came in childish accusation from the living-room: "Johnnie—you bad boy! What would mother say?"

"Aw, I don't believe she'd care—not this once."

"I don't, Johnnie, not this once. Only be careful." Her arms were about him as he slipped to the floor.

They entered the room together, her arm thrown across his shoulders, and he was grinning as though he had stumbled on something very near a joke that no one else had discovered. Little Bob and Anne were playing checkers, Dot was sewing doll's clothes, and Jean was deep in a book. The baby kicked about happily on a rug in his pen. Their father sat quietly by, doing nothing; that was the only strange thing about the home-coming—that and her taking the chair unnoticed beside him and sitting with folded hands instead of hurrying off to the kitchen or up-stairs.

Her coming seemed to hush them, even the baby. The room was very still for a long time, until she stooped and tickled the baby's toes, and he began to crow. Then little Bob snapped a checker across the table and shouted, "Beaten," and Johnnie, the inveterate tumbler, turned two somersaults in front of the baby, thereby reducing him to squeals of delight. All the others joined in, full-throated, as they always did when the baby laughed.

She slipped her hand into big Bob's and they sat as they had so often sat when they were first married and little Jean had been the baby rolling about in that self-same pen. She found herself listening for what big Bob always used to say:

"Let's have a dozen of them—just like little Jean."

And she whispered again the answer she had always made: "All right. Let's never let the cradle get empty." And they never had.

She was glad of it now, very glad. Didn't every baby mean more love left behind? Her husband must have caught her thinking from her, for he laid his other hand over hers—a way he always had—and said:

"Listen, children, just a minute. I've been thinking of something I want you to remember. Whatever you do—wherever you go—daddy wants you to remember that in every one of you there is a big, precious part of mother. That's the best part of you, and you are to keep it always as beautiful and happy as mother was."

Little Jean looked up from her book. "Not was—*is,* Daddy. Mother *is,* just as she always was." She dropped her book and came over to her father. "And yet it isn't just as she always was. You know, mother was always so busy. There was always something to do from the time we got up till time to go to bed. And now—" Little Jean wrinkled her forehead and stopped to think it out more plainly, "—now it just sort of seems as if all mother had to do was to be with us and love us. Close your eyes, Daddy."

She laid one hand over her father's eyes and the other over her own. "Now, doesn't it almost seem as if you could see mother sitting in her little rocker there and smiling? Doesn't it?"

She could see big Bob swallowing a lump in his throat, and she could feel the tightening of the hand under hers, but his smile never broke, and his voice was very steady.

"Of course I can see her, little daughter, smiling and happy—that's mother always."

All the children were listening now, games and dolls forgotten.

"Honest, Daddy, can you really see mother?" Little Bob sounded stifled with awe.

"I can't see her with my eyes, son. That's why Jean's closed them. But I can see her with my heart. Try it."

All but the baby closed eyes tight, and for safety's sake hands were clasped hard over them.

"I can see mother putting jam on our bread for supper. Gee, she's spreading it thicker'n Mrs. Libby does." Johnnie grinned in remembrance.

"I can see mother rocking the baby." Anne unconsciously swayed her little body back and forth in unison.

"I can see her picking up." Little Bob stole a surreptitious glance over his hands to the checkers spilled upon the floor. "I say, let's pick up and have a game of blind-man's buff."

Dot uncovered hers without telling anything, but she saw Jean's hand still clasped. "What do you see, Jean?"

"Oh, just mother."

The mother sat with them while they had their supper, and afterward she saw them all into bed. There was nothing calling her away, so she could take her own appointed time. She lingered over each crib or little cot until each child had gone to sleep, and then she made the prayer of all dear mothers there beside them for their safe-keeping. She went content, knowing she was leaving love a-plenty behind her and taking love with her whither she was going. She knew nothing else mattered.

THE LITTLE GOLD KEY *

Edith Barnard Delano

MARGARET HENDERSON stood before a window of her bedroom and looked across the dividing stretch of lawn at the men who were taking down the awning from the house next door. But it was not of the awning nor of the men that she was thinking; they were merely symbols of so much that was significant in her own household and her own heart. The morning papers had proclaimed the glory of Mrs. Whitney's ball, and the description had been read at the Henderson breakfast table; but the Henderson name had not figured in the list of those present. That had been two hours ago, but Margaret was still quivering at the memory of Anitra's tears and Mildred's scorching words, and the angry outburst of her husband.

Margaret Henderson was a little woman, and the house from whose windows she gazed was very large. She always felt oddly out of place in it; and indeed, its devising had been none of hers. For her the zenith of ambition had been reached when they had been able to move from the West Side flat into the suburbs and have a car, which Amos, her husband, drove, and when they could send Nita to the private primary school with the children of well-to-do parents.

That degree of luxury had been achieved quite suddenly. Only the autumn before they had found it none too easy to send Mildred East to college; then, almost overnight it seemed, Amos's business became spectacularly successful. Previously Margaret had always kept step with him, ever since the day when they had walked out into the world together from the little Vermont village of their birth. Sometimes, indeed, in the earlier years, when her courage had urged him over the difficult places, she had walked a pace or two ahead of him; but as their income mounted she had felt herself falling behind, and long before now she knew that Amos had passed her. If he had not quite left her far behind, she was miserably conscious that at least he felt her dragging on him, holding him back.

It was the same with the girls. She looked back now with tender longing upon the days when they had needed her, relied upon her, called on her for all their little necessities and had come to her with all their little joys. For them, and for their father, too, she had done everything; in those days her aching back and her tired hands had known the pull of the broom and the sting of hot suds.

She and Amos had waited long for the coming of the two girls. A boy had been born during the first year of their married life; he had looked like Margaret's people, slight and dark; but he had lived less than a year, and they had waited seven more years before Mildred came, and another six for Anitra; so that, by the time Anitra was home from the finishing school, her mother was beginning to feel middle-aged.

Yet that the years between Mildred's birth and Anitra's had held something of progress for their parents, their very names testified. Circumstances had become a little easier; Margaret occasionally heard music, had joined a woman's club; and Amos possessed a dress suit and wore it several times each winter. Those had been happy years, even with their worries; she had scarcely been happier when the coming of more money opened wider vistas; and now—

Margaret turned from the window. Now—ah! now they were all—husband and daughters—living in a world of which she seemed no least part. Not to be useful, not to be needed—that was bad enough; but for her there was an even greater sorrow. She failed them, she was in their way; she made mistakes which they held to be ineradicable. As she turned from the window she no longer felt only middle-aged, but as if life were done.

And that scene at the breakfast table! Mildred had been born during the years of her parents' realest poverty, and seemingly the acid of that anxious time had burned into the girl's character; now, at twenty-five, she was hard and bitter, as ambitious as she was handsome. She had precipitated the trouble that morning by a caustic taunt at Anitra; their neighbor had given a great ball the evening before, and her sister—Nita, they called her—who had caused herself to be announced as a débutante of the winter, had not been invited.

"Now, Milly," her mother had said, "you know very well we aren't even on calling terms with the folks next door. Why do you torment your sister so?"

At that Amos flung aside his paper. "And why weren't you invited?" he demanded. "You know I want you to be invited with the best. I provide you with everything, don't I? Then why ain't you invited, why don't you do your part, all of you? That's what I'd like to know."

Nita's eyes had filled with tears. "I do my best, dad," she had said. "A girl can't do everything—by herself."

"By herself! Don't I contribute something? What?"

"Yes. But—but other girls' mothers—"

Nita, with flaming cheeks and catching breath, had pushed back her chair and rushed out of the dining-room. "You contribute money enough, father," Mildred's cool, keen-edged voice had said, "but there really are things that money won't buy, you know!"

"What?" her father had asked truculently.

Mildred raised her eyebrows. "All the gold in the world wouldn't unlock Mrs. Whitney's door," she said. "And in this town our unknown neighbor is the reigning power in society."

For a moment her father frowned in silence. Then he asked: "Why not?"

"Oh, father!" Mildred protested, smiling. "Mrs. Whitney has everything in the world that any one could want—wealth, position, husband, the finest house in the city—oh, everything. There isn't anything we could offer Mrs. Whitney, really, that would make it worth while for her to open her doors to us!"

Amos Henderson considered. "If I thought it would do any good, I'd smash that husband of hers in the market. Then I guess she'd come down off her high horse. But I made Godwin send his wife to call last month, and what good did that do? Why didn't you get *her* to have you invited? Ain't she friends with this high-and-mighty next door?"

Again Mildred smiled. "Yes, Mrs. Godwin

called,'' she said. ''And mother came down, and talked recipes for gingerbread, and the best way of making pie-crust, and what she used to do for us when we had the croup. I fancy that's the end of our acquaintance with Mrs. Godwin.''

So it had been borne home to Margaret Henderson that she was not only no longer needed by her family, but that she was actually a hindrance to them in their desires. And oh, but the knowledge of it was hard! The old days were so far in the past!

She walked to her bureau and took from the back of the top drawer a little box. In it were some of her treasures, those foolish little things that every woman keeps—a crumbling spray of flowers that Amos had brought her on some early anniversary; some of Mildred's school reports; one of Nita's long yellow curls—they were cut off when she had scarlet fever; and a little cheap, worn, baby's shoe—still bulging and creased in the form of a tiny foot.

She held it to her cheek. Tears were far away from her that day, but suddenly the thought came to her that not for months, not for years had she been to that baby grave. Amos had caused the little body to be brought West, when they were able to afford the expense, and for a while they had gone to the cemetery together, occasionally, with flowers. Then she had gone alone; but it had been a long time, now, since she had gone at all. Back in Vermont it was the custom of the bereaved to go to their graves for comfort; she herself had found comfort in the custom in the earlier years.

She put away her little keepsakes, and dressed quickly for the street. The way to the cemetery was long, but she did not want to use one of the automobiles. Somehow, it seemed more natural to go in a street car, to stop at the florist's by the gate and buy flowers, and then to walk along the winding drives and paths to the lot where the little mound was, stopping now and then to read a name and date on a stone, or to admire a carving, or perhaps to speculate on some faded wreath or some newly made grave.

All this she did; then, having at last covered the little grave with the blossoms she had bought, she stood for a while dreaming. Would the little boy, she wondered, have been more like her than the girls were? Would he have understood her better; would he—would he have *needed* her more? But the brooding heart of a mother at such a moment may not be read. . . .

Margaret Henderson's eyes were open, but they saw nothing of the grass or the trees and sky, of the flowers and monuments all about her, until at length she was brought back to consciousness of the present by a low sound not far away. She half turned, and listened. Some one had sobbed, or had stifled a moaning cry.

Margaret's heart went out to whomever it was —suffering, perhaps, from a newer grief than hers, or an older one. She looked; and not twenty yards away there was another little grave, with a low and simple stone to mark its head; and on the ground a woman crouched huddled, pressing the earth as though she would touch what lay beneath it.

Only for an instant did Margaret hesitate, then swiftly crossed the intervening space and knelt beside the huddled figure. At her touch and the sound of her voice the woman looked up, and Margaret saw a young face, beautiful in spite of the marks of weeping and the look of dull and hopeless pain in the eyes.

"Child, child," Margaret breathed; and the other woman turned to her, and wept in her arms. Before the hour was out they had opened their hearts to each other, and told how in one grave was a young hope lost long years ago, and in the other a young hope never quite realized; and the younger woman had wept out, strangely, tensely, and with a fullness which would not have been possible except to a stranger, the soreness and bitterness of a heart denied its due of love, hurt to its quick by disloyalty and misunderstanding.

For a while Margaret felt as though the whole world had brought its sorrows and its disappointments, crucified, to her, and as though she, like one other mother of sorrows, held them tenderly, healingly, in her arms. . . .

Presently the younger woman—to Margaret she seemed scarcely older than her own Mildred, scarcely more than a child—looked up. "I think God must have sent you to me," she said simply. "Talking to you has been like what I suppose the confessional must be to those who believe in it—telling all one's sorrows to a great and silent sympathy—one that will never tell, but will always understand. I don't see how I am ever to let you go!"

"You need not, unless you want to," said Margaret quietly. Now they were standing, and the other woman threw her a swift glance, and then looked away. For the first time Margaret was aware of her slim elegance, of the richness of her furs, the modishness of all her apparel. At another time all this might have seemed a barrier, but now Margaret Henderson saw beneath it, felt the pulsing life which it covered, and the lonely, aching heart.

"I don't know what came over me, to talk so to a—a stranger," the other woman murmured. Then she smiled into Margaret's eyes. "I am very glad I did. I came here to the cemetery for comfort, and—I found it."

"We are not the first women who have done that, my dear," said Margaret, as they walked side by side back along the road to the gate.

"Where I came from, I can well remember my poor tired mother going up the hill to the quiet place, after my father left us, and coming down able to take up the burdens again. And there are many others—here as well as in Vermont."

"Vermont! You came from Vermont!" the younger woman said musingly. "Perhaps that partly accounts for the way I felt toward you. There is Vermont blood in me too. My mother came from there—from Meadow's Falls. Her name was Ellen—I am named for her—Ellen Williams."

Margaret stood still. "Ellen Williams—and she died when you were born—and I have her letters, my dear, just brim full of the joy of waiting for you! We grew up together, and were brides together! And you were just the age of—of my little boy back there!"

For a moment they looked deep into each other's eyes, then the younger woman's eyes brimmed with tears and her lips quivered. "I knew God sent you to me!" she said.

The shadows of twilight were lurking in the corners of the great square hall when Margaret Henderson walked past the butler through her own front door. She turned to speak to some one who had come in with her, and the butler had scarcely disappeared before a girl came running from the library at the back of the house.

"Mother!" Anitra cried. "Mother! We've been so anxious! You're so late, and no one knew where you were, and I was so horrid to you this morning—"

She stopped, for she had become aware that there was some one with her mother—some one standing a little back in the shadow. Anitra had the most curious feeling—it seemed as though they were not here in the city at all, but once more in the informal country neighborhood; for —with an effect of infinite oddness—the woman behind her mother was hatless, and wrapped in a great fur coat, quite as though she had just "run in," neighborly fashion. But her mother drew the hesitating figure forward.

"Nita, child, this is the daughter of an old friend of mine. I've been spending the day with her—most of it. And it's so nice that we live side by side."

Anitra's eyes opened very wide. She recognized the other woman now—but with recognition knew that there must be some mistake. And yet—

"I am Mrs. Walter Whitney," the other was saying, supplying the information that Mrs. Henderson had forgotten. She smiled—and not at all the sort of smile Anitra would have expected. "And we *are* neighbors, aren't we? I hope we are going to be very good friends!"

Before Anitra, speechless, could recover from

her amazement and bewilderment, a voice spoke from half-way down the stairs.

"Mother! Is that mother? Mother, do come up to father! He came home early with a cold, and he's been asking for you, and worrying so because—"

At the foot of the stairs Mildred also stopped, as Anitra had, in the surprise of the hatless figure at her mother's side. But Mrs. Henderson only smiled.

"Very well, Milly, I'll go right up to your father." Then she turned to Mrs. Whitney. "Ellen, my dear, you'll excuse me, won't you? I seem to be needed."

She and Mrs. Whitney smiled into each other's eyes, and kissed.

They watched her little figure mount the great winding staircase—a little figure which retained its homeliness amid all the sumptuous luxury of the house. Then Mrs. Whitney touched Anitra lightly on the arm, and said with a smile at Mildred:

"Your mother has the little golden key of sympathy. She knows how to open hearts, doesn't she?"

Anitra flushed. It was Mildred who answered. "Yes," she said. "Yes, I think she is—wonderful!"

"Oh, that, and more, much more! My friend, Mrs. Godwin, told me that she was wonderful, one of the 'real people'; but now I have found out for myself that she is much more than wonderful."

Anitra managed somehow to hear what Mrs. Whitney was saying as she moved toward the door. "We must be friends, as our mothers were," she said. "You will, won't you? Both of you? And don't you think you could run over to-morrow afternoon and help me for tea? There are some people coming, not too many—just a few I know rather well. Will you come?"

Again it was Mildred who replied, and Mildred who went to the door with their guest, ignoring the house-man who appeared, as though miraculously, to open the door, and retreated when he saw Miss Henderson at his duty. When she had closed the door after their departing visitor, Mildred leaned against it and looked at Nita. For a long moment neither spoke. Then Anitra said in a low tone: "I wonder what she meant by—'real people'!" Yet deep in the hearts of both—they knew.

MOTHER'S BUSINESS *

Juliet Wilbor Tompkins

THE girls were late this morning, and mother was in the hall when they flew off. She never offered good-by or greeting embraces herself; she simply was there, casually, if any one happened to feel like it. Mona and Betty always felt like it, being generous of embraces. They tumbled out the usual warnings:

"Mother, do be careful when you go out!"

"And don't try to read, muddie! Pussy Meadows adores to read to you."

"If you do have to cross the street—"

"Oh, go along with you!" Good-humored common sense scoffed in mother's voice. "You'll miss your train—"

She opened the front door and they flew out like birds from a cage. How pretty and how dear they were, with their robin brightness, their quick squabbles and their little murmurs and grunts of pure love! Flying daily from the old cage to the vast open sky of the city, into

* Reprinted from "Delineator." By special permission of the author and of the Butterick Publishing Company.

the glorious sun of success, yet faithfully flying home at night lest the cage should feel itself deserted, reading aloud somebody's "Life and Letters" with little consciousness of what the words said. They were leading life themselves and writing letters—what did those dead histories matter to Mona and Betty! But mother mattered. Not for their own sakes just then,—no one needs a mother very much at twenty-one and twenty-two,—but they wanted her to be happy, wanted it with passion. A reasonable mother will accept that as success.

Their fervor for work was her success, too. All their lives she had planned for just this—enthusiasm, ambition, anything that would glorify hard work and keep them from trying to do it on charm, like her poor Lawrence. While they were still little girls, she had begun spinning about the idea of work the glamour that novelists spin about love.

And it was mother who had suggested that they leave the old home for the city. The girls had been concerned about roots.

"You'll miss your church, mother!"

"My church," said mother strongly, "has bored me for thirty-five years. I go, because if I don't, Doctor Gracie comes and calls, and that bores me even worse."

They loved her for that; but—

"You'll miss your old friends," they warned.

"Some of them," she admitted. "But I can do without Flora Willey's gossip and Mrs. Van Dyke's symptoms, and it will be a relief not to have to shriek at Pussy Meadows. She says I am the only person who takes the trouble to speak distinctly to her, but she means who's willing to yell the skin off her lungs."

They loved her for that, too. Queer why the average mother will go on being so moral when it is her immoral impulses that bring her children closest. But—

"You've lived in this house for thirty-five years," they reminded her.

Mother looked about the living-room with a judging candor. She had come there as a tall wisp of a bride with drooping blond tendrils and a fine, high nose to give her an air of romance, and a mind as fresh and pungent and homely as the radishes she grew behind the barn. Doctor Tudor had always found roars of laughter in the contrast between how his wife looked and what she said. If he could have laughed over Lawrence, too, they might have saved their first-born; but he had fallen under the child's spell and could only worship, like every one else. No one but his mother ever criticized Lawrence; ever held him up in a clear light for his own inspection; and so he had built a wall on the side toward her. There was no possible way for her to have his love and yet keep her truth.

When the smash came and, in that very room Lawrence had had to face the cold daylight of judgment, he had known how to make his father break down and forgive him and his employer offer him another chance, but he had no way past his mother's tragic silence. He could not forgive them for having seen him stripped of his splendor, so he had walked out of his home, never to return. His father presently died of it all, and his funeral was one more scene stamped on the old room.

"Well, if we'd had any money to spare, I guess we'd have tried a few other homes," mother said. "Now, with you girls getting raised every Christmas, it won't hurt us to pay a little rent."

So it had been joyously settled. And then mother's eyes had begun to blur and falsify distances and change an approaching horse into some vague, vast terror, and the idea of her alone in the city streets was inconceivable, so the move was put off until she could be cured. One of the old family friends was an oculist—getting a little vague about the eyes himself, but full of encouragements and pattings. A good rest—that was what she needed. "All she needed," they made it.

Mother stood in the doorway, watching the two fade into the general brightness and beauty of the Spring morning, and it seemed to her they vanished sooner than they had even yesterday—certainly sooner than last week, when she had seen them as far off as the corner. She tried herself out in various tests, and they gave a startling certainty of lost ground. Her chill of fright took itself out in indignation against Doctor Bowen.

"Patting and blatting—I don't believe he knows much about eyes or anything else," she scolded. Her first thought was that she would go to town to-morrow with the girls and consult some big man, like Dr. Oscar Stein. The second thought, characteristically hers, was to dress in haste and take the next train. There was no sense in making the girls go to work wondering what the oculist would say.

"I never could see any use in three being worried because one had to be," she voiced her creed, stiffening herself against a weak desire for a confident young arm through hers. The distance between herself and the ground had grown uncertain, fluctuating. She put out a feeling foot even on a level pavement.

Patients usually had to wait for appointments with Doctor Stein, but as she had come from a distance she was sympathetically crowded in. Doctor Stein saw a tall, wispy woman, her face delicately lined and hollowed between gray tendrils but still lifted into romance by the fine, high nose; what he heard was the martial ring of common sense.

"I've been ordered to rest my eyes, and I've been patted and cheered and told not to worry, and I've had enough of all that. I want the truth. I sha'n't faint—I dare say I sha'n't even cry. Anyway, you needn't care if I do. Am I going blind?"

He gave her what she asked for. "Yes, I am afraid you are."

She did not cry, did not even seem shocked, or pause.

"How soon?"

He thought in about two months. He knew of no operation, nothing that would help.

"Well, after all, I'm not so surprised," she said in a surprised tone. "I guess I knew it, more or less, down underneath."

He tried to say something kind about her courage, but she was wholly outside of herself, as impersonal as a mechanician with a broken machine.

"The thing is, how not to be a nuisance," she told him, and went out more strongly than she had come in.

In the street, with lines of people swaying about her, she did feel a little giddy, and, looking about for a resting-place, saw the fluted shell-mouth of a moving-picture entrance.

"My mother would have looked up a church, but I guess this will have to do," she commented, pushing her money through a hole in a glass cage that held a hair-dresser's dream of feminine loveliness. She offered with it a remark about wanting to sit down for a while, longing for a human response, but the waxen beauty pushed back the ticket with a bored flip of manicured fingers, her gaze being permanently fixed man-high.

"If I'd told her I should be stone blind in two months, she'd have waked up," mother observed, and felt that she had a grim joke on the girl, who had missed the chance to see a soul under sentence.

In the sudden darkness of the auditorium she stopped short.

"This is the way it will feel," she told herself, and waited to see what would happen. An usher showed kindness in helping her to a seat. On the screen a heavily jowled magnate sat at an office desk, young men came and went with documents, a pretty girl in a moleskin wrap was shown in. Mother caught herself wondering what was afoot. For a moment she had forgotten that she was going blind.

"I guess it's only words to me as yet," she apologized, and tried over the central word—*blind*. It seemed to mean men with horrid eye-sockets, chins thrust forward, sticks tapping, pencils hung on their soiled fronts. Old Mrs. Pinkney had lost her sight before she died; when you were over eighty it wasn't blindness —you merely lost your sight. The young woman in moleskin was being locked into a room on the nineteenth floor and the rescuing young man sent off on a false clue; mother waited until he got her out of that fix, forgetting again. The memory this time came back more heavily; the weight on her heart had quite literally the slump of lead.

"Forgetting and remembering won't get me anywhere; I've got to think," she rebuked herself. "I guess a church would have been better, after all." Yet she felt no need of succor, of divine help to rest on; it never once occurred to her to pray. Her general feeling was that she would be perfectly adequate for dealing with this herself as soon as she got her breath. Where her mother would have dwelt on submitting to God's will and bearing her cross with resignation, she came back to the central doctrine of pure human gold that the doctor's verdict had struck out of her: "The thing is, how not to be a nuisance."

There it was: the eager little girls, tearing off to their work, believing in the righteous splendor of careers as young soldiers believe in the Cause, going headlong in the good direction where her hand had always pointed. Must one of them be jerked back to potter about with a blind woman? Either would do it, readily, pitifully, with her impatience very seldom bursting up through her goodness, and her desolation usually hidden in her own room. They would do their sturdy best, her Mona and Betty; but what would life be to her, knowing every day the full measure of what she was taking?

"Old nuisance," she said aloud, and had to cover it with a cough.

Her mother would have pointed out that sacrifice made character. "But they do sacrifice, every day, only they're so sweet and happy they don't call it that," she argued. "Their characters are getting all the development they need. Spoil a girl's life in order to make a fine character of her?—I guess not!" But how to help it.

The screen had shown the final fade-out embrace and gone on to orange orchards done in color, green and gold, fig-trees richly drooping, and run-away roses swarming old walls to dance in the eternal movie breeze. The orchestra played richly, sensuously. Mother turned dubiously to compensations: odors would still be good, and tastes, and pleasant sounds.

"But I never did like music, unless it was a little boy with a harmonica," she reflected, and saw her Lawrence so, smiling his intolerable charm up at her before he had walled her out. Those memories always brought such a twist of pain that she used to cry out "Don't!" before them, until the girls had laughed her out of it with their, "Don't what?"

"Well, I made him hate me, and I couldn't do any differently," she said to the subsiding pain. "What I need is a cup of tea."

She got her tea and a pretense of lunch at a dairy next door, vaguely surprised that she could see to help herself, for it seemed as though at least two months had gone by since she had received her sentence. The waitress was friendly, and the words nearly uttered themselves— "The doctor says I'm going blind!" She wanted to tell the gateman at the ferry, and when the conductor, standing by his train, recognized her by name, she stopped short, the news at her lips, and had to substitute some foolish question. With the awful need to tell went a sharp reluctance to having it known.

"I guess I want the fun of seeing them jump, but don't want to be offered consolations," she told herself. Then the sight of Pussy Meadows bearing down on her seat brought a flicker of forlorn humor. She could tell Pussy in perfect safety!

Pussy Meadows went to town a good deal, and in the streets she was a delightful young woman going about her important affairs; then the clock on the ferry struck and she went home, poor Pussy Meadows, who was getting deafer all the time. The sweet animation of her face, the smiling depths of womanhood that made strangers wish they knew her, were lost in a strident gaiety that oppressed and exhausted. Tired neighbors would resort to strategy or even miss a train in order not to share a seat with Pussy Meadows.

To-day her mood seemed abnormally strained; she chattered as though to keep out some sound, and her averted eyes were fever-bright. Mother watched her with a smiling fixity that held something in suspense, and Pussy presently became aware of it.

"I'm talking your head off," she admitted with a laugh that sounded breathless. "What have you been doing?"

Mother launched it in her usual quiet voice: "Pussy, I'm going blind. I shall be quite blind in two months."

Pussy might have caught the words, for she heard better on the train, but her attention had not really left her own inner state.

"Oh, that's fine," she said.

"I've heard how it sounds, anyhow," mother reflected, turning away. They were passing the outskirts of Newark, and to her thought, "I sha'n't see that after two months," came a brisk answer: "Well, I can't say it's much loss!"

Pussy was talking again, but disjointedly, inattentively. Suddenly she flung out an arresting sentence: "It's my birthday, to-day. I'm twenty-five."

Mother went straight for what lay back of the words. "Pretty dull for you," she said.

People did not speak of Pussy's deafness, for she was said to be abnormally sensitive. Perhaps they were too delicate about it, for she met this direct approach with a gasp of relief.

"Oh, Mrs. Tudor, no one knows!" burst from her. "It has been four years now. I've done my best—truly. And everybody has been kind; the girls ask me to play tennis and auction and all that. But I've known—I've always known— It is so terrible to feel yourself a nuisance!"

Mother's lips were closely folded but her eyes said, "I know."

Tears rained down Pussy's face. "I want to tell you," she whispered. "No one else. But with a secret as big as this, you have to tell some one!"

Mother understood that, too.

"The first year I was treated a lot, and hurt and hurt, and I only got worse," Pussy rushed on, "so I wouldn't stand any more. But to-day I have been to a new man, and he says the old treatment was all wrong, and that there is hope, there is good hope—oh, he thinks I can be cured!"

The eager young hands, burning hot through their gloves, were clinging to mother's. She made no bodily response and her words were, as always, calmly sensible: "Well, that's real nice for you, Pussy. I'm glad to know it." But no one ever found her unsatisfactory.

"It is only a hope," Pussy warned herself. "I won't breathe it to the family until we are sure—but I love your knowing it. You have been so kind! And you never told me about afflicted people who took to geology or bugs or electricity, and they were so happy when they found a beetle with a new stripe that they didn't mind if they were deaf. Beetles! Who cares how many stripes a beetle's got!"

"Men can care about things like that," mother said dubiously. "I don't know as we can. Though I do like to raise flowers."

Pussy heard only the last word. "I've hated flowers," she said. "They smelled like all the things I couldn't have. But now—oh, do you suppose it's true?"

"Good things can happen," Mrs. Tudor admitted and went home refreshed and steadied. "It's the young that matter. Old folks can get along," she told herself.

The house was as she had left it. Unmade beds and unwashed dishes gave a shocked air of bad news, and she hurriedly produced order. The girls must be told gradually, and after they had eaten a good hot dinner. As she worked she experimented in going without eyes, with poor success.

"The kitchen table's been on that spot for thirty-five years; you'd think I could walk around it in my sleep," she scolded, holding a bruised hip. "I guess I'm too tired to learn my business to-night. But you wait! I'm going to be the smartest blind woman in the country."

The prospect of telling the girls grew worse as their hour came. Mother trembled so that she could scarcely go about her work. They were so happy, the little girls! And so kind. The experience would enrich a thin nature, but they didn't need enriching. They were darlings just as they were. In her mourning over them she quite forgot that the hurt was, after all, to her.

They made it harder by coming home in tearing spirits. Both had had promotions in responsibility, and on the train they had conceived a scheme of going into business together half a dozen years later.

"I'll know the business from a to z by that time and Mona'll know the decorating," Betty explained, drying her face at her mother's door because she could not wait to talk. Mona was behind her, comb in hand.

"Tudor is a gorgeous name for a decorating firm," she added.

"You may have changed that name in six

years,'' mother pointed out. She had busied herself at her bureau so as not to face them.

Their nods admitted it. Both had abundant suitors.

''We could keep it for the firm name,'' they said. Betty added that if she married a man with an ugly name she would make him change it to Tudor anyway, and Mona said that a man who would do that was a poor fish, not worth marrying, and as Betty's best suitor was abjectly ready to change Funk for anything, there was a squally moment. Mother never troubled to pour oil. Thirty seconds later they were trying over Funk-Tudor and Tudor-Funk with gurgles of laughter, Betty's cheek squeezed against Mona's. They had always done that—squeezed their joyous faces together with a murmured ''Um-um!'' They would do it to her when she told them.

She had not often in her life said, ''I can't,'' but the words were saying themselves now: ''I *can't* tell them.'' It was like asking her to cut into their flesh. What if she simply waited until they saw for themselves? But they were planning, planning. They were sure her eyes would be well enough for town in the Autumn.

''Commutation is vexation,'' Betty chanted, and was secretly kicked by Mona, who declared that it was half the fun. Betty instantly agreed. The good children! Why must she, who had lived to further their lives, be now the dead weight that dragged them back?

She had meant to tell them when they finished the dishes. She had her casual beginning all arranged: "Oh, children, I went to town today and saw Dr. Oscar Stein—" But they were called to the telephone and then a neighbor came in, and then it was ten o'clock and bedtime.

"I'll tell them in the morning," she decided, and lay all night staring into the dark; but in the morning there was no time.

After all, Sunday morning would be better; they would have all day to get used to the idea and make their plans. Reprieved for five days, mother went briskly about her new business of becoming the smartest blind woman in the country. She learned the rooms and the garden paths by heart; she invented pricked labels for kitchen condiments; she spent hours mastering Betty's old typewriter; she simplified her clothes and did up her hair in the dark. She was busy from morning till night.

"I'm kind of enjoying it," she admitted to herself. "I always did like being smarter than other people!" The girls found her in her usual even spirits that week and told her that she was getting better all the time. They noticed that she moved more securely. She let them rejoice in it without comment. Sunday morning would be time enough.

Friday night they came in with the shout of good news. Mother, gathering "Europe" and "four months," sat down as though her knees had melted.

"She'll take you with her? For four months?" she repeated mechanically, and then, hating to kill their joy in its first splendor, she added a temporizing, "She must think you girls are pretty promising!"

"She thinks we're wonders," Mona declared, and Betty added, "Tudors," and they laughed richly over the old joke.

"But, of course, mother, we will find some one nice to stay with you," they said, and fell upon her with comforting arms and cheeks, then went into a rhapsody of what four months among Old World treasures would do for them professionally. "I'll bet she means to hand on the business to us when she retires," Betty declared.

They must be told; the moment had come. If they had looked into mother's face then, they would have known her news without words. But they were hauling out their clothes for inspection. Betty thought Mona's serge looked shabby and Mona retorted that it was a good deal fresher than Betty's crêpe, and there was a sharp spatter of "You always—" and "The trouble with you—" Then a gust of laughter cleared away wrath and the warm "dearest" and "ducky" were back in their speech.

"You know, muddie, we're sailing next Wednesday," they threw out.

Mother went to her room and closed the door. For a moment it almost seemed to her that she needed some outside help. One must stay home, one must go burdened with the other's loss as well as with the family sorrow.

"Old spoil-sport," she muttered, and even thought of death, but was too sensible to encourage the idea. "That wouldn't help much. But I might just wait till morning. They can't do much before morning," she decided, and again lay staring into the dark all night. What she saw there finally brought peace. She let the girls race happily off after breakfast, and as soon as her house was in order she telephoned for Pussy Meadows.

Pussy came with a lonely eagerness.

"It is too soon to tell yet, but he believes he can cure me," she began, her face lovely with its new light. "The family doesn't know a word about it—they think I'm gadding to town all the time. Oh, I am so happy!" Mother let her talk about it until Pussy herself remembered. "You wanted to see me," she broke off.

"Yes, I did," Mother meditated her beginning. "How would you like a job?"

Pussy sighed her desire. "Oh, if there were only something I could do!"

"There is. My girls are going to Europe for four months with their boss. If you want to move over here for that time, I'll call you a companion and manage a little salary. They don't just like leaving me alone."

Pussy was delighted and would not hear of a salary. She had a dozen reasons why it was just what she wanted most to do, but under them all lay the warm glow of being needed.

"And we can watch me get better, then spring it on the family," she exulted. "Oh, what good things are happening!"

"You know, I don't see very well," mother warned her. "You might call me half-blind. That will sort of tie you down."

"Well, I don't hear very well; you might call me half-deaf," Pussy returned with happy flippancy. "That will be a bore for you."

"I might go stone blind," mother insisted. "But I'm making it my business to get ready for that. It won't be much harder on you."

"If I go stone deaf, I'll drown myself, so that won't be any harder on you," Pussy said, and burst into a song about the owl and the pussy-cat.

Mona and Betty demurred a little at the idea of Pussy Meadows, but were too rushed not to accept any solution that satisfied mother.

They were counting the days, yet they ran home with a new eagerness.

"We'll miss you horribly, mother!" they kept telling her. When the last evening came, something unknown laid a cold hand on their spirits; they began to mean it so poignantly that it could not be said. They cried at good night.

Mother had no tears. She only looked at them, looked and looked into their faces as though she learned them by heart. When they were asleep, she stole in with a candle and stood looking down until they began to sigh and stir.

"I won't see them again, but that doesn't mean I won't feel them and have them," she scolded herself. "There's no sense in making such a fuss."

Her last sight of them was a blur of waving hands and laughing tearful faces.

"Do be careful, mother!" they implored.

"Go along with you. You'll miss your train," she said, as always.

Pussy was not to come until the next day. Mother allowed herself twenty-four hours of stark desolation, of great sighs bursting up from a sick heart; then she said, "Now, that's enough!" as she might have to a crying child, and went about her business. Pussy found her digging in the garden.

"We've always had pansies here, but I want

something that smells sweet,'' she said. ''Stocks, maybe.''

''We ought to have a bonga-tree,'' said Pussy.

The busy weeks flew past. Pussy helped in the garden, in the house, everywhere, and she looked like an ideal sweetheart—any man's ideal—in the bloom of her growing hope. Their two cases seemed to keep a mysterious balance: with every leap forward for Pussy there was a leap backward for mother. People were soon only shapes to her, a face was a pale blur. She had to hurry with her preparations, and became so deft at managing that Pussy still did not guess all her secret. The letters from the girls came tumbling in, three or four by every boat, loving, rapturous, full of sights and wonders. Her own letters, typewritten, ran about like this:

''Dear girls: You are good to write so often. I am glad you are enjoying it all. Pussy and I get along all right. She seems to like it here. We have set out some new roses. She wants to hire a boy to help with the vegetable garden. I don't know that I ought to let her, but Doctor Gracie knows of a young man who would be glad of the work. I miss you both, but I am glad you are having such a good time.'' And so on, down to ''Your loving mother.'' And yet they were not unsatisfactory letters. Something could be felt under the words—like the grip of a warm and steady hand.

It was two months to a day, a soft gray morning, and the world was little more than light and shadow. Pussy having gone to town, mother allowed herself rather more cane and fumbling than usual. There were days when she felt a great weariness, a longing to sit with hands folded, like any blind woman. It had taken scolding to get herself out into the garden, and even scolding could not keep her trowel going. She presently let it fall and felt her way to the seat under the old maple, sitting there with the lifted face of the blind.

"Well, I didn't suppose it would be any too easy," she said aloud. "I've had fun out of it, all the same." And then something made her aware of a presence. "Who is it?" she asked.

A husky little cough seemed to indicate a shy youth standing before her on the lawn.

"Oh, are you the young man who is coming to help me?" She spoke with new briskness.

His answer hesitated. "Yes; I've come to help you," he said at last. He did not sound like the lad she expected.

"Did Doctor Gracie send you?"

Again she had to wait for an answer: "I was sent to you." They were walking toward the vegetable garden and she could hear that he limped. She peered to see him, but could make out only a wavering shape. "You equal to the work?" she asked kindly.

"Oh, yes." He evidently wanted it very much, poor fellow. "I'm all right," he insisted.

He seemed to know by instinct where the tools were kept, and he worked so steadily and silently that mother decided to call it a full day, even though he had come so late. She sat within sound of him and her dark mood passed, leaving a new and rich content. The sun, coming through the grayness seemed to warm her to the soul.

"I guess I was lonesome," she decided. "Funny—he doesn't open his head, yet he's real good company."

She started to move her chair into the shade, and it was done for her. She dropped her cane, and as she felt for it it was placed in her hand. He was very thoughtful.

"I always did like a nice young fellow," she explained the growing anthem in her heart.

Toward noon she left him and went in to prepare lunch. Her ear had placed him as older than a boy, a gentleman, perhaps down and out and needing a good meal. She made her lunch of the things Lawrence had loved, hot muffins and bacon and cool salad and her own perfect coffee, and spread it on the veranda, then called him, sending him up-stairs to wash his hands.

"The end of the hall," she directed him.

"I'll find it." His voice was a mere thread,

and she could hear the drag of his lameness as he went.

"I guess I've worked you most to death," she apologized, and hurried to bring in the lunch. When he was seated opposite to her, the sunlight gave him a flickering outline. "Why, I can almost see you," she said contentedly.

"Are you here alone?" There was feeling, protest, in the question.

She told him about her dear girls and the trip and the young neighbor who was staying with her. Suddenly, not knowing how it had happened, she was telling him of her coming blindness.

"There wasn't any sense in spoiling their fun," she explained. "I can get about the house just about as well as I used to, so long as no one moves the furniture. Being blind isn't so bad—it makes other people kind. The way you are. Now, being deaf makes them cross. Queer, isn't it? I guess they like to put out a hand, but they hate to holler. Still, you could make a business of being deaf, just like I'm making a business of being blind. It's real interesting. I declare, I don't know when I've gabbled so," she broke off. "There's something about you—Are you eating your lunch?"

His answer was a sharp sigh. She knew that kind of sigh.

"You're in trouble," she said with her kindly directness. "You been sick?"

"Oh, yes—six months in a hospital." He spoke as though that were nothing.

"And I suppose you've come out without a cent?"

"No. I have—money enough." His voice trailed off as though speech were almost too difficult.

So the trouble was not health or money. There was loss, and there was also sin. She bent toward him, her eyes straining to see. "You want to tell me?" she urged.

"I want to tell you everything." He pushed back from the table, turning sidewise that he might rest his head on his hand, and at last she heard his full voice. "I don't know if I can. I've been broken to bits—body and soul."

She was listening rigidly, but as though to some far-off sound rather than to the words. "Go on— Go on—" she whispered.

"They patched up my body for me, but my soul had to find its own way." There was the sigh of sharp pain in every breath. "Back. Back through twelve years. Through layers and layers of rotten selfishness. Back to the good stock from which I had come. Back to—" He stopped.

Her hands, which had been checked in mid air, fluttered toward him.

"Who are you?" she cried.

He came and knelt beside her, letting her fingers touch his face. They found it wet with tears.

"I am no more worthy to be called your son," he said against her breast.

They sat together hand in hand all that afternoon. Lawrence told her everything, without flinching—not as he had seen it at the time, but as he had found it written on the hospital wall. But her heart was busy with its great feast of love and welcome. Her transfigured face was never turned away.

"Well, I'm real glad you came home," she said when he stopped, and for the first time Lawrence smiled.

"Blessed mother!" he said.

A joyous "Whoo-oo!" sounded through the house, and then Pussy Meadows stood in the doorway, lovely with happiness, a living sweetheart for any man's dream. Lawrence started up.

"Pussy, here's my son Lawrence," mother began. "He's come home—" Then she broke off with a cry. Over the sunset glow had come darkness, rolling down like a curtain. She turned her head in every direction but could find only the soft dark.

"Has the sun set?" she asked loudly.

"Not yet," Lawrence's voice answered, and

Pussy added: "Why, it's glorious!" Their hands were on her arms, they were questioning her lifted face.

"Glorious?" she repeated, then spoke on a deep breath: "Glorious. Well, so it is!"

A COOKY-JAR MOTHER *

Florence Hartman Townsend

THE new house next door was hardly as pretentious as any of its neighbors, yet it met the restrictions provided for the pretty suburb. And when Mrs. Elliott saw the family move in —she was watching discreetly from the folds of a sheer curtain—she decided the family exactly matched the house: plain, substantial, and quiet. The husband and father, whom she had learned was a doctor, was a good-looking, stalwart man, the wife of medium height, slender and even girlish appearing, and there were three children, two boys about ten and twelve and a little girl of seven or eight. She wondered if the children would prove suitable companions for her own twelve-year-old Don and eight-year-old Doris.

She wondered, too, if Mrs. Gates, the doctor's wife, would prove a valuable addition to their literary club. No doubt she would be delighted to join whether she had ever heard of Keats or Browning or Fröebel or Greek Myth-

* Reprinted by special permission of the author and of "The Christian Herald."

ology or Michelangelo or any other notable. Most women, she had discovered, harbored a fierce literary complex, and no doubt Mrs. Gates would prove no exception. If, after proper investigation, she should prove eligible she would present her name for membership in the Thursday Literary Club, of which she was president. Which trend of thought reminded her that she had a committee meeting at three that afternoon. She mustn't forget to tell Doris when she came in to luncheon that she would not be at home when she returned in the afternoon from school, and that she must remain at home until she returned. Don was quite capable of looking out for himself, and was usually off on his wheel as soon as he had put away his books.

Mrs. Elliott devoted the major part of the morning to household affairs, giving the maid instructions, ordering from the grocer and the butcher, then turning pridefully to the living portion of her attractive home. The entrance hall was tastefully formal with its Oriental rugs and gleaming mirrors. She went into the living-room with a dust cloth, removing imaginary flecks of dust, adjusting a pillow, moving a chair. It was a large, beautiful room, richly furnished and always in order. Mrs. Elliott took great pride in it. The furniture looked as fresh and new as it had six years before when the house had been built and furnished.

Mr. Elliott had rather insisted upon a nursery-playroom for the children at the expense of a considerably smaller living-room or the entire elimination of the tiled solarium, but his wife could not be persuaded and the playroom had had to be dispensed with. Sometimes Mrs. Elliott wondered if, after all, she had not made a mistake, for, of course, she couldn't allow the children to muss the living-room where callers were received, club meetings held, and bridge parties given. This applied to the solarium as well, for the larger parties frequently overflowed into it, and anyway it opened directly into the living-room and was green with potted plants and hanging ferns that the children might easily break.

Of course it was out of the question to have the entrance hall cluttered with toys, and so there really seemed to be no place for the children to play, especially in winter. The bedrooms were the only available place left and there they arranged their playthings, each in a corner of his and her little room, and there they—the toys—stayed. They seldom or never played with them. This in itself vexed Mrs. Elliott considerably, and though she frequently sent them to their rooms she knew they never really played with their toys as they might have done had they had them all together in a playroom. Nor did she realize that a child can not play with toys ranged in military precision along a wall, and, of course, they were not allowed to muss their dainty rooms by scattering things, willy-nilly, about the floor.

But as she gave the final touches this morning to the downstairs rooms she glowed with pride. She would welcome the day when she might invite her new neighbor into them. Mrs. Elliott liked to excel. Whether it was a matter of home or clothes or car or club paper or committee work, she was not happy unless she could excel. And, of course, her home excelled that of her neighbor in size, beauty, and richness, and she was filled with happy pride.

Mrs. Elliott returned rather late from the committee meeting to find the house quite empty. Neither Doris nor Don was to be found. The maid had not seen them. Don's wheel was under the porte-cochère. She had a sudden premonition but smothered it, and made another fruitless search of the place. Then she knew the premonition was correct—her children were calling upon the new neighbors! There were happy shouts from the rear yard next door.

Her cheeks flushed in vexation. How dared they become so intimate with the new family before she had had time to decide if they were eligible? She walked with great dignity to the front door of the Gates home and rang the bell.

Mrs. Gates answered her ring. She smiled cordially. Mrs. Elliott introduced herself and was invited in.

"Thank you, I just came to inquire if my children might possibly have strayed over here in my absence?"

"Yes, they are in the yard playing. Won't you come in?"

"Thank you, no, but I want to apologize for their intruding in this manner. I can't imagine what impelled them to do it."

"Please don't see it like that. Our children were delighted to have them, and they've had such a jolly time together."

"I hope they haven't been a bother. If you will be so kind I would like you to tell them to come home right away."

"Of course. I trust you will let them come again, and that you will come also."

"Thank you, I will."

Mrs. Elliott went home and walked the floor impatiently until the children arrived. She was inwardly raging with an unreasoning and unreasonable fury. She felt unaccountably humiliated and outraged. Not for anything would she have had this happen, not for anything! Why should children have so little idea of the eternal fitness of things?

The children came racing across the lawn, across the porch, and burst into the house. They were bubbling over with good spirits. Their mother came to meet them.

"Don! Doris! Why on earth—?"

"Say, mother, we had the best time! Those Gates kids have got the dandiest actin' pole."

"And a swing, mother," put in Doris, "and a—"

"Don! Doris! How dare you interrupt me when I am speaking? Doris, will you *please* not sit on that chair. There's sand all over your clothes. Don, tuck in your shirt—and your tie's all twisted, and your hands! Both of you go to the bathroom and make yourselves presentable at once!"

She herded them up the stairs. "Whatever possessed you to go to the house of a perfect stranger? The idea! When I had never even called and they had hardly gotten their household effects under the roof. I'm so mortified I don't know what to do!"

"I don't see what difference it makes," declared Don sullenly. "They're nice folks, all right. They're swell folks, I tell you, and the kids are straight shooters as ever was."

"Straight shooters!" his mother echoed in horror. "Don, where on earth do you pick up such language? From those new boys, I suppose."

"No, I didn't, either," he defended.

"Well, understand this, Don, and you too,

Doris, you are not to make another track in that Gates' yard until I grant you permission."

"Aw, mother—"

"That will do, Don. Doris, quit playing with the soap. Rinse your hands carefully."

"Oh, Don," Doris piped suddenly, "did you forget that book?"

"Yes, I did! Say, mother, Henry Gates loaned me a dandy book and I laid it down and forgot it. Let me run over—"

"No!"

"It won't take a minute, and Henry said it was a swell book."

"I said 'no,' Don. Strange you take such a sudden interest in books."

"Well, we ain't got any books for kids."

"Don, don't say 'ain't got.' Tell me what the book was and I'll buy it for you, but you sha'n't borrow it from the Gates boy. The idea, borrowing the first day they move in!"

"I don't remember what it was, but they've got hundreds of dandy books. I helped Henry and Ernest unpack 'em and put 'em on the shelves. You never saw the like of books. And they've got a—"

"Don, that will do. I've heard all I care to hear about them. Go to your room at once."

Mrs. Elliott wrestled with her new problem all alone. For some reason she could not bring herself to mention the matter to her husband.

There was the matter of the book. She stole a guilty glance at the elegant mahogany secretary that held a neat but limited collection of green and red volumes. A careful perusal of their titles would have shown them to be such as would hardly have interested children of eight and twelve. Mrs. Elliott frowned and sighed. There was a limit to their income, a very decided limit, and she had only a small amount to expend on books after their other rather heavy expenses were all paid. And there was nearly always a book she just must have in her club work.

Besides, one couldn't give one's children *everything!* They had a lovely home, exceptionally good clothes, good food, good training. Nevertheless, she bought Don a boy's book the next time she went shopping. She pictured, in her mind, the eagerness with which he would receive it, and had pleasant thoughts of Don's sitting quietly in the living-room reading. She wanted Don to grow up a dignified and cultured man, and she didn't like to have him running about so much.

But Don was off on his wheel somewhere when she returned, and she suffered an uncomfortable sinking of spirits. The Gates boys were playing handball in the yard next door, pausing occasionally to munch a cooky which they extracted from their pockets. It was a wonder, she thought, that their father, being a doctor, would allow eating between meals. *She* had never allowed *her* children to eat between meals, a mussy and disagreeable habit. Don had occasional stomach attacks as it was.

Don came in just before dark and his mother presented the book to him. He smiled in a pleased way and glanced through it.

"Thank you, mother. I'll begin it to-morrow. I have to get my lessons to-night."

The next day was her club day, and with the thought of Don enjoying his new book after school and Doris occupied with piano practice, Mrs. Elliott invited several of her friends for a drive in her car after the meeting, and it was late when she arrived home. As she turned into the driveway Don vaulted the hedge between the Elliotts' and the Gates' yard and entered the house by the rear door.

Mrs. Elliott's lips came together in a firm line. Don had disobeyed her! She had forbidden his going there without her permission, and this was how he obeyed! She walked very deliberately into the house and sought her son.

"Don, I had thought you would stay at home this afternoon and read your book. Instead I come home to find you have been over *there* again," she tossed her head toward the Gates' home. "And after I had forbidden you. I don't want you to do that again, Don. If you do I shall certainly punish you severely."

(Couldn't she imagine how desolate the house seemed with mother gone, and companionship just across the hedge?)

"But—aw, mother—"

"Not a word, Don. There is absolutely nothing further to be said about the matter."

Don sighed forlornly and went upstairs.

The little Gates girl had drifted over and she and Doris were sitting sedately on a veranda settee just outside the living-room window. Mrs. Elliott was preparing a club paper and their chatter was becoming annoying. She looked up from her writing.

"Doris, mother is writing a very important club paper and your talking bothers me. Won't you go somewhere else?"

Obediently the little girls arose and gathered something up from the seat between them. It was cookies! Mrs. Elliott frowned, but her frown changed to a pleased smile as she overheard her small daughter's boast.

"My mother's a club-woman. She belongs to the lit'rary Club and the Bridge Club, an' she's president an' chairman an' everything. Is your mother a club-woman?"

The other child shook her head. "I guess," she laughed as they ranged the cookies along the edge of the step, "I guess my mother's just a cooky-jar woman. That's what Daddy says."

"S-s-sh!" cautioned Doris. "Don't talk too loud about cookies. Mother doesn't allow me to eat between meals."

The conversation dropped to a whisper, and the paper was finished in peace, but the thought returned to tease her fancy as she straightened her desk. Just a cooky-jar woman! Hum. She was glad she was something the children could be proud of!

She decided, presently, to run over and call informally upon Mrs. Gates. She had really neglected the woman, and she must be quite lonely as she seldom went out and few had called.

Mrs. Elliott felt a little puzzled over the impression the visit had made upon her. She found Mrs. Gates reading. (She had, somehow, expected to find her baking cookies, and with a dab of flour on her nose.) Her frock was dark and soft and graceful. The living-room walls were largely devoted to bookshelves in which books, many in worn and faded bindings, new books, little books, big books, were ranged, row on row. There were two good paintings and a small print on the wall. A small grand piano, a table strewn with magazines, and several easy chairs completed the furnishings. Mrs. Elliott was impressed, perhaps by the books, and ventured the suggestion that Mrs. Gates join the study club.

"It's very kind of you to ask me," Mrs. Gates acknowledged, "but I can never seem to find time for club work. My family and household absorb all of my time and energy."

Mrs. Elliott was rather insistent that Mrs. Gates allow herself more time for recreation and release from home affairs, but Mrs. Gates was immovable. Perhaps when the children were older, she said.

Mrs. Elliott was disappointed. She liked Mrs. Gates and knew she would be a valuable addition to the club. Her call was prolonged to some length, and the children had come in from school before she rose to go.

When she reached home Don had come and gone, she knew not where, but he had taken his wheel. He returned an hour later and went upstairs to his room, Mrs. Elliott hoped, to read. Soon after his father came in, however, he came to the head of the stairs and said dismally, "Dad, I'm sick," then stumbled back to bed.

His parents hastened to him. He was quite ill, and Mr. Elliott, without a word to any one, went down and called in Dr. Gates, who had just driven into his driveway.

He found Don suffering with his stomach.

"What have you been eating, Don?" he asked kindly.

"Cakes," Don answered miserably.

"Cakes?" echoed Mrs. Elliott. "Where did you get cakes, dear?" knowing in her own mind that it was cookies from the Gates' pantry. Right here Dr. Gates would learn that his own children ate cookies between meals and had given them to her children!

"Got 'em at Tony's Delicatessen."

Mrs. Elliott started.

"Nice plain cookies, Don, or were they all dolled up with icing and cocoanut and pink and yellow meringue?"

"Um-huh," admitted Don.

"Why, Don!" Mrs. Elliott was white.

"Well, they ain't never any cookies here, and I was hungry!"

"But you know I've never permitted you to eat between meals, Don."

"Aw, gee!" muttered Don.

"Mother's pretty nearly right, Don, boy, but a fellow *does* come home from school powerful hungry, doesn't he?" Dr. Gates said. "And simple, home-made cookies are infinitely more wholesome than Tony's. Now, over at our house we've a big stone jar that Mrs. Gates tries to keep full, a futile task, I might add, but it's *never* empty. It's like the Biblical story of the widow's oil cruse, it never fails, though I hesitate to think of the many little pleasures Mrs. Gates sacrifices to it. Still, it's quite a matter of pride with her that the children know they can always depend on her and the cooky jar."

Mrs. Elliott flushed unaccountably.

"And the next time you just *must* have something to eat after school," the doctor went on, "why that cooky jar is open to you, if your mother will permit."

Mrs. Elliott choked. Her children have to go to a neighbor's for something to eat? She would *not* permit it!

By bedtime Don was quite easy, and it was then she noted her husband's drawn countenance.

"You are bothered, Frank. Is it just Don's illness?"

"No, it isn't. It's finances, my dear, bad as I hate to tell you. We are living beyond our means."

Mrs. Elliott patted his shoulder, staring out into the darkness. Out there she was seeing many things. The shadow was separating itself from the substance; things were ranging themselves in orderly rows, first things first.

"Frank, you are not to worry. Everything is going to be all right. I'm going to make them right. I—I've been such a—snob and a sham and a fraud. But from now on I'm going to be a—a cooky-jar mother, like our new neighbor."

And then he knew everything *would* be all right.

SO NOT TO BE ALONE *

Carolyn Hosmer Rhone

FROM the direction of the woodpile, outside Emma Guenther's kitchen door, came the sound of men's voices, quarreling: the even, brittle tones of Karl, her son, and the rumbling growl of Otto, her husband. Emma, working butter with energetic spankings of the broad wooden paddle, ignored the voices. Rivulets of oozy brine slid down the curved sides of the butter-bowl held firmly between her knees.

"Ach! Nodt so badt! Nodt so badt!" She patted the butter into a fat mound and marked it with a half-dozen little parallel creases. "Fifty cents a pound! Yah! Enough to buy the window-curtains, mebbe! The top-and-side kind. Silk, mebbe—and yellow!"

Emma lifted her eyes from the butter-bowl to the colored print above her dish-table, a picture of a rustic living-room clipped from the advertising section of a current magazine. Each detail of it—the beamed ceiling, the rich brown wainscoting of the walls, the winged chair by

* By permission of the author and of The Century Co.

the broad fireplace, the Indian rug on the floor, and the yellow curtains at the small-paned windows—she could see with her eyes shut tight.

Such a room! Ach! Such a room should be hers. For had she not, off the tourists, eating and sleeping them for two summers, saved seven hundred dollars that was hers to do with as she pleased? Soon no longer would she have to sit with visitors in the middle room where her husband slept. A company room should she have!

"Nodt so badt!" Before the heavy snows, it should be done. Yes, and the curtains and cushions! In the long winter evenings by the lamplight she should make them. A rug too! Not from Montgomery and Ward's should she buy a rug, when in the house she had old blankets which she could dye the yellow and old stockings for the black, to braid together into a round rug for the front of the fire.

And while yet the sleighing was good in the spring, she should have the company. The women of the club should sew their embroidery and play their cards of five hundred in her best room. She should no longer be a woman alone.

But no time was there to waste. Karl, her son, must this week begin to get out the logs on the hill. Ach! He and Otto were yet at their quarreling. Outside by the woodpile, their voices grew louder. She opened the door upon the stoop so that she might listen. Bitter were their words.

"Some day, I say to you, Karl, 'Gidt oudt, or I kick you oudt!' " From behind the kitchen window-curtain she could see Otto leaning against his ax, with scowls upon his face toward his son.

"Can't say it any too soon to suit me!" Karl's voice snapped like the breaking of the long icicles from the eaves in the spring sun.

Emma scalded her butter-bowl and paddle. She put the butter in the cooler.

Otto's voice answered Karl. "You go oudt onto the trail with the gun while it is yet September and the fall work to do! The wood not yedt ready for the winter! The logs nodt yedt down for the building! Ach! the work is nodt in you; only the lazinesses!"

Karl did not answer. Up the trail he went with his gun. Emma stepped out upon the stoop. The cat stirred lazily in the September sun. A squirrel scolded from a jack-pine by the door. Chickens scratched in the yard. The creek broke into a thousand voices beyond the hill. On the woodpile Otto's ax crashed once more upon the block. Emma took a few steps toward him. Stooped and drawn he was, with the hard work and the rheumatism, until his fifty years appeared as seventy.

"Otto!"

He moved out of the shade of a pine-tree so that the sunshine might warm his shoulders. "Yah?"

"We godt to keep Karl by us always. He cannodt go! If he is gone, we cannodt live. Is it nodt so?" Her face worked convulsively.

A dumpy little woman, Emma, her graying hair twisted hard at the top of her head; her close-set eyes, snapping, black as a girl's; her cheeks red with the red of the old country. She wore her gray calico dress gathered full at neck and shoulder and plump waist. Broad strings in a tight knot at the back held her ample blue apron, faded pale with the washing. Ten years younger than her husband, she looked twenty younger.

Otto bent his heavy body and rubbed the knee that the rheumatism had stiffened the worse.

"Karl! Ach! The loafer he is. So early he takes his gun and goes up the trail. Every day he gedts the more goot for nodtin. I drive him oudt some day!"

Emma waved both hands in a frenzy of argument. "Nein! Nein! You cannodt be left alone in the winter-time here on the mountain-side. You cannodt break the snows on the road. You cannodt tend the stocks in the storm. You talk foolishnesses! Do you nodt see? Karl, he forgedt soon his madt. He will get down the logs from the hillside and build the new room onto the house. Soon he do that! Yah!"

"Am I then no goot, no goot adt all? I? I ask nodt for Karl's help. I ask nodt for anybody's help!" Otto commenced to split wood with double energy, but the scowl of pain he could not keep from his face.

Emma turned back to the house where her work was nagging her, not yet done.

Karl *was* hard to manage lately; that she knew. But drive him, one could not. Sullen he was—sulky. Some day he would see the side of his bread the butter was on. Some day would not this ranch be his, when she and Otto were gone? And valuable it would be. When first the war, together with business failure in the city, had driven them out on the land, only a homestead it was, a homestead on the edge of the forest. But now it was growing into a resort, just because the fishing was here, and the hunting too, and the main road, the fine new road, not far away. Did not Karl know that he should be rich some day?

Emma entered the kitchen. She filled the scrubbing-bucket with water from the reservoir on the range, and, tucking her skirts high, she attacked the pine floor with broad rhythmic swishes of her scrubbing-brush.

What a handsome lad Karl was! And how the

girls took to him! That Abbie Wheelock down on the South Fork. A good housekeeper she would make, and an easy tongue would she have with the summer tourists.

Emma moved the long, oilcloth-covered table at which she served her boarders and scrubbed beneath it conscientiously, though never a sign of dirt could she find. Not for a week had she fed a tourist; the autumn weather already was scaring the motorist from the mountain passes.

Karl could do worse, much worse, than Abbie Wheelock. That chit of a Lassom girl who took in the money at the village drug-store of a summer. Always did she make the eyes at Karl. And often did he dance with her on Saturday nights. So often that people made talk about it. Ach! Karl! A heartache and a joy was Karl!

Around the stove where the wood-ashes grayed the floor, Emma scrubbed with quick parallel strokes.

When Karl married, he would be proud of the fine best room with the yellow curtains. The house as it now was, ach! such a house! Three rooms, end to end, like a train of cars, and the bedroom not even wall-boarded, only chinked between the logs to keep out the weather.

The scrubbing out of the way, Emma replaced the bucket on the bench outside the door. She did not have to touch one of the sleeping-cabins to-day. Easy work, in September. She went into the middle room, which served as bedroom and "settin' room" combined. It was dark in the middle room.

Right here should the door be cut into the best room. Right here!

Otto's bed she must tear to pieces and make from the feather tick up. A bad night he had had. See how the blankets were threshed and the pillowcase wrinkled. The pain in Otto's knee made the sleep impossible. Loud had she heard him groaning in the early hours.

With quick movements of her red, work-hardened hands, she finished the bed.

From here, when the door should stand open into the best room, the fireplace might be seen, and the window with the yellow curtains.

"Lazy I am! A fool am I, with a dream! Ach! Slow!" Emma hurried into the third room, where a curtain, pieced from flour-sacking, divided her bed from Karl's. Another curtain, hanging limply from a shelf in the corner, concealed her scant wardrobe. The room was as dark as north rooms always are, and as cold as a log house, shaded by a forest of pine, can be on a morning of early fall that has not yet bidden good-by to August.

Emma made quick shift of the beds. She lifted the curtain in the corner to look once again at her best dress. Taking it from its hook, she spread it on her bed.

"This sleeve must I make narrower here," she murmured. "And shorten it by the hem!" She picked a raveling from the skirt. "But it's nodt so badt! Nodt so badt adt all! Almost as goot as any!"

Yesterday she had worn that dress to the meeting. Karl had, with the team, taken her to the village. All the women together had had a club. The school-teacher, she had started it. And they called it—what was it they were going to call it? The Silver Creek Community Club. Some day would they save up money and build a house, a meeting-house for themselves. And such joy would it bring them all. Company for everybody, it would mean. Emma also should be a member. Had she not spoken up and said:

"You may come to my house. A surprise I will have for you. You may come to my house in the spring, while yedt you can ride in the bob-sleds. I will tell you when."

Had not Mrs. Spitzer, the wife of the cattle-man, said to her, "We can depend on you to come to every meeting, Mrs. Guenther?"

"As long as I have my Karl by me. I could nodt come the five mile alone. And the mister has the rheumatism so bad that often he can-nodt hitch up the team. Karl, he'll bring me always. He gedts excuses to come by the pool-hall. Is it not so?" Emma had answered.

Whipping-cream should she have thick on the

pudding, and sandwiches out of the breast of the chicken. Mrs. Spitzer, never could she make the raised bread like hers, Emma Guenther's.

She hung her best dress carefully on its hook and returned to her kitchen. She let the door stand wide open to the sunshine. Shading her eyes, she watched the hill trail. Karl? Returning so early? For sure! An easy swing had Karl in his walking.

Past the spring beyond the barn, past the corral, past the woodpile without a look at his father, came Karl, straight to Emma, in the kitchen.

He closed the door. Emma's eyes rested on him affectionately. He placed his gun carefully in the rack on the wall. Ach! Tall was Karl as the trees on the hill, and straight. His throat was brown where the red wool of his shirt-collar lay open. His chin was stubborn like that of a man who wins big stakes. But his black eyes were not steady. They shifted first to the floor and then to the window beyond which Otto was splitting wood.

"Here, Karl! The coffee simmers yedt in the pot at the back of the stove, and to-day's coffee-cake is yet warm from the oven. A sip? Jhust a crumb? Eh?"

Without a word, Karl sat down at the end of the long table and gulped the coffee. His frown was black upon his face.

"You godt troubles mebbe to-day, Karl?" Emma asked anxiously.

Karl grunted.

"Mebbe you begin to gedt down the logs from the hill for the new room, and you forgedt you godt troubles? Eh?" she suggested.

Karl sneered. "Yeuh! Fat chance, I'll say!"

"Jhust one more sip of the coffee?"

"Gosh, ma! Can't you see? I can't stand this damned country any longer! It's gettin' on my nerves. Can't even sleep nights!" He put the heavy white cup down with a thump upon the table. "I got to get out! See? Can't get along with the old man! Nothin' I do is right!"

Emma's voice broke in an effort to be casual. "Ach! Karl!"

He rose and paced the breadth of the room. "I got to get out, ma! Might as well go right off! I got to go!"

"But what I do without you? I cannodt plow the meadow, nor yet cut the timber! Karl!" she protested. Then, with dim hope, "You talk foolishnesses to tease me? Is it not that, you do? Say it is that!"

"God, no, ma! I've reached the end of my rope. See? You got money, ma; your money from the tourists. You can hire a good man cheap by the month. Pa could get along with a hired man!" Karl threw himself down again at the table, sprawling his elbows the width of it, and sinking his head into his hands.

Emma came close to him, but she did not touch him with her hand. "You godt a big future here yedt, Karl. Can you nodt see it? Tourists pay you the big money. Oudt there on the hillside are the trees for a hundred cabins, each with its white bed and its wash-stand and pitcher. Some day you marry and have here a nice home of your own, with much electricity for the lights and water for the white bath-tub. You have nice cars, and take trips. Can you nodt see? Away from here, you have only a job—only a job! It iss so!" Emma's voice rose shrill in excited argument.

Karl shook his head. "It ain't that, ma! A fellow goes stale as the devil in a hole like this. Who wants to be rich at the north pole? Nothing to do! Nowhere to go! Nothing to see! Nothing to hear! I want to see the world, all of it; and all I see is a fool squirrel in a jack-pine tree. All I hear is the old man growlin' by day and the coyotes yelpin' at night on the hill. Huh! I tell you I got to go! I got my own life to live, ma! I ain't mortgaged to a mountain-side!"

The tea-kettle crackled on the stove, and Emma filled it from a bucket on the wash-stand. Then she went to the window and stood with her back to her son.

"God, ma, but I'm sick of it all! I—"

"Karl," Emma interrupted, "suppose you

had a goot radio machine for to hear the world, speakings and music from everywheres—and suppose—and suppose you had a nice car to take your girl ridin' in, and down the valley of a Saturday night to the dance? Eh?" She rubbed an imaginary speck from the window-pane with a corner of her apron.

"Yeuh! I sure got a life-sized picture of it!"

Emma's eyes blurred. Somewhere in the distance she saw yellow window-curtains, top and side, fade out of a dream. Or were they transformed into yellow aspen-trees, away over there by the spring? She had not noticed yet that the aspens were turning. But overnight does the fall come!

"You—you—have them—them both," she faltered, "if you stay here by the ranch! I buy them for you! With my tourist money I buy them!" She did not look at her son. If she turned her face from the window she would see, over her dish-table, a picture.

"Gosh, that's different, ma! That's great! Could I go, right off, to Denver and buy them and drive the car home! Say, ma, could I?"

"Yah! I guess so! Mebbe. I'll see! Mebbe." The aspen-trees by the spring *were* yellowing. Yes. Otto must not split the wood for so long. He would be worse when the night came. "I guess so!"

Karl rose and strode in three steps across the

room to her. "Gee, ma, that's swell! That's swell!"

"You better not yedt tell your pa. The money is mine own, but— Better you not tell him I give you the check to get money from the bank!"

"Sure, ma; keep it dark. You're an old trump! You're great! He kissed awkwardly the knot of scraggly hair on top of her head.

"Nodt so badt! Nodt so badt!" thought Emma. But she turned straight to him now. "You stay, though; you stay by me for always! For that I do it, Karl!"

At first he did not answer. Then with a nervous shrug of his shoulders, "Oh, sure! Sure!"

"Then you go to-day. Go and get what makes you happy. I give it all to you, and you stay by me!"

"Right off? Can I start right off, ma?"

"If you can make the excuses that will keep your pa from gettin' madt!"

"Leave it to me, ma! I can hand him a line, I'll tell the cock-eyed world!"

He hurried out of doors. Emma picked up the scrub-rag and wiped the mud of the trail from the floor where his feet had stood. Then she stood dazed, in the middle of the orderly kitchen. Over her dish-table was there a picture? Yes. She stumbled into the middle room and returned with a gaudy art calendar of a girl picking cherries. She pinned it securely above the table, covering with it her dream of a best room.

"A calendar is a handy thing to have in a kitchen," she said.

Night came and Emma Guenther sat in the middle room with Otto. Karl had gone. He would stay the night in the village, and the next day he would get to the city. To-night would he be thinking kindly of her and the mountain ranch. Yes. She would mend a sock or two.

The coal-oil lamp gave off a faint sickly odor. The new blacking on the stove smelled like shoe-polish on fire. But one had to have the heat in September. The nights were chilly.

Opposite her sat Otto with his paper. His bad leg he had propped on a chair by the stove. He smoked noisily, and the strong tobacco-smoke from the old pipe mingled with the smell of the lamp and the stove.

Emma's needle felt its way through the heavy wool of Karl's sock. Thoughtfully she watched her husband. Should she prepare him for Karl's return? Just a hint? Yes.

"It is so quiet here of nights, pa."

"Ungh!" Otto's broad chin bristled with a week's growth of grizzly whiskers. One could almost see them in the shadow of his head over there on the wall.

"Sometimes I think, pa, a radio would be nice

up here in the winter nights. Music of a band mebbe? Speakings! I—''

''Nein! Nein! Radios! Foolishnesses! Foolishnesses to eat up the money!'' He turned a page of the paper with finality.

If once Karl had it, then what could he say? And such company would it be of a lonely night when the snow covered the windows and the pines moaned. Company? Ach, company!

And a car also. Except when the roads were deep with the drifts, quickly could Karl drive her to the meetings of the club. Never should she miss one; never one. Yah; company!

''Nodt so badt!'' She almost had joy inside her at the thought of Karl, happy—satisfied to stay by her on the homestead.

But of a sudden the joy turned bitter. She had not before thought such sorrow. Was she not proud? Then how could she, Emma Guenther, go to the meetings from house to house, if she had no room in which to have the club at her house? She would have to make the excuses. She could not belong with the women who had best rooms. And company? Never once more could she go. Proud she was. She could never lick the bone that she could not return with the meat upon it.

Otto dozed over his paper. The hole in the sock blurred. Mending was hard by the light of the lamp. She too would read. She put away the socks and picked up a magazine with a nice cover. It fell open at a picture of a bright room, a fine room with checked linoleum on the floor and yellow curtains at the window.

The lamp was too dim to read by. A bright lamp—a gasoline lamp—must she get some day. Her eyes were failing her. She laid the magazine back on the center-table.

Otto snored. His chin fell forward upon his broad chest. His paper dropped with a rustle to the floor.

Emma knew that she was the only person awake in all the world. Always does a woman struggle so not to be alone. For that she marries. For that had she not married Otto?—only to find that a man lives in his own land, apart.

For that does a woman have children, so that when she is old, she shall not be alone. Then they like not the home, and the mud of the trail is on their feet. Like Karl.

For that does a woman want a best room. So that she may make the pudding with the whipping-cream upon it—and the sandwiches of the breast of the chicken—for all the women of the club to come in their best dresses—and sew their embroidery and play their cards of five hundred. Company? So not to be alone.

The telephone clicked and then jangled.

What? Three long rings and two short? Yes. She was coming. Coming. Yes.

Could something be wrong with Karl? But no! Not until to-morrow would he get to the city where the danger was.

Otto roused from his nap. "Ungh?" he grunted and then sank back into the stupor of his sleep.

Emma's hand on the receiver trembled.

Karl's voice came over the wire, hearty, strong. Nothing wrong with Karl. Emma took a shuddering breath of relief.

"That you, ma? Say, ma, I got something to ask you, ma!"

"Yah?" she answered, her voice unsteady.

"Ma, you wouldn't care, wouldya, if I borrowed that tourist money off ya?"

Emma did not answer. What was he saying? Her mind was not quick to follow.

"You still there, ma? Say, I'd pay you good interest, sure. You see, ma, I want to get married, and I need the money."

Still Emma said nothing. Married? Then, surely, she would be no longer alone.

"Lissen, ma; it's—it's Sue Lassom. She won't live up there in the country, she says. I'm going to take her to the city, and get a job, and set up housekeeping. See? I sure need the money, ma!"

To the city? Emma leaned heavily against the wall beside the telephone.

"Don't get sore, ma! I'll pay it all back with big interest. Sure!"

Emma felt her life slipping from her—everything that she had lived for, hoped for; everything that she must have. She raised her voice in a frenzy of desperation.

"Nein! Nein! That you shall not do! You made the promises that you should stay by me always. Nein! Nein!" Hand and head shook in frantic gesture. "Nein! That you shall not do, Karl!"

"Aw, ma! Be a sport! Don't take it so hard! And lissen, ma; I'm married already and at the station. I already have got the money. But I'll pay it back some day, honest, with interest—with big interest. See? 'By, ma!"

Emma felt her way, chair by chair, across the room to the kitchen. She lit the bracket-lamp, holding the match until it burned out in her fingers.

Mechanically she took the bread-bowl from the shelf of the cupboard. She must set her sponge for to-morrow's baking.

Her eyes, out of habit, searched the wall above her dish-table—for a dream.

"It's handy," she faltered, "to—to have a—a—calendar in the kitchen!"

THE LITTLE MOTHER *

Ethel M. Colson

SHE was so little, always, so little and so timid and yet so daring. All her life long, although never a fool, she "rushed in"—albeit gently, and at the call of duty—where she literally "feared to tread." She came upon the scene somewhat earlier than she was expected, greatly to her mother's comfort and inconvenience. A friend of middle life, learning this circumstance, smiled quaintly.

"Just like Mary. Her mother was in sorrow, and somewhere back in the dim reaches of space the soul of Mary divined this and hastened to the rescue. She's been doing it, bless her! ever since."

She was the tiniest baby, and the quietest, with wide blue eyes that always looked a little frightened. The game of life scared her from the very beginning, but she never whined about it. Later, the nine big brothers who played with and teased her frightened her, periodically, al-

* Reprinted by special permission of the author and of "The Independent."

most out of existence, but she never let them suspect it. When the time came to part they missed and mourned her far more than the bigger, jollier sister who enjoyed rough play and "gave back as good as they sent." Responsibility scared her, but when the widowed mother suffered a paralytic stroke it was into Mary's girlish hands that the reins of restricted family management slipt—to be well handled. She dreaded the sight of pain, which made her sick with responsive misery, but hers was the tender task of "taking care of mother" until that mother died.

She was afraid of love, but it came early and she never hesitated to embrace it. She was afraid of loneliness, strange situations, but she married her John in an inland English village on a Monday, sailed with him for the South Seas on Thursday, and never saw another white woman for eight months. The ocean gales and the tropic tempests frightened her sorely, but she never said so. When, in South American ports, the young captain-husband went ashore without her, she was afraid of the Irish mate who looked at her so oddly, of "Portuguese Joe," the steward, who adored her, of the dark-faced port officials who sometimes came aboard in John's absence; but John never knew this, any more than he dreamed that she was timid of the fellow captains who found the shy little bride so sweet. Not given to self-analysis, introspection, she seldom questioned her feelings, sensations; put to the test, she would have admitted that she believed all women to be similarly afraid. Why, therefore, make a fuss about fear, any more than about any other difficult, uncomprehended rule of the game?

She feared, a year later, to take her babe so far away from doctors and more experienced mothers; but the women of her day rated no duty higher than wifely allegiance, and she never thought of not going back to sea with her husband. She kept him company—on a little sailing vessel, with an open fireplace down in the little cabin with a bunk built in its side and a hammock slung above for the baby—until she had more babies than could well be taken along.

It was not all smooth sailing. Captain John was a bold mariner, with a record for carrying sail and making swift voyages, and neither he nor Mary meant the record to be spoiled by her presence. Mary's land-reared heart dropt a beat, sometimes, when the rail was under water, but her calm face only betrayed this by its sun-softened pallor. Once the baby was very ill and only the homely wisdom of the sympathetic mate, whose odd looks she could not happily interpret, effected its salvation. Once Mary was ill herself, in mid-ocean, and more than once she and the willing steward nursed John, who was subject to attacks of fever, back to the life he had come so close to leaving. And there were incidents more nearly tragic.

One black night, for instance, a big "liner," tearing away from the home port for which they were headed, ran them down and cut the tiny *Pamlico* in two. The big ship rushed on, heedless of the fate of her insignificant victim, and Captain John, loyal shipmaster tho he was, sprang for a tense instant to the head of the "companion."

"Mary! For God's sake, come up!"

"Yes, dear," a quiet voice answered. "I'm coming. I was just getting a shawl for the baby."

But underneath its quietude the soft voice shook with fear.

The *Pamlico* did not sink, being loaded—and this is a true story!—with Para rubber, but nobody knew what might happen before morning. So all night long, while the men toiled at the pumps and Captain John did what he might in the interest of safety, Mary sat in the rigging, clad only in her night clothes—and it was raw November—hushing her swathed but shivering infant and smiling bravely whenever within the radius of Captain John's lantern. Daylight brought double luck in the shape of a sister ship willing to tow them to harbor, and the knowledge that the cabin, altho partially flooded, was at least as safe as the deck, also badly awash. So Mary clambered down again, the steward reverentially helping, and she scarcely noticed the cheer that the relieved sailors sent after her. The repressed terror of the long, silent hours was making her tremble, and besides, she was so conscious of her moistly clinging night-gown, so afraid that the now sleeping baby might have caught cold.

Another time, in a terrible storm, Mary saw three men swept overboard, and her husband flung against the rail with a broken shoulder. Still another time, out in Brazil, several of the sailors got drunk, got in a fight, got killed, and were, perforce, replaced with worthless Lascars. These trouble makers stirred up an incipient mutiny almost before the ship had cleared, and Captain John and the Irish mate had sore work to "hold" them. Mary, now well used to simulating courage, went in actual fear of her life, that time, and that, too, was the only time when she suffered violence from her husband. The little sleep John snatched he snatched with a revolver in his right hand, and, despite Mary's careful watch beside him, he formed the habit of hitting out with his big left hand if touched or too closely approached during slumber. The habit proved life-long, but before Mary suspected its existence she had tried to arouse John in her usual manner. Her face was still discolored when they drew to port. There was a fire, too, and the time when their little tender was nearly swampt in the Amazon River, and the time when they were held in port, the pitch starting from the vessel's seams, for fear of yellow fever. . . .

And there were other tests and trials. One voyage Mary could not accompany her husband. Liverpool "lodgings" do not form a cheerful prelude to the Valley of Death—into which Mary penetrated a long way in behalf of her second baby. John never saw this baby until she was more than a year old. His ship was lost off the coast of Newfoundland, and its penniless master was compelled to stay there until spring opened—when he worked his way home by means of another ship going to China. There was no telegraphic connection between Newfoundland and England in those days, so Mary did some troubled thinking, alone, in an unknown city with her two children, the money left her by her missing husband fast melting away. She would not, could not believe John dead, but supposing he should be. None of the nine brothers was wealthy, all, with true insular prejudice, had objected to Mary's marriage with a sailor. Mary herself had more than once helpt her sister, now on a Canadian farm with her family.

Mary herself recovered slowly, she knew no

way of earning a living, the new baby was delicate and difficult to keep alive. She only grew stronger when John returned and took mother and children with him on another long voyage. He had no ship of his own now, but a ship-owning friend had trusted him with mastership of the *Drake*.

Something of the same sort happened with the coming of the third baby, only this time the wreck was off the coast of France, with Captain John but three days out from Southampton. The storm which wrecked the *Drake* kept Captain John eight hours in the pounding billows, with the result that his heart was permanently injured. The news was carried to Mary so suddenly that she came near dying. But the subsequent good tidings helpt her creep back to life and smile courage back into her husband's sinking heart.

The ship-owning friend did not blame John, being himself an old sailor, but he decided that a wife and three babies were too many hostages for a master to have with him, and John hated leaving Mary behind, so he made but a few more voyages, to redeem his reputation and to save a little money. Then, taking the small legacy opportunely left Mary by an old aunt, they went to America, where the streets and the highways presumably were paved with gold.

John went first, to find a suitable investment

for their modest capital. He found it in a worn-out Missouri farm reputed to have coal mines beneath it. Mary, following with the children, found the journey from New York to Gixon very strange and alarming, and there was an accident that further distrest her. But, as always, she kept her fear hidden, and the bravely smiling little Britisher met with much kindness and many friends.

She arrived to find John deeply discouraged. The coal story proved a mere myth of the man who had sold him the land—in Boston. The land itself was hopeless, its long, bare stretches seemed especially dreary to eyes used to the trim, snug farms of England, the little graveyard just back of what had been the garden struck cold to Mary's heart—there were so many tiny graves in it. Years later, when they had sold the long-held white elephant for a song, silver actually was found beneath its fields and others reapt the benefit. But John and Mary, fearing starvation, fled within the year.

They fled to a small mining town of Southern Illinois, where a good-natured Missouri acquaintance had secured a "job" of sorts for John. The climate was torrid and unhealthful, the burning summer as hot as the Missouri winter had been cold, John promptly succumbed to fever. Again strange, cold fears clutched at the heart of Mary—now become "Mother"—worn thin and too old for her years by carking care. But she bore up bravely—what else was there to do?—nursing John with desperate tenderness, watching their little hoard melt away with terrible rapidity, scared of the future, scared of the unaccustomed "darkies" who thronged the mean little street outside her windows, scared of everything in the world but the kindly doctor and John. When the latter recovered he went to Chicago and found work as a sailor. Mother nearly died to see him go, but there was no work that he could do in Gaylord, and the doctor said that he could not stand the climate. And it was evident that the children must not go hungry. There were four of them by this time, all girls—the three sons came later. So John went back to sea.

He could not get a ship, of course, not yet being an American citizen, but a good old lake captain and owner helpt him to get out "first papers," gave him a job as mate on a boat going to Buffalo, and a letter of introduction that sent him to England as first officer of a rickety old tub that had the good luck, from the owner's point of view, to be run down, on the return trip, by a responsible steamer. John was rescued by a sailing vessel, en route for South America, and for long weeks he had no opportunity to send back word to Mother—suffering slow agonies in Gaylord, with two of her little ones ill of malaria and their purse all but empty, But:

"I won't have my children called fatherless!" she cried to the kind old gentleman who broke the news that the *Dunstan* was reported lost, with all on board. "If John were dead I should know it. But he'll come back; he will, he must!"

Twice a day, in the cool of the morning and evening, she trudged to the post-office, the tinier babies left in the care of the tiny eldest—not yet six years old. She took care of her children, she toiled, between times, at the fine sewing the kind old gentleman begged her to do for him, and always, at the bottom of her heart, she was praying. Mother never considered herself a religious woman. Later, when the children made mistakes, she was wont to feel that had she been more religious they might have done better. But always she said her prayers and read her Bible daily, and presently her faith that God had not forgotten them was rewarded.

One day the children were playing in the "side yard" with the kind old gentleman's dog—he would allow them to ride him until tired, then sit down gently, and, to their great glee, "shunt" them to the ground—when a man much thinner and more bearded than they remembered their boyish-looking father came thru the gate. He caught them up and kissed them, one after the other, and went slowly, almost timidly around to the side door. There was a piercing scream from Mother—to whom Father, after the long delay, had thought it best to bring tidings of his salvation in person—and the children wondered why she should sink down on the step and weep so terribly, she whom they never before had seen to shed a tear. Father wondered too, a little, but the kind old gentleman was wiser.

"Let her have her cry out, my son," he told Father. "She's a fine, brave creature, but she's been thru a bitter deal."

Father went no more to sea. The Chicago ship-owner got him work at an adjacent watering-place and there the family stayed until the youngest son had been born and buried. Then they went to Chicago for the sake of the children. Mother's health had grown so poor that sometimes she feared she might die and leave them, but she said nothing. She was used to keeping her fears under, and the children went untroubled and happy. Practically alone and unaided, since faithful Father was none too successful and "no manager," she battled with and vanquished the dragon of poverty. It took hard work and for years Mother went shabby, but they were all neatly clothed and comfortable, and the children never suspected that they were poor. Somehow or other they were educated, drest, supported. Then Father, who had developt a latent talent for engineering, was sent West to install the water system of a new penitentiary. The promised salary was tempting, but by the time Father got to work a new political party was in power and a Kansas City firm got the new contract. Mother and the children arrived to find that they need not have come at all.

The Chicago company recalled Father, but nothing was said about bringing back his family. Mother and the children stayed West nearly three years before enough could be pinched and saved to pay railway fares to Chicago. The penitentiary prisoners escaped sometimes, and Mother lived in terror of them. Also, she feared that the boys might become rough and unruly in such a strange place and away from Father. Once all the children had first measles, then chicken-pox, with no one to nurse them but Mother. When, at last, they got away, the eldest girl—and she was but seventeen!—insisted upon marrying a Missouri farmer, so they left her behind them. And she was the only one of the children to have a family as it turned out.

One by one the children grew up, became self-supporting or married. One or two made unhappy ventures and came back home. One was unhappy, but tried not to show it. Mother's fears and cares for them all tried her, but presently all the minor anxieties that had seemed so great were merged in a greater. Father's health, as Mother's, had become uncertain. The fear of a helpless old age tugged at his soul and communicated itself to Mother, altho she would not admit the possibility. But the doctor told her privately that the old man's over-taxed heart was liable to "give out" at any time.

Thereafter Mother lived in fear of having Father brought home to her lifeless—and one day the awful fear came true.

It was a fearful shock to Mother, despite her long dread, and at first it was feared that she might not survive it. Night and day her sick heart yearned and hungered for the lost companion who had protected her as she had mothered, comforted him.

"You can't understand it, my dear," she said, with gentle pathos to a friend who tried to suggest consolation. "I've lived with Father more years than you've yet dreamed of; nearly fifty years we've been together, and I was engaged to him before that. I can't seem to realize life without him at all."

But she found comfort in the thought that Father had died too suddenly to remember that he was leaving her all but penniless—it had never been possible to do more than carry a minute insurance—and, being still needed, she rallied bravely. There were the children to consider. One of the sons was in sorrow, the daughter out West was having trouble over one of the grandchildren, one of the daughters still at home was acting strangely—this was the daughter born when Father was first lost at sea, and Mother always believed her "marked" by that time of stress and trial. Mother smiled down the grief that turned her soul to ashes, crushed down the new fear that was springing up in place of the fruited old one, and took up the task of caring for that nervous, middle-aged child.

After that things changed rapidly. The family was small and Mother was persuaded to move into an apartment. And she was very lonely. The work of the outgrown house had been too much for her; its rent too big for her slender income. But the old house had been rife with memories of Father and the children, the cozy little apartment had no memories. The children who still lived at home were out all day and Mother had much time for sorrowful thinking, for the new, groundless fear of dependent old age.

Sometimes, too, when she allowed herself to acknowledge it, her childhood fear of death returned to torment her. Of course, if she were quite sure she were going to Father and the long buried baby—but the babe had been so innocent, Father such a good man! And she'd been too busy, always, to be as good, as religious as she should have been, surely. As always, Mother took great comfort in saying her prayers and reading her Bible, but she could not, she never had been able to relate the religion that so helpt her to live to the thought of dying, and now, for some time, she suffered severely. She was too much alone.

But, as always, she kept busy, she refrained from allowing her fears to trouble those about her, and one day comfort came. Death, after all, she reflected, is but an unknown journey, an untried experiment, and of these she had made and taken so many. Surely it could not be more to be dreaded than the long, lonely journey from New York to Missouri, that awful, subsequent sojourn in a strange country with four hungry little ones at her knee and no news of her husband. She had lived through all this, every one had been so kind, and the Good Lord had made everything right in the long run. In Missouri, Father had met her—

After that, her fears died a natural death, somehow. Mother did not yet know it, but the Great Fear had been banished never to return.

One day one of the distant living sons came West on a business trip and stopt for a brief visit with Mother. He had not seen her for some years, and he was imprest by the grave beauty of her appearance. Mother had not been a beauty in youth, and she had never cared for the tricks and assistance whereby some women hold back the encroachments of time. She had been too busy, always, to think much of her looks, outside of exquisite cleanliness and neatness. But she had grown old as simply and frankly and sweetly as she had done everything else. Time and experience had carved her face into wonderful lines, her smile was sweet beyond expression, her eyes like the gates of Heaven. Her son, too, found her strangely full of charm.

Mother had never seemed to talk much, perhaps because there always had been so many others to do the talking. But she had thought much and clearly, and now, sitting alone with her in the evening, her son wondered why he never before had recognized her conversational ability. She knew so many things, so deeply, that he had been at such pains, such cost, to learn. He learned a lot that night.

The talk turned on a recent disaster, with the varied heroism thereby engendered. The son, praising a certain man's brave conduct, opined that he could never have so acted. Mother smiled.

"Oh, yes, I think you could, dear," she answered. "We think we can't do and bear lots of things that are quite possible when they come to us. I think human beings can always do and bear what they must, and it isn't the doing or the bearing that hurts; it's the being scared and complaining. I've always tried not to complain, but if I had my life to live over, I'd try not to be so frightened. So many of the things I've dreaded have never come to me, and I've managed to endure the others. Of course," with the slow, sweet blush of old age, "I never could have done anything heroic, but I've had some hard things to go through.

"Your sister Alice and I were talking, the other day," she went on, presently, "and she thinks she could never bring herself to go so far from home with any man as I went with your father, that she couldn't stand what I did when we were first married. But I tell her she could if he had to, and it wouldn't be too hard if she had love enough to sustain her. That's why I've had such a happy life, sonnie; I loved your father so much, and I've been so happy in you children, so proud of you! Life isn't too hard, unless we're trying to shirk things, or are lonely. I've always kept going because I've had so much to do."

Silence fell between them, and by and by Mother, tired with the unwonted talk and excitement, dropt into the light, easy sleep of advanced years. Son, watching her, smiled oddly. It had come to him suddenly, how much he was losing in not seeing more of his mother, how little he had really known her all his life.

The Benjamin of the family, born when the hardest times were over, he had not shared in the severest household struggles, and Mother always had believed in keeping trouble from the children. But, of course, he had known, vaguely, of those hard early trials, and now, like a panorama, he saw what his mother—this little, delicate mother—had borne and endured.

He thought of his own luxurious life, steam heated, rubber tired, cushioned, and contrasted it with the life that had so ripened and sweetened Mother. He dreaded heat and cold alike, managed never to be long subjected to them; she had suffered freezing cold on the Missouri farm and the small country house of his infancy, suffered awful heat in the tropics, in western Kansas, in that Illinois mining town where she had so bravely battled with poverty and despair. He shrank from an hour's loneliness, took a drink or went to the theater if even threatened with depression, he had known no crucial bereavement or sorrow; she had been soul sick, heart hungry, lonely—starvingly, smilingly lonely—thru long years.

He demanded "something to deaden the

pain'' of the merest toothache. What had she not suffered in silence? Fire, shipwreck, child-bearing, operations, long terms of rheumatic misery, of dragging weakness and weariness, of recurrent agony balanced by alternations of dull distress, but who had heard her moan or grumble? He loved his work, but he insisted upon frequent holidays, and the bugbear of ''overwork'' was ever before him. She had never loved housekeeping—somehow he knew it!—but when had she rested at all?

Suddenly he knew, too, the secret of her cool courage, the smiling bravery he had always believed instinctive if not unconscious. Suddenly he realized what that quiet courage had cost her, how in her secret heart she had always been afraid.

Soldiers are pensioned, justly enough, for the brave deeds they are paid to render. But mothers—splendid heroism at their hands is unrecognized because so general, so unassuming, ''as natural as life.''

A great wave of tenderness swept over Son, sitting there regarding Mother's quiet face and folded, work-worn hands, tenderness mixt with new and reverential comprehension, tenderness not unmixt with wonder. Mother looked so little fitted for her long tale of doughty deeds. Yet he knew that, should need arise, her future would be as silently brave and unselfish as her past.

"And she's always been so little," he pondered, watching her calm breath rise and flow gently, "so little and so scared!"

THE MOTHER *

Robert Haven Schauffler

All day her watch had lasted on the plateau above the town. And now the sun slanted low over the dull, blue sheen of the western sea, playing changingly with the angular mountain which rose abruptly from its surge.

The young matron did not heed the magic which was transforming the theater of hills to the north and lingering lovingly at last on the eastern summit. Nor had she any eyes for the changing hue of the ivy-clad cubes of stone that formed the village over which her hungry gaze passed, sweeping the length and breadth of the plain below.

She seemed not much above thirty: tall, erect, and lithe. Her throat, bared to the breeze, was of the purest modeling; her skin of a whiteness unusual in that warm climate. Her head, a little small for her rounded figure, was crowned with a coil of chestnut hair, and her eyes glowed with a look strange to the common light of

* By special permission of the author and of The Century Co.

every day. It was her soul that was scanning that southward country.

From time to time she would fondle something hidden beneath the white folds of her robe. Once she threw her arms out in a passionate gesture toward the plain, and tears overflowed the beautiful eyes. Again she fell on her knees, and the throes of inner prayer found relief at her lips:

"Father, my Father, grant me to see him ere the dusk!"

Once again she sank down, moaning:

"He is in Thine everlasting arms. But Thou, who knowest times and seasons, give him to me on this day of days!"

Under the curve of a shielding hand her vision strained through the clear, pure air,—strained and found at last two specks far out in the plain, and followed them breathlessly as they crept nearer. One traveler was clad in a dark garment, and stopped presently, leaving his light-robed companion to hasten on alone toward the hungry-eyed woman on the plateau.

All at once she gathered her skirt with a joyous cry and ran with lithe, elastic steps down through the village.

They met on a low, rounded hill near the plain.

"My son, my darling!" she cried, catching him passionately to her bosom. "We have searched, and waited, and agonized,'' she continued after a pause, smiling at him through her happy tears. ''But it matters nothing now. I have thee again.''

''My mother,'' said the boy as he caressed her cheek, looking at her dreamily, ''I have been with my cousin. Even now he waits below for me. I must bid thee farewell. I must pass from thy face forever.''

His lip trembled a little, but he smiled bravely. ''For it is the will of God, the Father.''

The mother's face went ashen. She tottered and would have fallen but for his slender arm about her.

Her thoughts were whirling in wild confusion, yet she knew that she must decide calmly, wisely, quickly.

Her lips moved, but made no sound.

''Oh, lay Thy wise and gracious hand upon me!'' was what she breathed in silence.

Then her voice sounded rich and happy and fresh, as it had always sounded for him.

''His will be done. Thou comest to bid farewell to thy brothers and father?''

''It may not be,'' he answered. ''My lot henceforth is to flee the touch of the world, the unsympathetic eye, the ribald tongue of those like my brothers—the defilement of common life.''

The mother pressed him closer.

"Say all that is in thine heart," she murmured. "We will bide here."

They sank down together on the soft, bright turf, facing the brilliance of the west, she holding her child as of old in the hollow of her arm.

He began to speak.

"For long and long a voice within me said, 'Go and seek thy cousin.' So I sought and found, and we abode together in the woods and fields, and were friends with our dear brothers the beasts, and the fishes, and the birds. And there, day by day, my cousin would tell me of the dream that filled his soul and of the holy men who had put the dream there."

The mother's eyes grew larger with a swift terror, but she held her peace.

"And at the last, when the beauty, the wind, the sun, the rain, and the voice of God, had purified me in some measure, my cousin brought me to visit these holy men."

The clear, boyish voice rose and began to vibrate with enthusiasm.

"Ah, mother, *they* are the chosen ones of God! Sweet and grave and gentle they are, and theirs is the perfect life. They dwell spotless and apart from the world. They own one common purse, and spend their lives working with their hands and pondering and dreaming on purity, goodness, and the commands of the great law."

He sprang up in his excitement from her encircling arm and stood erect and wide-eyed before her.

"Ah, mother, they are so good that they would do nothing on the Sabbath, even to saving the lives of their animals, or their brothers, or their own. They bathe very often in sacred water. They have no wives, and mortify the flesh, and—"

"What is their aim in this?" the mother interrupted gently.

The boy was aflame with his subject.

"Ah, that is it—the great goal toward which they all run," he cried. "They are doing my Father's work, and I must help! Hear, hear what is before me: When a young novice comes to them they give him the symbols of purity: a spade, an apron, and a white robe to wear at the holy meals. In a year he receives a closer fellowship and the baths of purification. After that he enters the state of bodily purity. Then little by little he enters into purity of the spirit, meekness, holiness. He becomes a temple of the Holy Spirit, and prophesies. Ah, think, mother, how sweet it would be to lie entranced there for days and weeks in an earthly paradise, with no rough world to break the spell, while the angels sing softly in one's ears! I, even I, have already tasted of that bliss."

"Say on," she breathed. "What does the holy man do then?"

"Then," the inspired, boyish tones continued —"then he performs miracles, and finally—" he clasped her hand convulsively—"he becomes Elias, the forerunner of the Messiah!"

From far out in the wilderness came a melancholy cry.

"It is John, my cousin," said the boy, radiant, half turning himself at the sound. "I must go to him."

She drew in her breath sharply, and rose to her feet.

"Bear a message to John," she said. "Not pourings of water, nor white robes; not times and seasons, nor feasts in darkness and silence, shall hasten the kingdom of heaven; neither formulas, nor phylacteries, nor madness on the Sabbath. Above all, no selfish, proud isolation shall usher in the glorious reign of the Messiah. These holy men—these Essenes—are but stricter, sterner, nobler Pharisees. Tell thy cousin to take all the noble and fine, to reject all the selfish and unmeaning, in their lives. Doctrine is not in heaven. Not by fasts and scourgings, not by vigils and scruples about the law; not by selfishly shutting out the world, but by taking all poor, suffering, erring, striving humanity into his heart will he become the true Elias."

There was a breathless, thrilling moment of perfect silence as the glowing eyes of the mother looked deep into the astonished, questioning eyes of the son.

Then she rested both hands on his shoulders and spoke almost in a whisper.

"As for thee, the time is now come. Does my son know what this day means?"

He looked at her wonderingly and was silent.

The mother spoke:

"For many years I have kept these things and pondered them in my heart. Now, *now* the hour is here when thou must know them."

She bent so close that a strand of loosened hair swept his forehead.

"In the time before thou wert born, there came as in a dream a wondrous visitor to me straight from the Father. And that pure, ecstatic messenger announced that the power of the Highest would overshadow me, and that my child was to be the son of the Highest, who should save His people from their sins—the Prince of Peace—the Messiah!"

From the wilderness came a long, melancholy cry, but the rapt boy heard not.

The mother continued in the soft, tender voice that began to tremble with her in her ecstasy.

"This day is thy birthday. Twelve years ago this eventide, when thou camest into the world of men, men came to worship and praise God for thee,—the lowliest and the highest,—as a token that thou wert to be not only Son of God but Son of Man as well. Poor, ignorant shepherds crowded about us in that little stable where we lay, and left the sweet savor of their prayers, and tears, and rejoicings. And great, wise kings from another part of the earth came also."

From beneath the folds of her robe she drew forth by a fine-spun chain an intricately chased casket of soft, yellow gold.

The boy took it dreamily into his hands, and as his fingers opened it, there floated forth upon the air of the hills of Nazareth the sacred odor of incense mingled with a perfume indescribably delicate and precious.

"Read!" whispered the mother.

The boy held his breath suddenly.

There, on the lower surface of the lid, graven in rude characters, as if on the inspiration of the moment, stood the single word

LOVE

She flung aside her arms as if to embrace the universe.

"Love! Love! Love!" she cried in her rich, mother's voice. "It is the greatest thing in the world! It is the message of the Messiah!"

The heavens over the sea were of molten gold, and a golden glow seemed to radiate from the boyish face that confronted them. In their trance-like ecstasy the wonderful eyes gazed full into the blinding west—gazed on and on until day had passed into night.

One iterant sound alone, as it drew closer, stirred the silence of that evening: it was the voice of one crying in the wilderness.

MOTHER HARVEY'S STRATEGY *

Olive Higgins Prouty

"OH yes," sighed Mrs. Harvey, "you have to keep after this modern generation of ours, Mrs. Jesse. That's what mothers are for, I think. I don't know anything about Mr. Jesse, but you see my husband is a very practical sort of person. Most men are. It's we women who have to keep alive the sentiments."

Mrs. Jesse, bending over embroidery rings, looked up and smiled. She hadn't been living in the little town very long, but already she had heard of Myron Harvey's "practicalness." It had been he, she recalled, who had spoken so strongly in the town-meeting about the foolish extravagance of spending money on the Fourth of July for public fireworks.

"Poor Myron!" Mrs. Harvey went on. "It sort of riles him all up—bands, and flags, and flowers, and speeches—such things. Yet he'd be among the first to enlist, if his country needed him to fight. That's how Myron is. My

* Reprinted from "Delineator" by special permission of the Butterick Publishing Company and of the author.

goodness! I can't remember when he last gave any of us a Christmas present. It sort of irritates him somehow—buying presents, wishing people Happy New Year. 'Tom-fool nonsense,' he calls it. But he wouldn't see any of his family in trouble, Myron wouldn't."

She looked up thoughtfully, letting her sewing fall.

"At first," she concluded, "I tried to make Myron over according to my pattern. But I gave it up after a while as a bad job. It's better not to try to mold husbands too much, Mrs. Jesse. I do all my molding on the children. They're the clay God sent me. And you'd better get down on your knees and thank God *you've* got some clay to work on too. Women are awful empty-handed without it."

She nodded, bit off her thread with a snap, reeled off a fresh length of cotton, skilfully rethreaded her needle and continued running rapid little rows of stitches along a tiny petticoat.

"I tell you, Mrs. Jesse," she continued, "I was bound that my children should feel some of the joy I do about bands and fireworks and anniversaries. I was bound to pass on to them some of the good old customs *my* folks passed on to me. I've succeeded, too! Of course it's meant a lot of fuss and bother, with a holiday always around the next corner to get ready for.

"But it's paid—it's paid, Mrs. Jesse! I don't put any stock at all in this modern-mother, simple-holiday talk. I tell you, you simply can't preach the spirit of anniversaries into people's hearts without a few of the symbols. Now my children, Mrs. Jesse, feel all the sweet old sentiments there are to feel, about Christmas and Easter and Thanksgiving; and it's because I haven't been lazy and told 'em I hadn't time for colored Easter eggs and Christmas trees, and flour paste and valentines—such things." She drew a long breath, then added:

"The result is, grown-up as they are, they're all just counting on their big Fourth of July dinner here at the house next Thursday, with salmon and peas and ice-cream, and the fireworks at night in the empty lot. Edna and Elsie are coming home especially. You see, we Harveys would feel as if the bottom had dropped out, without our celebrations. We do have the best times together!

"Oh, I tell you, Mrs. Jesse, keeping up old customs together is what makes a family strong, and rich in traditions, I think; or a country either, for that matter. But there! I'm preaching. Myron says I'm like a victrola: set the needle on one of my half-dozen records, and I'm started, and no stopping me."

She broke off gaily into a laugh, fastened her thread with three repeated little jerks, stuck the needle, point down, into the front of her waist, and held up the petticoat.

"For Linda's baby," she announced, "this is. Those girls of mine won't have a stitch of machine work on any of their babies' clothes. Nonsense, I say. Why I remember how proud I was of my first machine-hemmed ruffles. But there! I've started off on another of my records!"

"I've never heard any of them. I enjoy them, Mrs. Harvey," little Mrs. Jesse protested.

"No, it's six o'clock and I've got to go along. It's my baby's birthday. He's seventeen, and I've got to put the candles on his cake, and get up into my gift trunk in the attic, before supper. Junior and his wife are coming over, and I'm sort of afraid Junior's forgotten about Roy's birthday.

"You do have to keep after this modern generation a little. I have a supply of presents on hand for just such emergencies. I've got a nice little Longfellow birthday-book that will be just the thing for Junior to give Roy. I picked it up, marked down, just after last Christmas. Good-night, Mrs. Jesse. Come over on the Fourth. You must know us Harveys."

The Fourth of July proved to be a very warm one that year. Mrs. Harvey was downstairs early, closing blinds and drawing shades, in the hope that a little of the cool night air might be preserved in air-tight and darkened rooms against another day's attack of burning heat and scorching sun. Bare-footed, still in her short nightgown, she picked her way out to the back hall to see how the ice had held out. As she was returning, the telephone rang. She bustled into the coat-closet and took down the receiver.

"Hello, mother," called a fresh, wide-awake voice. "Were you up? It's Linda. Ed has just looked at the thermometer and it's up to eighty-four even now. It's going to be a regular old scorcher, Ed says, and I don't think you ought to have us all over there. It's too much for you."

"Nonsense, Linda!"

"No, I mean it. That's why I'm calling so early. Really, mother—"

"Nonsense—nonsense!" repeated Mrs. Harvey. "Why, the peas are shelled already, and the salmon on the ice. You get dressed and you'll feel better."

At ten o'clock there was a telephone call from Mary. Mary was Mrs. Harvey's youngest daughter and had been married six months. She lived in the next town, six miles away. "It's ninety-two degrees, mother, in the shade," she called. "I've been talking to Phil. He's out in the hammock now, just about *all* in, poor boy! We've talked it over, Phil and I, and we think it's too hot for you to bother with a big dinner. You've got Elsie and Edna there and that's plenty, such weather. We'll be over for the fireworks this evening, though."

"You'll be here at one o'clock, and don't be ridiculous, Mary," snapped Mrs. Harvey. "Why, there's a lovely breeze here, and I'm setting the table on the side porch. Tell Phil to move around and keep away from the thermometer." She hung up the receiver. "Too hot! I declare!" She scoffed under her breath, and bustled out on the porch to continue her table decorations with tiny flags and tissue-paper. Elsie, tall, slight, languid, in a thin dressing-sack of dotted muslin, stood by the long, extended table with a bunch of flat silver in her hands. Elsie was the Harvey daughter who had gone to college and was now a full-fledged librarian in New York.

"That's right, Elsie," said Mrs. Harvey briskly. "Lay them around."

"Oh, mother," sighed Elsie. "Why do you bother so? Why do you make them all come, when it's so hot and no one wants to?"

Mrs. Harvey glanced up quickly, then: "They do want to come, child," she disputed emphatically. "They do. They're only afraid it will be too much for me. Why, I like it. Come, come, Elsie, do show a little Fourth of July spirit. Do, dear."

At half-past twelve, the thermometer registered ninety-seven on the side porch. Mrs. Harvey, in the kitchen, prodding the salmon gently with a long fork was singing softly to herself.

It was nine o'clock before the last rocket in the empty lot beside the Harveys' shot skyward, burst into three floating blue stars, and fell with a muffled thud in the long grass. It was half-past nine before a troop of timid breezes came stealing up from the meadow, and stealthily found their way to the Harveys' side porch.

The Harveys were all there, the boys stretched full length upon the closely cropped lawn, the girls leaning languidly back in the big porch-chairs, the grandchildren, too tired even for occasional firecrackers, gathered on the steps, arms clasped about their knees—they were all there except Mr. Harvey. He, as usual, had disappeared immediately after the sandwich supper, "out of patience," he had remarked, "with such nonsense." He had been sound asleep now for nearly two hours.

At present the rhythmic squeak of Mrs. Harvey's chair was the only sound to be heard upon the porch as she rocked energetically back and forth in her corner by the railing. She was the only one of the little group who didn't seem utterly exhausted.

"Why, there's a breeze!" she ejaculated

cheerfully. "Sure as anything. It'll be cooler now. We always do get the breeze on this porch! Now you children all stay here as long as you want. I guess I'll go up now, if you don't care." She got to her feet. "The fireworks were lovely, boys," she called down to them. "I believe that was the finest pinwheel I ever saw! We've had a lovely day, I think," she went on. "The salmon never was better, or the peas either, and the table looked real pretty, I thought, with those streamers. Haven't we had a nice day?" she asked pleasantly.

"Very nice, mother," sighed Linda.

"Very nice," conceded Junior wearily from the lawn, where he sprawled full length.

Mrs. Harvey moved over toward the door.

"I declare I believe I shall sleep to-night!" she said, with a satisfied little sigh. "I believe I shall. It's been such a grand old Fourth, and such a happy one too—with all my children here. I hope you'll always keep up these family reunions after I'm dead and gone," she said. "I believe in them. Well, good night. Sweet dreams to you all. Better not stay up *much* later."

The screen door slammed behind her. She stood a moment at the foot of the stairs, then before going up glanced into the parlor to see if everything was all right; squeaked down the hall to the sitting-room and back again; and looked into the dining-room. One of the little breezes from the meadow was stirring the window-curtain. Mrs. Harvey went over to the couch just beneath the window and sat down. "I declare," she whispered, turning her forehead toward the breeze, "that feels good. I'll lie here just a minute."

She fell asleep almost instantly. She didn't know how long she had been dozing when she woke to find the window-curtain brushing her cheek. It could not be very late, though, because the children were still up; she could hear them talking just outside on the porch. That was Linda speaking now.

"Well, now that we've sent the chicks off home to bed," she was saying, "let's go on with what we were discussing about mother."

"It's not only," broke in Mary's crisp young voice, "that mother is wearing herself all out with all this fuss, but she's wearing us all out too. Phil and I were just crazy for a day all by ourselves this year."

"So were we, Mary," said Sally, "last Thanksgiving, Junior and I. We had it all planned to run off to New York and have a little honeymoon time all by ourselves, but when Junior spoke to Mother Harvey about it—why, she wouldn't hear of it. It seemed like sacrilege to her. We just had to give the idea up."

"It was terribly inconvenient for me to take my vacation just now," sighed librarian Elsie.

"And I had to travel three hours to get here from Portland," said Edna. "Of course it's nice to be here at the house with mother for a day or two, but there's only one bathroom, as you all know. I didn't have the courage to disappoint poor mother, however."

"Here we've all been just miserable and hot and unhappy all day long, and she thinks we like it!" sputtered Mary.

"She set the alarm-clock for me at 5 A. M. this morning," contributed Roy. "I told her the fellows I went with weren't kids to get up early any more."

"Exactly," took up Mary. "It was like that about my wedding. I wanted it quiet and simple, but it would have broken her heart not to have seen me duded-out in white satin and a wedding-veil."

"It makes me just weary to think about Christmas," broke in Linda. "Mother never wants any presents for *herself*. *That* isn't the difficulty. In fact, the poor thing never gets any of much account, but she makes the rest of us hustle. She finds out what we're all giving to each other, lists the things up, and then if any one of us seems to appear neglected, she gets after the others. I found her list, one year. Why really, when I select a present for you, Elsie, for instance, I'm wondering if it's good enough to suit *mother.* Oh, she makes Christmas a terrible burden—so many presents, such a lot of work and expense. Father hates it, too."

"I think," said Elsie, "one of the reasons father hates celebrations so is because mother celebrates so hard. It's making us all hate them—that is what it's doing. Mother is a dear, but I do wish she'd leave us alone for a little while."

"Oh, well," said Junior, "don't feel too strongly about it. We've got to remember that mother is getting older. It won't hurt us, I guess, to humor her a little. We'll have time enough to celebrate our holidays according to our own notions. Mother is nearly seventy, you know."

Junior was sitting on the porch now, in a chair tilted back against the casement of the dining-room window. Mrs. Harvey, just inside, could have touched her son's shoulder except for the screen. She lay very still, flat on her back, eyes wide open, her plump hands clasped over her breast. She was afraid Junior could hear her breathe. She didn't care to raise her hand and push aside the curtain brushing her cheek. They mustn't know she had been listening. She must spare them that. She couldn't risk rising and stealing up-stairs, because there was a spring in the couch that groaned sometimes. She lay imprisoned for nearly an hour.

It was when the children were finally breaking up, pushing the chairs back against the house, and calling out good-night, that Mrs. Harvey rose at last, crept noiselessly out to the kitchen, and threaded her way up the back stairs to her room. She didn't sleep very much that night. As she lay and listened to Myron, snoring steadily hour after hour in the adjoining room, her bright little eyes peered through the dimness to the row of white cardboard squares stretched along the back of her bureau. They were the pictures of the children. She couldn't see their features, but she felt that they were all conspiring together there on her bureau, just as they had downstairs on the porch, repeating over and over again the things she had heard them say—the cruel things that had stabbed and hurt.

She didn't cry. That was characteristic. She had learned not to. She only lay and stared, and turned over at intervals of every ten minutes. Once in a while she would whisper out loud, "So that's the story," or, "I must warn Mrs. Jesse," or, grimly, "Well—well, wrong all these years!" and finally before she fell asleep, just before dawn, "I'll do it if it kills me," she declared.

Three nights later, Elsie, braiding her long hair before the mirror in the guest-room, remarked to Edna, lolling on the bed, "I wonder if mother is feeling well. Did you notice anything queer about her to-day?"

"Queer? No. What do you mean?"

"Oh, nothing, only—well—I happen to be thirty years old to-day, and—"

"That's so. Of course—the seventh!" interrupted Edna, "and no one, poor child, no one—"

"Oh, I didn't expect *you* to remember, all by yourselves, but mother—well, it's the first time *she's* forgotten. It's the first year of my life that I haven't had a present, and a nice preachy little sermon, and a cake with candles on it from mother. Seems queer to have *her* forget."

Edna sat up straight.

"It does seem queer—*awfully* queer," she exclaimed. "I don't like it, Elsie. I'm afraid Junior was right. Mother's getting older. Why she *never* forgot before. Poor mother! How it will hurt her tender heart when she does recollect! You must let her down just as gently as you know how. She'll be terribly contrite. Tell her birthdays don't count for much when you're older, anyway."

Two weeks later it was Junior's birthday that Mrs. Harvey "forgot." To Sally, his wife, Junior asked at dinner, "Nothing come over from the house yet?" (The Harvey children all referred to their old home as "the house"), and later, "No word at all from mother to-day?" and at 10 P. M., anxiously, "Do you suppose mother's sick?"

But she wasn't, just a little tired, after getting Elsie off to New York she explained over the 'phone.—So it was! His fortieth birthday! Well—well! she hoped it was a happy one—and there! she hadn't made him a cake, had she? Had he missed it very much?

"Not a bit—not a bit, mother. Glad enough you didn't bother. Glad enough!" he assured her emphatically. But to Sally he remarked gravely, after hanging up the receiver, "Mother's getting older, Sally, I'm afraid. Mother's getting older."

In September it was Mary and Phil's wedding anniversary day that mother failed to observe by a little dinner at the house. In October it was the grandchildren's Hallowe'en party that she explained she was a little too tired after the church supper to arrange.

On Thanksgiving, for the first time since any of the children could remember, there was no family reunion at the house. Mother had decided in mid-November to spend Thanksgiving week with her only sister, Julia, who lived in Bangor. Aunt Julia had not been well all the Fall, and each of her letters urged Martha's long-deferred visit more and more impatiently.

Mrs. Harvey mentioned her intentions one night to Linda, when the oldest daughter had dropped in on her way home from church.

"Of course," she said, "I do feel dreadfully not to be home Thanksgiving, but I am sort of anxious about Julia, and I think she'd appreciate my going up to spend Thanksgiving with her. I thought your father and Roy could have dinner with you, or with Junior—either one. I don't know as I've ever visited on Thanksgiving Day, and think I'd like to for once. What do you think?"

"Why," said Linda, perplexed, "if you really want to go, mother, of course we can manage all right."

"I thought you could, too," went on Mrs. Harvey pleasantly. "Perhaps Junior and Sally could take that New York trip of theirs this year. And if Elsie comes home you could take care of her at your house, couldn't you?"

"Yes, indeed, mother. Oh, we'd all get on all right. Don't worry. You mustn't think you've got to look out for us all that way. It will seem strange to have you away at Thanksgiving. We'll miss you, but we've all been afraid you needed a change—or a rest, or something. You've seemed sort of tired and different this Fall. Perhaps it will do you good."

"Perhaps," Mrs. Harvey replied brightly. "Well, I'll write Julia to-night, then. Dear me, Linda, see if *you* can thread this needle."

Linda stopped at Junior's on her way home from the house that night. She found Mary and Phil had been there for supper, and that father had "gone around" after prayer-meeting, to continue a business discussion with his oldest son. Linda made her announcement in regard to mother's plans for Thanksgiving as soon as she entered the big living-room where they were all assembled. A silence followed her news, a silence of amazement, bordering on fear. Sally dropped her sewing in her lap and stared, Junior got up from his chair abruptly, and shoved his hands into his pockets. Mary reached over and pushed her fist into Phil's. Phil gave a long, low, subdued whistle.

"No Thanksgiving dinner at the house!" finally exclaimed Sally.

"Oh, dear, is mother going to be sick?" cried out Mary.

"It doesn't seem as if I could bear it—mother losing all her enthusiasm, this way," almost sobbed Linda.

Mr. Harvey got up and walked out into the hall without a word. He reappeared a moment later, hat on, overcoat buttoned to his chin.

"You make me tired, the whole lot of you!" he blurted out. He stopped at the doctor's on his way home.

Idle hands were Mrs. Harvey's all November,

with no surprises to prepare for the children at the Thanksgiving reunion, no muslin curtains to be freshly laundered for the guest-room, no new cretonne hangings to be added here and there, no especially mixed mince-meat to be stewed and stirred, and tenderly administered to for hours and hours on the back of the kitchen range. Idle hands, too, that later busied themselves nimbly with no bit of fancy ribbon or embroidery; that jotted joyfully down no lists of children's names followed by an array of gifts; idle hands, and idle thoughts that did not plan during the long night hours how a hundred dollars could be evenly distributed, and lovingly, between the children and their children at Christmas-time. For when Mrs. Harvey came back from Aunt Julia's, the week after Thanksgiving, she took out all her best nightgowns from her best-clothes trunk, brought them downstairs, laid them near at hand in her bottom bureau-drawer, and prepared for an illness. She could devise no other scheme for avoiding the big Christmas celebration. The children must not suspect her of subtle motives; besides, it was easier for her.

The shop windows, trimmed now with Christmas red and evergreen; the counters laden with holiday gifts and children's toys galore; the sidewalks crowded with bare little fir-trees, ready for the joyful trimming and starring and candle-lighting— Oh, no! she could not bear to witness all the happy getting-ready time, and take no part. It was easier to stay in bed; besides, perhaps something really was the matter with her—all the children seemed to think so; perhaps there was.

"That's right, Mrs. Jesse," she would smile wanly and longingly from her pillows at the younger woman, as she sat and sewed beside her in mid-December, "that's right. Just you get all the happiness and joy you can out of these holidays when your children are young. Just you do. I've changed my ideas some this summer. When your babies are all grown up you mustn't try to drive them too hard. You've got to just leave them alone some. Remember that, my dear. I haven't been feeling quite up to snuff this Fall, and do you know what I've discovered? Why—I've discovered it was sort of a relief to my children not to have me bothering around all the time with birthdays and celebrations. Yes, sir—a sort of relief. No," she went on cheerily, "no, we aren't having a tree this year. It's the first time since Junior was a tiny little baby. Just think—forty years. But I'm just too played out! Do? Oh, I've no idea what they are going to do. I imagine there won't be any present-giving though. No presents seems to be the modern idea. By the way —you can have all our Christmas-tree trimmings if you want, Mrs. Jesse. I don't believe Linda or Junior will bring their children up on Christmas trees. They won't want them."

Neither did the Harvey children know what they were going to do. The rudder to their little world seemed to be lost, with mother upstairs sick in bed. Mother had never been sick at Christmas before. What were they going to do? They didn't know. First the little Harveys began to ask; then Elsie from New York; then Edna from Portland. Do? Do? Why, what *could* they do, with mother sick, and fear that approached consternation possessing their hearts?

"Well," grumbled father, "I'd do something, seems to me—brought up as you were. You act like heathen around here—no Thanksgiving, no Christmas—no Sundays next, I suppose. Is that the way your mother and I brought you up? You disgust me—the whole lot of you. It's about as dismal as a grave around this house lately, and I keep out of it all I can."

"But, father, we thought that you hated—"

"You thought—you thought—you thought—Do less thinking and get your mother well," he flung back crossly.

When Christmas was but seven days away, and the yawning prospect of another dreary holiday like the preceding Thanksgiving stared the Harveys in the face, Linda said to Mary: "It's like losing mother before she really goes

—no Thanksgiving, no Christmas, no getting-together of us all. It's unnatural and it's horrid! Oh, Mary,—let's ask Dr. Mason if it would hurt her—a tree, I mean, and presents here at the house, just as always."

"Oh, let's, dear Linda. Let's!"

"Why it may be the very thing to rouse her," said Dr. Mason; "can't tell. No harm anyhow, as I see. Happiness, you know. Nothing like it for a cure. Do everything you can think of to please her. That's the idea."

"Everything you can think of to please her." That night Father Harvey stole out after supper, and returned an hour later bearing with him a small white pasteboard box in his vest pocket.

Christmas morning dawned very bright and sunny that year. Mrs. Harvey, lying quietly awake, flat on her back, hands folded idly, waited patiently for the arrival of the little flickering square of sunlight on the counterpane. To-day her eyes filled with tears at sight of it. Why, this was the first Christmas morning since she could remember that she had not risen very early, before the sun itself, bobbed her head into every occupied bedroom in the house and called out an explosive "Merry Christmas!" She wiped the tears from her eyes with a corner of the sheet. Her thoughts descended to the picture of the empty sitting-room below.

"Just as if our Christmas tree had been sick and died," she sighed.

She breakfasted at eight—or tried to. "Don't seem to have any appetite, Delia," she said in explanation of the untouched pile of toast and hardly disturbed omelet. "I declare," she added, when Delia had gone out, "I believe I'm not so well to-day. I don't know as I'm ever going to get up." Then she folded her hands again in their listless fashion on top of the white sheet, neatly folded back over the blanket. Her eyes began their daily pilgrimage up and down the hilly track made by a crack in the white plaster overhead.

Thus she was lying at nine o'clock when the Harvey children and grandchildren, having assembled in the hall below, crawled stealthily up the stairs, suppressing whispers, forefingers pressed upon lips, eyes a-twinkle, and stood ready all in a huddled bunch outside mother's closed door. Then Junior whispered, "Ready!" and opened the door. A chorus of Merry Christmases burst like a dozen stars from a giant rocket.

Mrs. Harvey sat bolt upright in bed. Then they were upon her—all the children, all the in-laws, all the grandchildren—all the dear, dear family, all but Myron. Secretly hidden behind the door of the adjoining room, one eye shut, the other held close against the open crack by the hinge, stood Myron Harvey, on tiptoes now, better to observe the expression on Martha's face, as upon the counterpane, where two hours before had lain the solitary little square of sunlight, now began to grow a mound of packages, all shapes and sizes.

As he gazed he heard the children's tumultuous voices: "I made this, every stitch"; "Got to get well to wear mine"; "Wonder if you like jewelry"; "Hope you need what I chose," and intermingled in the turmoil, he caught Martha's gentle ejaculations, "Well, well!" "I declare!" and "Did you ever!"

"Now you're not to worry with all this or get excited, Mother Harvey," ordered Mary's fresh young voice.

"Dr. Mason said," put in Linda, "that we were just to pop in and pop out again. We're all going right downstairs, and while you're opening your things up here, we're going to be opening ours on the tree downstairs."

"We just had to have our tree, mother," burst forth impetuous Mary.

"We traced the trimmings to Mrs. Jesse, night before last," said Elsie, "and she said she *understood perfectly* the sentiment we felt about the dear old things. She was glad to give them back. They're all fastened on in the same old places. We did it last night when you were sound asleep."

"And, by the way, we're staying to dinner," remarked Junior as casually as he knew how, "but don't worry about that—the girls have it all planned and half cooked already, I guess. Delia was told about it a week ago. I selected the turkey myself.

"You know Thanksgiving was so dismal!" pleaded Elsie.

"And the grandchildren would have been heartbroken," put in Sally.

"And we're all sort of dependent on Christmas here at the house," apologized Linda.

When the door finally closed on the last of the noisy troop Mrs. Harvey sat staring straight in front of her. She said nothing, only kept on rolling and unrolling a bit of the top edge of the sheet, back and forth, back and forth, between her thumb and forefinger, as she had throughout the entire scene. The reflection of her face in the mirror, as Mr. Harvey caught it through his crack, made him look away, so bright and heavenly it was. Martha had looked like that on their wedding-day, and then again when their first baby was born. He moved one of his feet.

She glanced toward the door. He appeared on the threshold. She opened her mouth to speak, but he interrupted her.

"I'm no hand at presents myself," he grumbled. "Foolishness, I think—but here's something or other I picked up." Flushing and very ill at ease, he tucked his little box beneath the pile of bundles on the bed, turned quickly and left the room. Mrs. Harvey dropped the edge of the sheet then, reached for the package, and unwrapped it with fingers trembling.

Within the box lay an ugly little brooch made of jet. Mrs. Harvey remembered now, with a little stab of tenderness, that Myron used to admire jet forty years ago. He had given her a velvet cape covered with it when Junior was born.

An hour later Mrs. Jesse, knocking gently on the door, discovered Mrs. Harvey sitting before her bureau doing up her hair. There was a sparkle like bright steel in the sunshine in Mrs. Harvey's eyes. There was the determination of a proud flag in a stiff breeze in the poise of her head. The bed behind her was ripped wide open, the bedclothes stretched back over a chair at the foot. The pillows, stripped now of their white cases, perched atop the turned-back clothes. An array of many-colored Christmas gifts lay in confusion on the table. A pair of patent-leather shoes stood at attention upon a near-by chair.

Mrs. Harvey jerked her head into an emphatic little nod at sight of Mrs. Jesse.

"Good morning, Mrs. Jesse," she staccatoed. "Merry Christmas, dear. I'm up, you see. Come in. Do! Sit down! I've got fifteen coming to dinner,'' she boasted. ''Tell you what—I've got to get downstairs and see about my table—surprise the children. You can hook me up. Seems my children had to have their tree anyhow! Those are my presents on the table there. Did you ever see such a show? I want you to go upstairs to the attic and bring down all there is in the third trunk on the left. Guess I got enough to just about go round. Nothing like the convenience of a gift trunk, Mrs. Jesse. Always said so. You better start one. Awful handy.''

Mrs. Jesse closed the door behind her and quickly went over to Mrs. Harvey.

''I'm so glad—'' she began, tears stood in her eyes—''oh, so glad that—''

''There, there, dearie, I know you are. You don't need to tell me. Listen.'' Then taking the younger woman's hand in hers she repeated, head tilted playfully to one side:

> ''Little Bopeep has lost her sheep,
> And doesn't know where to find them.
> Leave them alone, and they'll come home,
> Bringing their tails behind them.''

She paused. ''I 'left them alone' all the Fall, 'and they've come home' now, Mrs. Jesse—all of my sheep. Even Myron,'' she added tenderly.

THE RASPBERRY DRESS *

Ada Jack Carver

EUGÉNIE LASTON was nearly sixty.

When she was in her early forties she had put on deep black—a kerchief tied under her chin at home, and many veils when she went abroad—and had become an old woman. This was the custom among the people with whom she had lived since her marriage, a stocky, blue-eyed peasant folk who, in the days before the war, had drifted to the Louisiana bayous from Burgundy and the north of France. To these people the kerchief and the veils are a symbol: they signify that a woman has forever renounced the world, the flesh, and the devil.

But Eugénie hated her black clothes. They were irksome, distasteful to her. She hated the very smell of black. She could even taste it, a dull dyed color against the tongue. From the folds of the black kerchief her face, still beautifully pointed, looked out with rebellion. Her eyes, with yellow flecks in them, were sullen,

* Reprinted from the Century Magazine by special permission of the author and of The Century Co.

lit at times with the flash of secret laughter.

In the community where Eugénie lived, women treasure innumerable bags and boxes. These boxes are filled with the trinkets, the fripperies of their youth. In one of her most secret places, hidden away under layers of ragged old quilts, Eugénie, unknown to her family, hoarded her savings, nearly two hundred dollars in greenbacks and silver; money which, in old-woman ways, she had earned through the years: crocheting and knitting, piecing quilts, embroidering altar-cloths. . . . Eugénie had hoarded this money for a purpose.

When long ago she had put on a kerchief, she had said to herself, rebelliously: "Tchick! In a year or two, as soon as I get money enough, I'm going back to New Orleans, dressed fit to kill. I shall go and visit my good friend, Jeanie Jomette." . . . That was nearly twenty years ago. Life on the bayou was hard; and Eugénie had buried one child after another, with yellow fever and smallpox, little sickly blue-eyed girls. Now the two that were left to her were married and had girls of their own. But the prospect of her journey still lent purpose, direction, to Eugénie's days. She would go down by boat. That is the only way, of course, to approach New Orleans, in some sort of river craft. She would buy herself a silken dress; and when she was out of sight, beyond Martin's Ferry, she would throw her kerchief overboard, into the black bayou water.

Every spring on Fat Tuesday Eugénie would say to herself, "I should have gone down for Mardi gras." And during the Lenten season, when people think of their sins, Eugénie muttered: "I better go down this Easter. I'm getting old."

And now the spring had come again; and for the first time in years Eugénie's two daughters were up and about, with no new baby on the way, and none underfoot. It would be a good time to go. Some fine day she would say to her daughters, Silla and Rose: "Me, I'm going away for a little trip. . . . A week or so. I'm going down to the city."

They wouldn't ask any questions. They had never understood their mother (they took after their father's folks), but they were respectful and dutiful girls. "Poor mama," they would say, "her mind's on the river." By which they did not refer to the sluggish stream that crawled in front of the door; when a Louisianian speaks of "the river" he means the Mississippi.

Eugénie was not of peasant stock. . . . In her youth she had drifted about from one houseboat to another. There were tales told of her birth; of how she was not really born at all, but was found by an old bayou ferryman curled up in the reeds, like Moses, wrapped in a gorgeous Spanish shawl . . . and crowing with delight at the blue, untroubled, monotonous drift of the water-hyacinths. . . . Later, when she was in her twenties, Eugénie had kept a "house of entertainment" on the river, below New Orleans. The big boats used to stop at her place; and the townspeople and the wealthy sugar-planters, when they had guests from the North, brought them out for gumbo and bouillabaisse suppers. On such occasions Eugénie would dance for them. One time, she remembered, an artist had painted her in a red dress. "The Red Dress," he had called the picture. Eugénie remembered the dress well. It was made of pigeon-throat silk, and it dropped off of one shoulder. In one hand she had held a red fan. She had looked as if she were about to dance the Spanish fandango. . . . People had said that the artist was in love with her. Eugénie wondered sometimes what had become of the picture, and of the painter.

Perhaps because Eugénie's youth had been spent on the river, she remembered it so vividly. The Mississippi is queer. It does something to you. At times old Eugénie was vague, *distrait;* and her sons-in-law would say she was daft. Then her Madonna daughters would get angry, offended. "You let mama alone! Her mind's on the river."

The goings-on of Eugénie's youth would have filled a book; for Eugénie had loved all over the State, clear down to the Ouachita River. Her past was in layers. Once when she was seventeen she had had a brief infatuation for a sailor from Buenos Aires. Ah, well, life was as tranquil, as meaningless now as an old outworn shoe. For Eugénie had been an old woman going on twenty years; and there were no steamboats any more, and no wine and no whisky. And the sun was too hot, and the moon was too cold, and she had too many granddaughters.

Holy Jesus! What a noise and to-do they made, swarming like flies, here, there, and everywhere, so a body could scarcely sleep. "Grandmama, you is forget," they would say, "how people feel when they young."

Ah, but had she forgotten?

Eugénie's granddaughters began with little Fleurette, who was six, on up to Aline, sixteen and a half. Aline looked as Eugénie had looked when she was a girl—all French and Spanish, all languor and insolence, with the same red mouth and mournful eyes. What lying eyes the child had! "What's the matter with you, Aline?" the river boys would ask. "What's eatin' on you, honey? I reckon you need some lovin'."

Eugénie lived with her two daughters and their families in a rambling, rickety two-story abode made out of an old river steamboat. One daughter lived on the upper deck, and the other one down. Their husbands—shiftless, improvident, sleepy-eyed—picked moss and fished for a living and raised a little rice and sugar-cane. Across each deck of the house, upstairs and down, a clothes-line was flung. What a lot of clothes it took for ten growing girls! It seemed to Eugénie that her two daughters did nothing but make dresses and wash them, so those chits would look decent and clean. The dresses were fashioned just alike, and of a grayish material bought by the bolt from the store. The girls, to look at them, might have been orphans, out of an orphan asylum. Sometimes Aline would rebel, with tears in her eyes. "I wish I had a dress made out of some other color."

At such times old Eugénie, where she would be sitting smoking her corncob pipe, would smile to herself. "Aline, she gets that from me." And sometimes, when her daughters were out of earshot, Eugénie would call Aline to her side. "Come, *chére.*" She would feel the girl's slim thighs, and pinch her smooth round arm. "Wait. Maybe I got two bit, hid away . . . for a new ribbon, *hein?*"

Aline and the priest were the only fun and excitement old Eugénie ever had. The priest was very old too, and when he came to call, her daughters turned him over to Eugénie to be entertained. They had a feeling that there was something between these two, a common bond —because Eugénie and the father had both loved the old steamboat days; because Eugénie for her part had known life and living, and the father the white way of heaven. They were great cronies, these two, Eugénie and Father Brochet. The father had little creases in his cheeks, and a sense of humor. And somehow Eugénie felt that this good man, so close to God and the devil, understood her better than any one else on the bayou. Well, he ought to, of course. Had she not confessed all her sins, and become a good Catholic?

Eugénie's sins, purple and gold and scarlet, hung furled and tattered like battle-scarred flags in the arsenal of her heart. Sometimes, weeping, she took them out and looked at them, and put them away again. Such beautiful sins! —sins so near to goodness you could scarcely tell them apart; you could scarcely tell where the good left off and the bad began.

. . . .

One bright morning, during this Lenten season, Eugénie's sons-in-law brought her a letter. "Who's writing to you from the city?" they asked. Eugénie hurried to her little room to read it. Her hand shook. . . . The letter was from her old friend, Madame Jeanne Jomette.

"How are you getting along, Eugénie? . . . You remember the artist who painted you? He is boarding with me, and we sit and talk of old times. . . . I have a nice, fine house now, with plenty of room. If you ever come to the city . . ."

This letter decided Eugénie, filled her with yearning. She would go down and visit Madame Jomette. On Easter Sunday morning she would take the train for Baton Rouge, and catch the excursion boat. . . . She set about at once making her preparations. She was as shameless, as secretive as an old mammy-cat. The week after next would be Easter. Already John Politte, who kept the meat and fish market in town, was grooming his Easter beef, the finest in all the country-side, which, on Easter Sunday, would be paraded through the streets in garlands of flowers. . . . Eugénie got her clothes in order; her petticoats, her "josies," her stockings, and her kerchiefs. When they were all ready she packed them into a bundle. Then she took her darning out to the deck. "I'll patch up them children's clothes before I go 'way," she said. She sat and thought of her trip; of how she would buy for herself a fine silken dress; of how pleased Jeanne would be to see her again.

Upstairs Eugénie's daughter Silla was running her sewing-machine—*hum, hum, hum, hum!*—making Easter dresses for her children.

Downstairs her daughter Rose was running *her* sewing-machine, making Easter dresses for *her* children. Scraps of dull grayish cloth littered the place. "Bah! The color of river-bilge!" Eugénie said to herself. Eugénie, dozing, had Easter thoughts. "Look here!" she called once, shrilly, to her youngest granddaughters, who played near by with their dollies. "Look here; you must be good children. Good little girls. I raised your mamas right."

The little girls looked up at Eugénie with pretty, intense, yellow eyes. Their little gold faces were eager, and Eugénie grew more vehement. "What long legs girls have these days," she thought, darning, "and how tall my granddaughters are getting! Soon they'll all be grown, and I'll be an old, old woman." Aloud she said: "Look here, Fleurette, you and Marie. You must never let the boys kiss you!"

"No, grandmama," the little girls answered, in shocked voices. And Marie, who was ten, piously clasped the hands of her dolly together as if it were praying. "No, granny."

Eugénie blinked at Marie, very fast, striving to keep her eyes open. "Marie," she said sternly, "is you been to catechism this week? Is you been to confession?"

Marie's voice was drowsy. She dropped her demure yellow eyes. "Yes, grandmama. I say to the father: 'Father, I accuse myself of—of slapping my little sister; of sassing my good kind grandmama, what darn all my clothes.' "

Eugénie grunted. The baby, with her sly little baby sins! She slapped at the gnats and the flies. The scent of sweet-olive stained the air; and along the bayou, wild plum and haw lifted their bloom, like white lace spread out in the sun. . . . Presently there was talk from the little girls, excited, staccato. "Yonder come Aline and her beau! I saw 'em first!"

Eugénie peeped through the shrubbery. It was nine o'clock in the morning, and that Jules, that lazy *garçon,* he ought to be out in the fields, instead of making love this time of day. Well, it wasn't like it used to be. Girls used to stay indoors till sundown to take care of their skins; nice, well-mannered young ladies. They waited for the moon to do their courting. Eugénie peered, and the little girls peered. The eyes of the old woman and the eyes of the children were dark with excitement. Aline's beau parted from her lingeringly at the gate and went on down the road, playing on his mouth-organ. He played the lazy drawling grumble of a train, far off in the Indian pine-woods. He played the lonely mournful whistle of a steamboat. Well, he was just the sort of boy Eugénie used to like when she was young; tall, untroubled, indolent, with a lilting sway to his shoulders.

Once he turned and threw a beautiful careless

kiss to the girl Aline. Eugénie could feel it in the air as it passed over her head. You could see at a glance that Aline was in love. She seemed to have bloomed overnight. It was just as if an artist had touched her up in places, a high-light here, a shadow there. Even the children could sense it. They looked at her and drew in their breaths. "Oh, Aline!" they screamed. Aline's slim hands strayed to the flowers; her eyes laughed in the face of the sun. She put her arms around her grandmother's neck. "Grandmama," she asked, "were you ever in love?"

Eugénie shook her off. Bah! The question was an insult. She began to rock very fast. "I don't think much of that boy, that Jules. How come he ain't at work, out in the field?"

But already Aline had forgotten Eugénie. She stepped over and through her little sisters, humming; and Eugénie, left to herself, laughed softly. In love! What did Aline know about love, such a baby? But for some reason Eugénie felt happy inside. Aline was just like she used to be, all Spanish and French. She would have to talk to Aline, give her a little lecture. "Look here, Aline," she would say, "you must never let the boys kiss you, *chére.*" Eugénie felt pleasantly stirred, awakened. She liked to watch people in love. Time was when she had had a hand in every love-affair in the parish. She could no more help dabbling in love than she could help breathing.

. . . .

The next morning at breakfast, upstairs with Silla, there was a heated discussion. Silla was the mother of Aline, and one day Eugénie took her meals with Silla upstairs, and the next day with Rose below. Eugénie, from her crowded seat far down at the foot of the table, heard Silla and Aline at it, having it nip and tuck. She listened. Aline, it seemed, wanted a store-bought dress for her Easter. There were tears in her voice; it seemed to be a life-and-death question. There were tears in Silla's voice too. "Look what done happen to her, since Aline go out with the boys! She got all kind of notion!" Aline's mother threw out her hands, with a knife in one and a fork in the other. "Nothing don't suit her no more. Now she got to go gad about and dress like a fancy woman."

"Oh, but mama!" Aline threw out *her* hands, with a violet in one and a rose in the other—she had no use for a knife or a fork; she ate nothing at all any more. "Oh, but if you could see, mama, the so-pretty frocks in the stores! Red ones and pink ones, all trim in ruffle!"

Eugénie listened with interest and strained her old ears. She could just see those dresses the child described, fluffy and fussy, like crêpe-myrtle trees. She had raised her own daughters religious, but her grandchildren were different. She hadn't had much to do with them, with their upbringing; she had served her time when they came along. . . . Little lovely, secret things were always cropping out in them, things that puzzled their mothers. But Eugénie knew, understood. So the stores in town were full of dresses, dresses with ruffles! She got up from her place at the table, sly like a cat. "I believe, me, I go spend the day with Tante Antoinette," she said to her daughters, yawning. She went and washed her face and hands, and put on a fresh black "josie." She got out her black cotton gloves, her veils, and her Sunday shoes. And into her bag went some of her savings, sixty dollars in greenbacks.

Eugénie walked along the bayou until she reached Martin's Ferry. There she waited for the bus that would take her to town. She had not long to wait; it was Saturday, and the buses ran every hour, taking the country-folk in to trade. . . . It is no uncommon sight in the streets of this town to see a little old black-garbed woman gazing wistfully in at the shop-windows, and holding tight to a worn black purse, as if afraid it will fly away.

The pretty town spread out along the bayou, under trees that were gold in the sunshine and purple deep in the shadows. Against mossy old walls and the sides of houses the crimson rambler splashed; in the gardens were red japonicas and rich double poppies. Through the heart of the spring ran crimson, the keynote, the motif. The earth is old, thought Eugénie, older than I am, older than any one is; yet it bedecks itself in scarlet twice a year, and in purple and gold. This year was a red season. Holy Mother! It would be a red Easter! Hats and frocks and parasols, petticoats and purses. Raspberry red, the shopgirls called it. Eugénie walked about, peering and gazing, dragging her tired, still sprightly old body.

Once, as she walked about, she passed the church, the beautiful gray-walled cathedral. Girls and young men and children passed in and out. Some, Eugénie knew, went in to confession—oh, the beautiful sins of youth! Eugénie went into the church to rest. Her back ached with the unaccustomed walking, and her old feet were tired. In the vestibule she paused and dipped her yellow fingers into the holy water, which an angel proffered her from a gold-fluted shell. In the church she knelt before a pew and then sat down. Near her, the plush curtains of a confessional stirred, were drawn closer together; and Eugénie sighed. It had been so long since she had known remorse, contrition. She felt for her prayer-beads.

"Bless me, father, for I have sinned. I accuse myself, I an old woman, of desiring a raspberry dress.'' . . . She peeped about her, through her fingers. Well, purple and scarlet, pontifical colors, were not unknown to the church. Almighty God! Even the Virgin Mary was all in purple and crimson! . . . Eugénie got to her feet, and passed out of the church. It lacked but a day and a week until Easter; and Eugénie could see herself, all dressed up in red, going down to New Orleans. . . . What would the artist say? Would he remember? Her heart beat high with excitement; her still lovely pointed face grew flushed with laughter.

. . . .

It was hard to pick out the right one among so many. And they were all so different from the frocks she had loved and worn long ago. Eugénie would enter a store and stand about, pointing. ''How much is that?'' she would ask. ''*Mais non*, and that?'' At last she beheld a red dress and knew it as hers. A raspberry dress, with ruffles. It had a bodice and a rippling skirt, and the dress was forty-nine dollars—a fortune. ''That one I want, that one,'' she whispered to the startled young clerk. She opened her bag, with the money tied up in a black cotton handkerchief. ''And me, I want a pretty red fan.''

Eugénie rode home on the bus, through drifts of flowers that lay along the marshes. The sky above the bayous changed from glory into glory. God made the heavens and earth, she thought, and mixed scarlet in with the dying sun. God likes purple and scarlet. Well, when she had come back from New Orleans she would put away her finery, lock it up in her *armoire*. She would save it to be buried in, some far-distant day. How pleased the sweet angels would be!—so much white must grow tiresome in heaven.

When she reached Martin's Ferry, Eugénie got out of the bus. She went into the bushes and took off one of her three petticoats. In this she wrapped her dress and her fan. If she should encounter her daughters, she would say, "Just some old quilt-scraps that Tante Antoinette gave to me."

That night, when she was alone, Eugénie took out her raspberry dress, as she took out her sins, and looked at it and touched it and put it away again. How beautiful it was! As she lay in her narrow widow's bed she dreamed of it. How shocked they would be, the other old women, if they knew of her raspberry dress! Along the bayou, where old women wear black, there can be no sin like the sin of desirous and unholy age. Once in the night Eugénie got up and counted her money: more than enough to buy her a ticket down to the city and back, and have a big time in the bargain. She would go and stay at Madame Jomette's. How glad Jeanne would be to see her! "You are looking young," Jeanne would say. "The years have been good to you, *chére.*"

Nights like these Eugénie could not sleep very well, with a moon as broad as a whisky-barrel, coming up out of the bayou. The bayou water was high this spring. It came up and took all the windows, each little window a picture, moving with blue water-hyacinths. Eugénie got up and stole out to the gallery, to the sagging deck of the old river steamboat. Trees closed about it; vines hung around it. It was moored and anchored to the earth, with its wanderings over forever. . . . Once as Eugénie sat there, she thought she heard some one sobbing. She got up and tiptoed to the little room where Aline, her granddaughter, slept. She peeped in at the one little window. "Aline, Aline . . . honey?"

But no sound came from within, only the deep breathing of a young girl asleep.

The next morning, a Sunday, it seemed to Eugénie that Aline looked pale. And her eyes were so mournful. "Aline, honey, what's the matter with you? I reckon you need some lovin'."

Well, whatever the trouble, it was something to do with that Jules, that lazy *garçon.* The two had quarreled, perhaps, and to-morrow the child would be happy again. Eugénie was annoyed, and tried not to think of Aline. "Humph!" she said. "It ain't my affair, no!"

But on the morrow Aline was more pale than ever. She was silent and very still, and Eugénie missed her laughter. "Look here, Silla," Eugénie said to her daughter, "how come you don't put a ruffle or two on Aline's little Easter dress?"

Silla gazed at her mother with her thin, tired smile. "Dour" is not a French word. It is Scotch. But it describes the way Silla looked. . . . "God in heaven, mama!" she cried. "A ruffle? For s'pose I put a ruffle on each one of them children's dresses? I wouldn't have time to do nothing else, just make ruffle." Silla looked into her mother's still lovely, discreet old eyes. "And beside, mama, you reckon Aline would have Easter thoughts, in a ruffled dress?"

Eugénie blinked. "Easter thoughts? Well, a girl like Aline needs a ruffle," she grumbled. "They go together, ruffles and girls."

Later that same morning Eugénie sought out her youngest granddaughters, Fleurette, and Marie who was ten. Children keep up with what's going on. They spy around and eavesdrop. "What's the matter with Aline?" their grandmama asked. "What's ailing your sister?"

The eyes of the little girls grew round. "Oh, don't you know, grandmama? Jules, he ain't been around for a week. She want him to come back and kiss her." Eugénie shooed them away, like flies. Such children! But that night she sat up and listened. This time she knew; she was certain she heard Aline sobbing. She got up and crept to Aline's window, soft like a cat. Eugénie knew the sound of a girl's broken heart. Her own had been broken many a time, long ago. . . . The moon trailed a shimmering path on the water, like a lady with a long satin train. Eugénie crouched low and listened. Bah! She could spank Aline, pining away because of a boy's lazy laugh and the insolent shrug of his shoulders. Ah, but *she* knew! She knew how it was!

Eugénie crept back to bed. Perhaps to-morrow that Jules would come. But Jules did not come. Wednesday's sun rose and set, and still no Jules. Then Thursday, Good Friday, and Saturday. On Saturday night, after every one had gone to bed, Eugénie walked boldly into Aline's room and lighted the little oil-lamp. This would be her last chance at Aline, for to-morrow she, Eugénie, would be gone; already her things were packed, in a bundle. Aline's Easter dress hung against the wall, a little gray slip of a thing, the color of bilge-water. Eugénie, grumbling, sat down by her granddaughter's bed, in the one little rickety chair.

"Me, I don't think much of that Jules," she began, hurriedly, "a boy that is like to die of the laziness. And beside—bah!—love, it ain't everything, *chére.* It is nothing."

But Eugénie knew she was lying, she, a priestess of love; and she knew that her granddaughter knew it. She stared at Aline. How lovely and pale the child looked, in her tumbled-up bed, her dark hair spread out on the pillow! From under Aline's pillow the beads of a rosary crept, bead by bead, like vicious little blue bugs. . . . So the child had been praying! Beside the bed was a little prie-dieu; so the child had been down on her knees! Eugénie felt indignant, afraid. What awful thing had happened, that Aline had had to go and tell God the Father about it?

Aline sat up in bed, her hands clasped about her bare knees; one shoulder was bare, and her round brown arms. This child, thought Eugénie, is my very own; more mine than my own two daughters. . . . "Love, it ain't nothing," she said hypocritically, slapping out at the flies. "Bah! It is less than nothing."

But Aline seemed not to hear her. "Grandmama." The girl's voice choked, grew husky. "I—I—she's a mean old hateful *town* girl, granny, all dress up in a pink ruffled dress."

Eugénie puffed on her pipe. She felt gladness, relief. So that was it!—another girl, a town girl. She looked at Aline and saw herself as she had looked long years ago. Then, lifting her eyes, she saw herself in a little cracked mirror above her head; saw herself as she was now, with a yellow, still beautifully pointed face, and old mournful eyes. Why, she'd look like a Mardi gras, all tricked out in red! Suddenly it seemed to Eugénie that nothing in the world mattered but to see this child's proud head again unbowed; to hear her laugh once more, in the face of the sun. . . . She was startled to hear herself saying: "Bah! What does a boy care for a pink dress, if there's a red one around?"

She blinked very fast, and got up, and reached for the little oil-lamp. She seemed to be somebody else, not herself. Feet that were not her own carried her to the door. "Come," she whispered, "come with me, *chére*. See what grandmama got, lock up in her press."

As she slipped the dress over Aline's head, there in the dead of night, it seemed to old Eugénie that strength flowed into the girl with those silky red ruffles. "My daughter Silla is a fool," thought Eugénie. "*Mon Dieu!* How is a girl to flirt properly without a red ruffle or two?" Aline in the red-ruffled dress looked tall as a princess. Her eyes were round and shining; her red mouth smiled. She unfurled the fan and used it, as fans are meant to be used. She looked as if she were about to dance the Spanish fandango.

"Granny," she whispered, "granny . . . is you buy these so-pretty things just for *me?*"

Eugénie found herself nodding. "*Mais oui,*" she said, "just for you."

She stared at Aline. Why, the girl was her very image, herself grown young again! But as she stared, some dim troubled memory stirred Eugénie's old unquiet heart. She began to cackle, her voice very thin.

"Aline, *chére,* you must be good girl. I raise your mama religious. Aline—" (What was this that she heard herself saying?) "Me, I'm saving some money for you, *mon enfant*, if you is good girl. For when you get marry, *hein?* To help buy a trousseau, and linen perhap; when time come for marry with Jules."

But Aline seemed not to have heard her. The girl's eyes were mournful, and strange. . . . And Eugénie grew more vehement. "Aline—you must never let the boys kiss you. . . ."

. . . . . .

The sun shone on the bayou, on the drifting and tedious hyacinths. And Eugénie, adjusting her kerchief, thought she had never seen so many lilies in bloom in the garden. There was something in Eugénie's blood, something French, that adored the lily. She went out to gather an armful to take to Easter service.

Ah, well, she must go to confession; she must be absolved from her sins, before she could receive the body and blood of the Christ. Not that she had very much to confess; just a few little colorless baby sins, like the sins of Marie who was ten. The old priest would go to sleep as he listened. "Holy Father, I accuse myself of finding fault with my two kind daughters, who provide me a home. I accuse myself of—of telling a lie, a little white lie, concerning a raspberry dress—"

The breath of the lilies was so thick, so intense, that Eugénie nodded above them.

THE MOTHER IN PARADISE *

Eugene Field

A MOTHER came to the gateway of Heaven. She was aged and weary. Her body was bowed and her face was wrinkled and withered, for her burden had been the burden of care and trouble and sorrow. So she was glad to be done with life and to seek at the gateway of Heaven the fulfilment of the Promise that had been her solace through all the hard, bitter years.

An angel met the Mother at the gateway, and put her arms about the drooping figure, and spoke gracious, tender words.

"Whom seekest thou?" asked the angel.

"I seek my dear ones who came hither before me," answered the Mother. "They are very many—my father, my mother, my husband, my children—they all are here together, and for many and weary years I have lived in my loneliness, with no other thing to cheer me but the thought that I should follow them in good time."

* From "Second Book of Tales"; copyright, 1896, by Julia S. Field: published by Charles Scribner's Sons. By permission of the publishers.

"Yes, they are here and they await thee," said the angel. "Lean upon me, dear Mother, and I will lead thee to them."

Then the angel led the way through the garden of Paradise, and the angel and the Mother talked as they walked together.

"I am not weary now," said the Mother, "and my heart is not troubled."

"It is the grace of Heaven that restoreth thee, dear Mother," quoth the angel. "Presently thou shalt be filled with the new life, and thou shalt be young again; and thou shalt sing with rapture, and thy soul shall know the endless ecstasy of Heaven."

"Alas, I care not to be young again," saith the Mother. "I care only to find and to be forever with my beloved ones."

As they journeyed in their way a company came to meet them. Then the Mother saw and knew her dear ones—even though the heavenly life had glorified their countenances, the Mother knew them, and she ran to greet them, and there was great joy to her and to them. Meanwhile the angel kept steadfastly at her side.

Now the Mother, when she had embraced her dear ones, looked at each of them separately once more, and then she said: "Ye are indeed my beloved—my mother, my father, my husband, and my children! But there is one who should be of your company whom I do not see

—my babe, my little helpless babe that came hither alone so many, many years ago. My heart fainteth, my breast yearneth for that dear little lamb of mine! Come, let us go together and search for her; or await me here under these pleasant trees while I search and call in this fair garden for my dear, lost little babe!"

The others answered never a word, but the angel said: "I will go with thee, Mother, and together we shall find thy child."

As they went on their way the angel said: "Shall I tell thee of myself? For I was a little helpless babe when I came hither to this fair garden and into this heavenly life."

"Perchance thou knowest her, my precious lambkin!" cried the Mother.

"I was a babe when I came hither," said the angel. "See how I am grown and what happiness hath been mine! The compassion of divinity hath protected and fostered me, and hath led me all these years in the peace that passeth all human understanding. God hath instructed me in wisdom, and He shall instruct thee, too; for all who come hither are as children in His sight, and they shall grow in wisdom and in grace eternally."

"But my babe—my own lost little one whom I have not held in these arms for so many weary years—shall she not still be my little babe, and shall I not cradle her in my bosom?" asked the Mother.

"Thy child shall be restored to thee," said the angel; "for she yearneth for thee even as thou yearnest for her. Only with this difference, dear Mother: Thy child hath known, in the grace of heavenly wisdom, that at the last thy earthly sorrow should surely be rewarded with the joys of the endless reunion in Paradise!"

"Then she hath thought of me and longed for me to come!" cried the Mother. "And my lost babe shall be restored and shall know her mother again!"

"Ay, she loveth thee fondly," said the angel, "and she hath awaited thy coming, lo, these many years. Presently thine eyes shall be opened and thou shalt see her standing before thee in her heavenly raiment whiter than snow, and around her neck thou shalt see her wearing most precious pearls—the tears which thou hast shed, oh lonely Mother! and which are the pearls the little ones in Heaven gather up and cherish as an adornment most pleasing unto God and them."

Then the Mother felt that her eyes were opened, and she turned and looked upon the angel. And the Mother saw that the angel was her lost beloved child whom she was seeking: not the helpless babe that she had thought to find, but a maiden of such heavenly beauty and gentleness as only the dwellers in Paradise behold and know. And the Mother spread her arms, and gave a great cry of joy, and folded her very dear one to her bosom.

Then presently they returned together to the others. And there was rapturous acclaim in Paradise, and it was to God's sweet pleasance that it was so. For a Mother and her beloved communed in the holy companionship of love everlasting.

THE REVOLT OF "MOTHER" *

Mary E. Wilkins Freeman

"FATHER!"

"What is it?"

"What are them men diggin' over there in the field for?"

There was a sudden dropping and enlarging of the lower part of the old man's face, as if some heavy weight had settled therein; he shut his mouth tight, and went on harnessing the great bay mare. He hustled the collar on to her neck with a jerk.

"Father!"

The old man slapped the saddle upon the mare's back.

"Look here, father, I want to know what them men are diggin' over in the field for, an' I'm goin' to know."

"I wish you'd go into the house, mother, an' 'tend to your own affairs," the old man said then. He ran his words together, and his speech was almost as inarticulate as a growl.

* From "A New England Nun and other Stories," by Mary E. Wilkins Freeman; Copyright, 1891, by Harper & Bros. Reprinted by special permission.

But the woman understood; it was her most native tongue. "I ain't goin' into the house till you tell me what them men are doin' over there in the field," said she.

Then she stood waiting. She was a small woman, short and straight-waisted like a child in her brown cotton gown. Her forehead was mild and benevolent between the smooth curves of gray hair; there were meek downward lines about her nose and mouth; but her eyes, fixed upon the old man, looked as if the meekness had been the result of her own will, never of the will of another.

They were in the barn, standing before the wide open doors. The spring air, full of the smell of growing grass and unseen blossoms, came in their faces. The deep yard in front was littered with farm wagons and piles of wood; on the edges, close to the fence and the house, the grass was a vivid green, and there were some dandelions.

The old man glanced doggedly at his wife as he tightened the last buckles on the harness. She looked as immovable to him as one of the rocks in his pasture-land, bound to the earth with generations of blackberry vines. He slapped the reins over the horse, and started forth from the barn.

"*Father!*" said she.

The old man pulled up. "What is it?"

"I want to know what them men are diggin' over there in that field for."

"They're diggin' a cellar, I s'pose, if you've got to know."

"A cellar for what?"

"A barn."

"A barn? You ain't goin' to build a barn over there where we was goin' to have a house, father?"

The old man said not another word. He hurried the horse into the farm wagon, and clattered out of the yard, jouncing as sturdily on his seat as a boy.

The woman stood a moment looking after him, then she went out of the barn across a corner of the yard to the house. The house, standing at right angles with the great barn and a long reach of sheds and out-buildings, was infinitesimal compared with them. It was scarcely as commodious for people as the little boxes under the barn eaves were for doves.

A pretty girl's face, pink and delicate as a flower, was looking out of one of the house windows. She was watching three men who were digging over in the field which bounded the yard near the road line. She turned quietly when the woman entered.

"What are they digging for, mother?" said she. "Did he tell you?"

"They're diggin' for—a cellar for a new barn."

"Oh, mother, he ain't going to build another barn?"

"That's what he says."

A boy stood before the kitchen glass combing his hair. He combed slowly and painstakingly, arranging his brown hair in a smooth hillock over his forehead. He did not seem to pay any attention to the conversation.

"Sammy, did you know father was going to build a new barn?" asked the girl.

The boy combed assiduously.

"Sammy!"

He turned, and showed a face like his father's under his smooth crest of hair. "Yes, I s'pose I did," he said, reluctantly.

"How long have you known it?" asked his mother.

" 'Bout three months, I guess."

"Why didn't you tell of it?"

"Didn't think 'twould do no good."

"I don't see what father wants another barn for," said the girl, in her sweet, slow voice. She turned again to the window, and stared out at the digging men in the field. Her tender, sweet face was full of a gentle distress. Her forehead was as bald and innocent as a baby's, with the light hair strained back from it in a row of curl-papers. She was quite large, but her soft curves did not look as if they covered muscles.

Her mother looked sternly at the boy. "Is he goin' to buy more cows?" said she.

The boy did not reply; he was tying his shoes.

"Sammy, I want you to tell me if he's goin' to buy more cows."

"I s'pose he is."

"How many?"

"Four, I guess."

His mother said nothing more. She went into the pantry, and there was a clatter of dishes. The boy got his cap from a nail behind the door, took an old arithmetic from the shelf, and started for school. He was lightly built, but clumsy. He went out of the yard with a curious spring in the hips, that made his loose home-made jacket tilt up in the rear.

The girl went to the sink, and began to wash the dishes that were piled up there. Her mother came promptly out of the pantry, and shoved her aside. "You wipe 'em," said she. "I'll wash. There's a good many this mornin'."

The mother plunged her hands vigorously into the water, the girl wiped the plates slowly and dreamily. "Mother," said she, "don't you think it's too bad father's going to build that new barn, much as we need a decent house to live in?"

Her mother scrubbed a dish fiercely. "You ain't found out yet we're women-folks, Nanny

Penn," said she. "You ain't seen enough of men-folks yet to. One of these days you'll find it out, an' then you'll know that we know only what men-folks think we do, so far as any use of it goes, an' how we'd ought to reckon men-folks in with Providence, an' not complain of what they do any more than we do of the weather."

"I don't care; I don't believe George is anything like that, anyhow," said Nanny. Her delicate face flushed pink, her lips pouted softly, as if she were going to cry.

"You wait an' see. I guess George Eastman ain't no better than other men. You hadn't ought to judge father, though. He can't help it, 'cause he don't look at things jest the way we do. An' we've been pretty comfortable here, after all. The roof don't leak—ain't never but once—that's one thing. Father's kept it shingled right up."

"I do wish we had a parlor."

"I guess it won't hurt George Eastman any to come to see you in a nice clean kitchen. I guess a good many girls don't have as good a place as this. Nobody's ever heard me complain."

"I ain't complained either, mother."

"Well, I don't think you'd better, a good father, an' a good home as you've got. S'pose your father made you go out an' work for your livin'? Lots of girls have to that ain't no stronger an' better able to than you be."

Sarah Penn washed the frying-pan with a conclusive air. She scrubbed the outside of it as faithfully as the inside. She was a masterly keeper of her box of a house. Her one living-room never seemed to have in it any of the dust which the friction of life with inanimate matter produces. She swept, and there seemed to be no dirt to go before the broom; she cleaned, and one could see no difference. She was like an artist so perfect that he has apparently no art. To-day she got out a mixing bowl and a board, and rolled some pies, and there was no more flour upon her than upon her daughter who was doing finer work. Nanny was to be married in the fall, and she was sewing on some white cambric and embroidery. She sewed industriously while her mother cooked, her soft milk-white hands and wrists showed whiter than her delicate work.

"We must have the stove moved out in the shed before long," said Mrs. Penn. "Talk about not havin' things, it's been a real blessin' to be able to put a stove up in that shed in hot weather. Father did one good thing when he fixed that stove-pipe out there."

Sarah Penn's face as she rolled her pies had that expression of meek vigor which might have characterized one of the New Testament saints.

She was making mince-pies. Her husband, Adoniram Penn, liked them better than any other kind. She baked twice a week. Adoniram often liked a piece of pie between meals. She hurried this morning. It had been later than usual when she began, and she wanted to have a pie baked for dinner. However deep a resentment she might be forced to hold against her husband, she would never fail in sedulous attention to his wants.

Nobility of character manifests itself at loopholes when it is not provided with large doors. Sarah Penn's showed itself to-day in flaky dishes of pastry. So she made the pies faithfully, while across the table she could see, when she glanced up from her work, the sight that rankled in her patient and steadfast soul—the digging of the cellar of the new barn in the place where Adoniram forty years ago had promised her their new house should stand.

The pies were done for dinner. Adoniram and Sammy were home a few minutes after twelve o'clock. The dinner was eaten with serious haste. There was never much conversation at the table in the Penn family. Adoniram asked a blessing, and they ate promptly, then rose up and went about their work.

Sammy went back to school, taking soft sly lopes out of the yard like a rabbit. He wanted a game of marbles before school, and feared his father would give him some chores to do. Adoniram hastened to the door and called after him, but he was out of sight.

"I don't see what you let him go for, mother," said he. "I wanted him to help me unload that wood."

Adoniram went to work out in the yard unloading wood from the wagon. Sarah put away the dinner dishes, while Nanny took down her curl-papers and changed her dress. She was going down to the store to buy some more embroidery and thread.

When Nanny was gone, Mrs. Penn went to the door. "Father!" she called.

"Well, what is it!"

"I want to see you jest a minute, father."

"I can't leave this wood nohow. I've got to git it unloaded an' go for a load of gravel afore two o'clock. Sammy had ought to helped me. You hadn't ought to let him go to school so early."

"I want to see you jest a minute."

"I tell ye I can't, nohow, mother."

"Father, you come here." Sarah Penn stood in the door like a queen; she held her head as if it bore a crown; there was that patience which makes authority royal in her voice. Adoniram went.

Mrs. Penn led the way into the kitchen, and pointed to a chair. "Sit down, father," said she. "I've got somethin' I want to say to you."

He sat down heavily; his face was quite stolid, but he looked at her with restive eyes. "Well, what is it, mother?"

"I want to know what you're buildin' that new barn for, father?"

"I ain't got nothin' to say about it."

"It can't be you think you need another barn?"

"I tell ye I ain't got nothin' to say about it, mother; an' I ain't goin' to say nothin'."

"Be you goin' to buy more cows?"

Adoniram did not reply; he shut his mouth tight.

"I know you be, as well as I want to. Now, father, look here"—Sarah Penn had not sat down; she stood before her husband in the humble fashion of a Scripture woman—"I'm going to talk real plain to you; I never have sence I married you, but I'm goin' to now. I ain't never complained, an' I ain't goin' to complain now, but I'm goin' to talk plain. You see this room here, father; you look at it well. You see there ain't no carpet on the floor, an' you see the paper is all dirty, an' droppin' off the walls. We ain't had no new paper on it for ten year, an' then I put it on myself, an' it didn't cost but ninepence a roll. You see this room, father; it's all the one I've had to work in an' eat in' an' sit in sence we was married.

There ain't another woman in the whole town whose husband ain't got half the means you have but what's got better. It's all the room Nanny's got to have her company in; an' there ain't one of her mates but what's got better, an' their fathers not so able as hers is. It's all the room she'll have to be married in. What would you have thought, father, if we had had our weddin' in a room no better than this? I was married in my mother's parlor, with a carpet on the floor, an' stuffed furniture, an' a mahogany card-table. An' this is all the room my daughter will have to be married in. Look here, father!"

Sarah Penn went across the room as though it were a tragic stage. She flung open a door and disclosed a tiny bedroom, only large enough for a bed and bureau, with a path between. "There, father," said she—"there's all the room I've had to sleep in forty years. All my children were born there—the two that died, an' the two that's livin'. I was sick with a fever there."

She stepped to another door and opened it. It led into the small, ill-lighted pantry. "Here," said she, "is all the buttery I've got—every place I've got for my dishes, to set away my victuals in, an' to keep my milk-pans in. Father, I've been takin' care of the milk of six cows in this place, an' now you're goin' to build a new barn, an' keep more cows, an' give me more to do in it.''

She threw open another door. A narrow crooked flight of stairs wound upward from it. ''There, father,'' said she, ''I want you to look at the stairs that go up to them two unfinished chambers that are all the places our son an' daughter have had to sleep in all their lives. There ain't a prettier girl in town nor a more ladylike one than Nanny, an' that's the place she has to sleep in. It ain't so good as your horse's stall; it ain't so warm an' tight.''

Sarah Penn went back and stood before her husband. ''Now, father,'' said she, ''I want to know if you think you're doin' right an' accordin' to what you profess. Here, when we was married, forty year ago, you promised me faithful that we should have a new house built in that lot over in the field before the year was out. You said you had money enough, an' you wouldn't ask me to live in no such place as this. It is forty year now, an' you've been makin' more money, an' I've been savin' of it for you ever sence, an' you ain't built no house yet. You've built sheds an' cow-houses an' one new barn, an' now you're goin' to build another. Father, I want to know if you think it's right. You're lodgin' your dumb beasts better than you are your own flesh an' blood. I want to know if you think it's right.''

"I ain't got nothin' to say."

"You can't say nothin' without ownin' it ain't right, father. An' there's another thing—I ain't complained; I've got along forty year, an' I s'pose I should forty more, if it wasn't for that—if we don't have another house. Nanny she can't live with us after she's married. She'll have to go somewhere else to live away from us, an' it don't seem as if I could have it so, noways, father. She wasn't ever strong. She's got considerable color, but there wasn't never any backbone to her. I've always took the heft of everything off her, an' she ain't fit to keep house an' do everything herself. She'll be all worn out inside of a year. Think of her doin' all the washin' an' ironin' an' bakin' with them soft white hands an' arms, an' sweepin'! I can't have it so, noways, father."

Mrs. Penn's face was burning; her mild eyes gleamed. She had pleaded her little cause like a Webster; she had ranged from severity to pathos; but her opponent employed that obstinate silence which makes eloquence futile with mocking echoes. Adoniram arose clumsily.

"Father, ain't you got nothin' to say?" said Mrs. Penn.

"I've got to go off after that load of gravel. I can't stan' here talkin' all day."

"Father, won't you think it over, an' have a house built there instead of a barn?"

"I ain't got nothin' to say."

Adoniram shuffled out. Mrs. Penn went into her bedroom. When she came out, her eyes were red. She had a roll of unbleached cotton cloth. She spread it out on the kitchen table, and began cutting out some shirts for her husband. The men over in the field had a team to help them this afternoon; she could hear their halloos. She had a scanty pattern for the shirts; she had to plan and piece the sleeves.

Nanny came home with her embroidery, and sat down with her needlework. She had taken down her curl-papers, and there was a soft roll of fair hair like an aureole over her forehead; her face was as delicately fine and clear as porcelain. Suddenly she looked up, and the tender red flamed all over her face and neck. "Mother," said she.

"What say?"

"I've been thinking—I don't see how we're goin' to have any—wedding in this room. I'd be ashamed to have his folks come if we didn't have anybody else."

"Mebbe we can have some new paper before then; I can put it on. I guess you won't have no call to be ashamed of your belongin's."

"We might have the wedding in the new barn," said Nanny, with gentle pettishness. "Why, mother, what makes you look so?"

Mrs. Penn had started, and was staring at

her with a curious expression. She turned again to her work, and spread out a pattern carefully on the cloth. "Nothin'," said she.

Presently Adoniram clattered out of the yard in his two-wheeled dump-cart, standing as proudly upright as a Roman charioteer. Mrs. Penn opened the door and stood there a minute looking out; the halloos of the men sounded louder.

It seemed to her all through the spring months that she heard nothing but the halloos and the noises of saws and hammers. The new barn grew fast. It was a fine edifice for this little village. Men came on pleasant Sundays, in their meeting suits and clean shirt bosoms, and stood around it admiringly. Mrs. Penn did not speak of it, and Adoniram did not mention it to her, although sometimes, upon a return from inspecting it, he bore himself with injured dignity.

"It's a strange thing how your mother feels about the new barn," he said, confidentially, to Sammy one day.

Sammy only grunted after an odd fashion for a boy; he had learned it from his father.

The barn was all completed ready for use by the third week in July. Adoniram had planned to move his stock in on Wednesday; on Tuesday he received a letter which changed his plans. He came in with it early in the morning. "Sammy's been to the post-office,'' said he, ''an' I've got a letter from Hiram.'' Hiram was Mrs. Penn's brother, who lived in Vermont.

''Well,'' said Mrs. Penn, ''what does he say about the folks?''

''I guess they're all right. He says he thinks if I come up country right off there's a chance to buy jest the kind of a horse I want.'' He stared reflectively out of the window at the new barn.

Mrs. Penn was making pies. She went on clapping the rolling-pin into the crust, although she was very pale, and her heart beat loudly.

''I dun' know but what I'd better go,'' said Adoniram. ''I hate to go off jest now, right in the midst of hayin', but the ten-acre lot's cut, an' I guess Rufus an' the others can git along without me three or four days. I can't get a horse round here to suit me, nohow, an' I've got to have another for all that wood-haulin' in the fall. I told Hiram to watch out, an' if he got wind of a good horse to let me know. I guess I'd better go.''

''I'll get out your clean shirt an' collar,'' said Mrs. Penn, calmly.

She laid out Adoniram's Sunday suit and his clean clothes on the bed in the little bedroom. She got his shaving-water and razor ready. At last she buttoned on his collar and fastened his black cravat.

Adoniram never wore his collar and cravat except on extra occasions. He held his head high, with a rasped dignity. When he was all ready, with his coat and hat brushed, and a lunch of pie and cheese in a paper bag, he hesitated on the threshold of the door. He looked at his wife, and his manner was defiantly apologetic. "*If* them cows come to-day, Sammy can drive 'em into the new barn," said he; "an' when they bring the hay up, they can pitch it in there."

"Well," replied Mrs. Penn.

Adoniram set his shaven face ahead and started. When he had cleared the door-step, he turned and looked back with a kind of nervous solemnity. "I shall be back by Saturday if nothin' happens," said he.

"Do be careful, father," returned his wife.

She stood in the door with Nanny at her elbow and watched him out of sight. Her eyes had a strange, doubtful expression in them; her peaceful forehead was contracted. She went in, and about her baking again. Nanny sat sewing. Her wedding-day was drawing nearer, and she was getting pale and thin with her steady sewing. Her mother kept glancing at her.

"Have you got that pain in your side this mornin'?" she asked.

"A little."

Mrs. Penn's face, as she worked, changed,

her perplexed forehead smoothed, her eyes were steady, her lips firmly set. She formed a maxim for herself, although incoherently with her unlettered thoughts. "Unsolicited opportunities are the guide-posts of the Lord to the new roads of life," she repeated in effect, and she made up her mind to her course of action.

"S'posin I *had* wrote to Hiram," she muttered once, when she was in the pantry—"s'posin' I had wrote, an' asked him if he knew of any horse? But I didn't, an' father's goin' wan't none of my doin'. It looks like a providence." Her voice rang out quite loud at the last.

"What you talkin' about, mother?" called Nanny.

"Nothin'."

Mrs. Penn hurried her baking; at eleven o'clock it was all done. The load of hay from the west field came slowly down the cart track, and drew up at the new barn. Mrs. Penn ran out. "Stop!" she screamed—"stop!"

The men stopped and looked; Sammy upreared from the top of the load, and stared at his mother.

"Stop!" she cried out again. "Don't you put the hay in that barn; put it in the old one."

"Why, he said to put it in here," returned one of the haymakers, wonderingly. He was a young man, a neighbor's son, whom Adoniram hired by the year to help on the farm.

"Don't you put the hay in the new barn; there's room enough in the old one, ain't there?" said Mrs. Penn.

"Room enough," returned the hired man, in his thick, rustic tones. "Didn't need the new barn, nohow, far as room's concerned. Well, I s'pose he changed his mind." He took hold of the horses' bridles.

Mrs. Penn went back to the house. Soon the kitchen windows were darkened, and a fragrance like warm honey came into the room.

Nanny laid down her work. "I thought father wanted them to put the hay into the new barn?" she said, wonderingly.

"It's all right," replied her mother.

Sammy slid down from the load of hay, and came in to see if dinner was ready.

"I ain't goin' to get a regular dinner to-day, as long as father's gone," said his mother. "I've let the fire go out. You can have some bread an' milk an' pie. I thought we could get along." She set out some bowls of milk, some bread, and a pie on the kitchen table. "You'd better eat your dinner now," said she. "You might jest as well get through with it. I want you to help me afterwards."

Nanny and Sammy stared at each other. There was something strange in their mother's manner. Mrs. Penn did not eat anything herself. She went into the pantry, and they heard her moving dishes while they ate. Presently she came out with a pile of plates. She got the clothes-basket out of the shed, and packed them in it. Nanny and Sammy watched. She brought out cups and saucers, and put them in with the plates.

"What you goin' to do, mother?" inquired Nanny, in a timid voice. A sense of something unusual made her tremble, as if it were a ghost. Sammy rolled his eyes over his pie.

"You'll see what I'm goin' to do," replied Mrs. Penn. "If you're through, Nanny, I want you to go upstairs an' pack up your things; an' I want you, Sammy, to help me take down the bed in the bedroom."

"Oh, mother, what for?" gasped Nanny.

"You'll see."

During the next few hours a feat was performed by this simple, pious New England mother which was equal in its way to Wolfe's storming of the Heights of Abraham. It took no more genius and audacity of bravery for Wolfe to cheer his wondering soldiers up those steep precipices, under the sleeping eyes of the enemy, than for Sarah Penn, at the head of her children, to move all their little household goods into the new barn while her husband was away.

Nanny and Sammy followed their mother's

instructions without a murmur; indeed, they were overawed. There is a certain uncanny and superhuman quality about all such purely original undertakings as their mother's was to them; Nanny went back and forth with her light loads, and Sammy tugged with sober energy.

At five o'clock in the afternoon the little house in which the Penns had lived for forty years had emptied itself into the new barn.

Every builder builds somewhat for unknown purposes, and is in a measure a prophet. The architect of Adoniram Penn's barn, while he designed it for the comfort of four-footed animals, had planned better than he knew for the comfort of humans. Sarah Penn saw at a glance its possibilities. Those great box-stalls, with quilts hung before them, would make better bedrooms than the one she had occupied for forty years, and there was a tight carriage-room. The harness-room, with its chimney and shelves, would make a kitchen of her dreams. The great middle space would make a parlor, by-and-by, fit for a palace. Upstairs there was as much room as down. With partitions and windows, what a house would there be! Sarah looked at the row of stanchions before the allotted space for cows, and reflected that she would have her front entry there.

At six o'clock the stove was up in the harness-room, the kettle was boiling, and the table set for tea. It looked almost as home-like as the abandoned house across the yard had ever done. The young hired man milked, and Sarah directed him calmly to bring the milk to the new barn. He came gaping, dropping little blots of foam from the brimming pails on the grass. Before the next morning he had spread the story of Adoniram Penn's wife moving into the new barn, all over the little village. Men assembled in the store and talked it over, women with shawls over their heads scuttled into each other's houses before their work was done. Any deviation from the ordinary course of life in this quiet town was enough to stop all progress in it. Everybody paused to look at the staid, independent figure on the side track. There was a difference of opinion with regard to her. Some held her to be insane; some, of a lawless and rebellious spirit.

Friday the minister went to see her. It was in the forenoon, and she was at the barn door shelling peas for dinner. She looked up and returned his salutation with dignity, then she went on with her work. She did not invite him in. The saintly expression of her face remained fixed, but there was an angry flush over it.

The minister stood awkwardly before her, and talked. She handled the peas as if they were bullets. At last she looked up, and her eyes showed the spirit that her meek front had covered for a lifetime.

"There ain't no use talkin', Mr. Hersey," said she. "I've thought it all over an' over, an' I believe I'm doin' what's right. I've made it the subject of prayer, an' it's betwixt me an' the Lord an' Adoniram. There ain't no call for nobody else to worry about it."

"Well, of course, if you have brought it to the Lord in prayer, and feel satisfied that you are doing right, Mrs. Penn," said the minister, helplessly. His thin gray-bearded face was pathetic. He was a sickly man; his youthful confidence had cooled; he had to scourge himself up to some of his pastoral duties as relentlessly as a Catholic ascetic, and then he was prostrated by the smart.

"I think it's right jest as much as I think it was right for our forefathers to come over from the old country 'cause they didn't have what belonged to 'em," said Mrs. Penn. She arose. The barn threshold might have been Plymouth Rock from her bearing. "I don't doubt you mean well, Mr. Hersey," said she, "but there are things people hadn't ought to interfere with. I've been a member of the church for over forty years. I've got my own mind an' my own feet, an' I'm goin' to think my own thoughts an' go my own ways, an' nobody but the Lord is goin' to dictate to me unless I've a mind to have him. Won't you come in an' set down? How is Mis' Hersey?"

"She is well, I thank you," replied the minister. He added some more perplexed apologetic remarks; then he retreated.

He could expound the intricacies of every character study in the Scriptures, he was competent to grasp the Pilgrim Fathers and all historical innovators, but Sarah Penn was beyond him. He could deal with primal cases, but parallel ones worsted him. But, after all, although it was aside from his province, he wondered more how Adoniram Penn would deal with his wife than how the Lord would. Everybody shared the wonder. When Adoniram's four new cows arrived, Sarah ordered three to be put in the old barn, the other in the house shed where the cooking-stove had stood. That added to the excitement. It was whispered that all four cows were domiciled in the house.

Towards sunset on Saturday, when Adoniram was expected home, there was a knot of men in the road near the new barn. The hired man had milked, but he still hung around the premises. Sarah Penn had supper all ready. There were brown-bread and baked beans and a custard pie; it was the supper that Adoniram loved on a Saturday night. She had on a clean calico, and she bore herself imperturbably. Nanny and Sammy kept close at her heels.

Their eyes were large, and Nanny was full of nervous tremors. Still there was to them more pleasant excitement than anything else. An inborn confidence in their mother over their father asserted itself.

Sammy looked out of the harness-room window. "There he is," he announced, in an awed whisper. He and Nanny peeped around the casing. Mrs. Penn kept on about her work. The children watched Adoniram leave the new horse standing in the drive while he went to the house door. It was fastened. Then he went around to the shed. That door was seldom locked, even when the family was away. The thought how her father would be confronted by the cow flashed upon Nanny. There was a hysterical sob in her throat. Adoniram emerged from the shed and stood looking about in a dazed fashion. His lips moved; he was saying something, but they could not hear what it was. The hired man was peeping around a corner of the old barn, but nobody saw him.

Adoniram took the new horse by the bridle and led him across the yard to the new barn. Nanny and Sammy slunk close to their mother. The barn doors rolled back, and there stood Adoniram, with the long mild face of the great Canadian farm horse looking over his shoulder.

Nanny kept behind her mother, but Sammy

stepped suddenly forward, and stood in front of her.

Adoniram stared at the group. ''What on airth you all down here for?'' said he. ''What's the matter over to the house?''

''We've come here to live, father,'' said Sammy. His shrill voice quavered out bravely.

''What''—Adoniram sniffed—''what is it smells like cookin'?'' said he. He stepped forward and looked in the open door of the harness-room. Then he turned to his wife. His old bristling face was pale and frightened. ''What on airth does this mean, mother?'' he gasped.

''You come in here, father,'' said Sarah. She led the way into the harness-room and shut the door. ''Now, father,'' said she, ''you needn't be scared. I ain't crazy. There ain't nothin' to be upset over. But we've come here to live, an' we're goin' to live here. We've got jest as good a right here as new horses an' cows. The house wasn't fit for us to live in any longer, an' I made up my mind I wa'n't goin' to stay there. I've done my duty by you for forty year, an' I'm goin' to do it now; but I'm goin' to live here. You've got to put in some windows and partitions; an' you'll have to buy some furniture.''

''Why, mother!'' the old man gasped.

''You'd better take your coat off, an' get

washed—there's the wash-basin—an' then we'll have supper."

"Why, mother!"

Sammy went past the window, leading the new horse to the old barn. The old man saw him, and shook his head speechlessly. He tried to take off his coat, but his arms seemed to lack the power. His wife helped him. She poured some water into the tin basin, and put in a piece of soap. She got the comb and brush, and smoothed his thin gray hair after he had washed. Then she put the beans, hot bread, and tea on the table. Sammy came in, and the family drew up. Adoniram sat looking dazedly at his plate, and they waited.

"Ain't you goin' to ask a blessin', father?" said Sarah.

And the old man bent his head and mumbled.

All through the meal he stopped eating at intervals, and stared furtively at his wife; but he ate well. The home food tasted good to him, and his old frame was too sturdily healthy to be affected by his mind. But after supper he went out, and sat down on the step of the smaller door at the right of the barn, through which he had meant his Jerseys to pass in stately file, but which Sarah designed for her front house door, and he leaned his head on his hands.

After the supper dishes were cleared away and the milk-pans washed, Sarah went out to him. The twilight was deepening. There was a clear green glow in the sky. Before them stretched the smooth level of field; in the distance was a cluster of hay-stacks like the huts of a village; the air was very cool and calm and sweet. The landscape might have been an ideal one of peace.

Sarah bent over and touched her husband on one of his thin, sinewy shoulders. "Father!"

The old man's shoulders heaved: he was weeping.

"Why, don't do so, father," said Sarah.

"I'll—put up the—partitions, an'—everything you—want, mother."

Sarah put her apron up to her face; she was overcome by her own triumph.

Adoniram was like a fortress whose walls had no active resistance, and went down the instant the right besieging tools were used. "Why, mother," he said, hoarsely, "I hadn't no idee you was so set on't as all this comes to."

THE RETURN *

Dorothy E. Norman-Smith

ANN REDFERN stood at the door of her cottage, gazing down the silent strip of street.

So motionless was her attitude, one gnarled leaf-brown hand shading her fierce blue eyes from the glare, she might have been a part of the square stone cottage itself that stood, high and aloof in its green and scarlet patch of garden, above the handful of drab dwellings and meager shops that made the village.

None could have guessed at the emotions that surged through her frail body, as she waited, motionless, for the first glimpse of Robert's girl. . . .

There was nothing in sight. The horizon was as empty as the stony sun-washed street, silent in its noon-tide sleep. Not a child's cry broke the stillness. Not a woman clattered at her door-step or called to her frowsy neighbor over the way. Yet Ann Redfern knew that Cadney was very much awake. Its doors might be shut and

* Reprinted by special permission of the author and of The Century Co.

its voice hushed. But there was not a slatternly window-curtain that did not hide a curious pair of eyes and wagging tongue.

Cadney; a mean dry name and a mean dry nature. How she hated the place! Her fierce old eyes left the empty horizon and swept derisively along the whispering houses. They were talking her over, in there, those loutish men and drab hostile women who had hated her for thirty years; hated her because she was not of them; because Bob Redfern, for all his drink and his poverty, was a gentleman; because Robert, the son, was a gentleman too, had made a name for himself in cities, and was going to marry a fine lady; hated her because for thirty years Ann Redfern had kept herself aloof, her cottage in shining contrast to their cluttered hovels.

But they had never hated Ann Redfern as she hated them! . . .

She had thought her heart must break when Bob brought her, fresh from a smiling Kentish orchard, to this stark, hostile, north-country village, a mere handful of sullen houses thrown together on the writhing ribbon of road, down to the edge of which crowded the dun illimitable stretches of moor, pricking away into eternity. . . . She never forgot her first impression of the place, nor how she had hugged Robert, a sleeping baby of a few months old, hard against her lean breast, for comfort.

She had not been a young woman when Bob had married her. Above the drab planes of her unfulfilled ambitions, this marriage with a gentleman had seemed God-sent. That he was a drunkard, shiftless, weak, and penniless, mattered less than nothing. She could work still, as she had always had to work; and perhaps marriage would steady Bob. . . . After a year of desperate striving she had given up any hope of that. She followed Bob's coffin with the same sullen apathy as she had followed the living man to Cadney. She made no attempt to leave the place. Bob had brought her here. Here she would bring up Bob's child, and her success in this should be proportionate to her failure in the other.

She had worshiped the child.

Just at first she had shown little interest in him; she was too old for children, she had said. . . .

Standing at her door, tremulous for his return, she could remember the moment when first the wells of her love had been reached. He had been sitting, a scrap of a thing in a blue crawler, on the hearth-rug, while she ironed the clothes. "Ma . . . ma . . ." he had uttered proudly, in imitation of the other children.

Turning on him swiftly, she had rebuked him. "Don't call me that. Nasty! Say mother."

"Mother," he had said clearly; and she had

caught him up in her arms, ablaze with sudden determination. He was hers—all she had. And he was a gentleman's son! She was the wife of a gentleman! She would show them, these slatternly hostile women, how great a gulf lay between her and them, between their tattered brats, yelling in the littered back yards, and Robert Redfern, a gentleman's son!

To this end she had dedicated her life. She had urged him to his books that he might win scholarships, and when he had won them, worked her fingers to the bone so that lack of clothing and pocket-money should not mark him out from his fellows.

The day that he went to Cambridge she had locked the door of her cottage and gone, for the first time voluntarily, out on the purple spaces of the moors, tramping the whole day through, exalted, foodless, like a woman possessed. . . . Not until she returned, exhausted, at nightfall, did she realize she had lost him. . . .

Across the street a door creaked, and a woman emerged, wiping dirty fingers around the base of her nose.

"This'll be a great day fer you, missis!" she called, wrapping her great arms in her apron.

"It is," was the laconic reply.

"Nothing in sight yet?"

"Not yet."

"Reckon yer never thought to see 'im again, did yer?"

"He's always written regular, has my Robert," Ann defended deftly.

"Aye, but writin's easy. Us old 'uns gets forgotten sometimes. Goin' to marry a lady, ain't he?"

"He's going to marry into his own class," returned Ann briefly, her heart beating high with triumph. This was indeed her day of days! "They must be coming by the four ten, or the car would 'a' been here by now."

The other woman's jaw dropped.

"Car? What—all the way from Scartop?"

"Well, ye didn't suppose my son 'ud come in the baker's cart!" was the quiet reply.

Having dropped her bombshell, Ann Redfern turned indoors and had the satisfaction of seeing the woman scuttle through her neighbor's door to impart the thrilling titbit.

But a cloud, no bigger than a man's hand, had sailed across the horizon of her joy. They were so late! Suppose after all Robert's girl had refused to come. . . .

In a corner of the dark spotless parlor lay a pile of thin pink-covered books. Ann knew them almost by heart, knew and respected and passionately understood the pale superior heroines who strewed their pages with scorn of all that was low, common, and base. "Esmerelda's Evidence" . . . "Lady Louisa's Love" . . . "A Heart for a Coronet" . . . each pink cameo contained at least one real lady, with whose thoughts, words, and actions Ann's heart beat in unison. Those books were her one solace in life now. Her fingers mentally stroked the fine silks and laces of the gowns; her nostrils savored the bountiful banquets; her eyes appraised the sumptuous appointments of castle and town house. For the stories she cared not at all. In every tall courtly hero she saw Robert; in every scornful trailing beauty she recognized Robert's wife. . . .

Her eyes snapped fanatically. A real lady! . . . How she would loathe Cadney and despise its trolloping women, with their coarse slow voices! How she would pick her way down the littered cobbles of the street, glancing neither to the right nor the left. Her jewels would glitter softly at neck and wrists; her silks would swish and rustle about the dark gleaming cottage; her high sweet voice would echo about the rooms long, long after Robert had said good-by and taken her back to the great cities. For Ann knew that the visit would be but a thing of hours—at most a precious day and night. Robert's lady would be gracious to her; but she would not stay; Ann did not expect that. It was more, far more than she had ever hoped for, that Robert should return to his humble home, bringing with him the lady of her dreams.

A sound broke upon the listening silence; and with the rumble of the baker's cart-wheels, the village woke to sudden shrill life. From her window Ann Redfern saw two women descending clumsily from the cart; for the baker from Scartop acted as carrier too. A little group closed about the new-comers. From the babel of broad voices there presently emerged shrill laughter, and words that caused Ann's heart to falter and then race.

"Didn't reckernize him at first, for dust, but there was no mistakin' that walk. My! they looked hot!"

"Owd Ann'll freeze 'em cool enough!"

" 'Ere! They're comin'! Sound yer hooter, man!"

They stared and sniggered and drew back into their dark doorways. One wit barked out a few bars of the national anthem. Another gave an imitation of a motor-horn. A score of eyes fastened on Ann's door, as it opened to emit her frail stiff-backed figure.

She stared up the dusty ribbon of road to where two figures swung along side by side beneath the glaring sky. Both had their coats over their shoulders; little eddies of white dust rose from their feet with each step. . . .

Without a glance at her neighbors, Ann went

indoors again and set the kettle on the stove. Her back was as stiff as ever, but her hands shook violently, and her eyes burned with unshed tears.

Walking! . . . Robert's girl had walked the five miles from Scartop station! After all she had boasted! Mrs. Lunn and Mrs. Ketley had passed them in the baker's cart; had spattered their hot bodies with the dust from its wheels. . . . Walking . . . Robert's lady. . . .

As the footsteps stopped outside the little gate, Ann forced her lips to a stiff smile and went to meet them.

She saw Robert first. . . . For that first moment of aching sweetness, when her body felt the remembered strength and tenderness of his arms, there was nobody in the whole world but Robert. Then it was over, and he was drawing forward the smiling girl at his side; and life and Cadney became real again.

"This is Mary, mother," he said simply.

The girl stooped and kissed her on the cheek.

She was as tall as Robert, with the shoulders of an athlete and sensible feet cased in dust-smothered brogues; her rough tweed skirt, short and spare, was neatly darned in two places. Her white shirt-blouse hung open at the neck, showing the damp sturdy base of her throat. A comfortable felt hat, crammed down over gray honest eyes, shadowed a tip-tilted nose, liberally powdered with freckles.

"My aunt, it's hot!" she exclaimed, flopping gratefully down on Ann's newly scoured doorstep. . . .

Somehow or other they got through dinner. It was an uncomfortable meal, between the enormous quantities of hot food and the strange impenetrable depths of Ann's silence. But at length Ann rose and began collecting the plates.

Robert's girl sprang up immediately.

"No, I'm going to do that," she said eagerly. "I know you and Bob are just dying to talk. You'll see how quick and clean I can be!"

Ann shot her a look of dull anger.

"You'll want to rest after yer walk," she answered firmly. "I'll show you the room."

Surprised into obedience, the girl followed her up dark twisted stairs into the cool white-draped little bedroom above. Everything was quiet, spotless, vaguely scented. A fat yellow rose tapped gently on the window-sill. Between the wide-flung panes the moor stretched in unbroken expanse of brown and purple, as far as the eye could see.

"Maybe it's not what ye've bin used to," Ann uttered slowly, "but it's the best I have." She was proud of this room. Yet had Robert's girl shuddered delicately at the patchwork quilt, the coarse snowy pillows, and the cheap crockery, nothing would have pleased her more. It was no room for a delicately born lady. But Robert's girl did not shudder.

"It's lovely!" she exclaimed with real pleasure. "And if you saw what I *have* been used to! D'you know, my bedroom looked on to a mews! I love horses, mind you, but—" Her nose wrinkled comically. "I absolutely love your moors! I know I'm going to be awfully happy here. All this quietness and beauty, and Bob, and you." With a movement half shy, half eager, she bent and kissed the glazed brown cheek of the old woman. "I do want you to love me—mother!" she said softly. "I've never known a real mother, and it means such a lot to me, this visit. Bob's told me all about how fine you've been, working and scraping—oh, I think it was more than wonderful! You must be so proud of him!"

Ann stiffened.

"Robert was bound to succeed," she said clearly. "He's different from the folks round here. His father was a gentleman!"

"Of course!" the girl agreed quickly, conscious of having said something wrong.

Old Ann descended the stairs slowly, one hand pressed against her heart.

In the kitchen Robert was filling his pipe, whistling a soft rag-time melody.

"It's true, I suppose," she asked him abruptly, "what you wrote in your letter about her being a lady?"

Robert glanced up with a slight frown.

"True? Yes, of course. But don't you worry about that, mother. There never was any one with less side than Mary. You didn't suppose I'd fall in love with a girl who had a permanent turn-up to her nose, did you?"

Ann carried the dirty plates to the sink and set bowls and towel in readiness.

"She tells me her bedroom looked on to a stable," she continued slowly.

"I dare say. You see, she works in the East End, among the dockers; works hard too, and the people adore her. Her own folk died when she was a kid, and the uncle who brought her up was as poor as a church-mouse. So as soon as she left school she had to choose between work and marrying money. And—thank God!—she chose to work. But I'm going to alter all that. I've got a rather nice little house out Hampstead way, and as soon as I can persuade her—" He struck a match and lit his pipe with long slow puffs. "We both want you to come and live with us, mother. I've got a photo of the place in my bag. I think you'll like the look of it. By the way, our luggage ought to be here now," he ended, glancing at his watch.

"Your luggage? Are you goin' ter stay?" Ann asked tonelessly. Robert looked surprised.

"Well—of course! Don't you want us to stay? We sha'n't make any extra work. Mary can cook like an angel and loves messing about in a house. I believe the prospect of helping you is half the joy of this holiday for her."

There was a long pause, filled only by the rattle of crockery and the slow *tack-tack* of the clock in the corner.

"What's her name again? Her title, I mean."

"Oh, she is the Hon. Mary Evangeline Victoria Tawlish, I believe," Bob grinned. "I do wish you'd forget it though, mother dear. If you're afraid she'll put the neighbors' backs up with her finicky ways, it only shows you don't know Mary yet. She's a darling!"

The frail stiff figure at the steaming sink never turned or bent. He wished she would turn and look at him, smile or even rebuke him in the old way, so that he could break the ice between them and tell her something of his love and admiration for her, of his gratitude, of his shame for the years he had allowed to slip by without coming to see her. . . .

But old Ann continued to wash up; and the hot silent kitchen was full of an indefinable sense of failure. . . .

Ann rested her weight on the wet wash-tub and looked her visitors straight in the face.

"This is an unexpected honor!" she remarked

dourly, in the prim voice she kept for Cadney villagers.

The three women—Mrs. Ketley, fat and lacrymose; Mrs. Lunn, fat and vacant; and Mrs. Moseley, like a shriveled bird, whose poisoned tongue was at once the delight and dread of the village—disposed themselves awkwardly about the shining kitchen.

"Just dropped in for a word with Bob and his gal," announced Mrs. Lunn.

"Only neighborly," amended Mrs. Moseley, her bright hard little eyes darting about the room in pitiless curiosity.

Ann wiped her wrinkled steamy hands on her sacking apron. It was war to the knife, she knew. An hour ago Robert and Mary had wandered away over the moors, with books tucked under their arms. All the village had seen them go.

"You're rather late in coming. They've bin here a full week now."

Mrs. Ketley and Mrs. Lunn looked for support to Mrs. Moseley, who passed her tongue over her thin lips and prepared to enjoy herself.

"We didn't hardly like to come afore, after all you'd said about her being a fine lady. My word, missis, you had it on us that time! You're a rare one fer a joke. Most on us thought you meant what you said. But when I see her flop down on't door-step, same as what I'd do meself, I says to our George, 'Ee, I'm right pleased,' I says, ' 'at it was only Mrs. Redfern's joke. Pore thing,' I says, 'where'd she 'a' been with a grand madam trapesing about th' 'ouse?' "

"Happen it were Bob's joke, an' Mrs. Redfern were as relieved as we was," put in Mrs. Ketley, employing a handkerchief with extraordinary frankness.

"And then," Mrs. Moseley continued with relish, "when I see her hangin' out a bit of washing, day afore yesterday, I says, 'Well, that settles it,' I says. 'An' rare an' pleased the poor creeture must be that it *was* only a joke.' I declare I quite envy you, missis, with a strapping daughter-in-law like 'yond; and her so willing and capable an' all. For you aren't as young as yer used ter be, not by a long chalk. You've looked a bit peaky these months back."

"Ah!" moaned Mrs. Ketley, with melancholy relish, "as soon as Mary Tawlish is made Mary Redfern, I should go and live along of her, missis. Then when anything happens yer—" And her watery eyes gazed covetously round the well kept kitchen of the cottage she had long desired for her ever-increasing family.

"Her name," said Ann slowly and clearly, "is the Hon. Mary Evangeline Victoria Tawlish."

Exaggerated symptoms of mirth greeted the announcement.

"Eh, missis!" quavered Mrs. Moseley, "to think of you living here all these years an' us never guessing what a card you was! That's as good as the bit about the car she were going to bring!"

"She never brought her car, because of the roads bein' so bad. I'd ought to thought of that," Ann lied desperately.

This threw her audience into further paroxysms. The steaming kitchen creaked and writhed with their mirth. Ann stared at the rocking women with baleful desperate eyes. They would never go until their hateful joke was exhausted. They had come to bait her, and they would stick there until they had seen the thing through. True, she might order them from her kitchen; but they were three to one—and they might choose to regard it as another bit of buffoonery. . . . Somehow, she wasn't sure of her power. . . . For thirty years hers had been the whip-hand. Slowly, confidently, she had built up her glittering palace of pride; steadfastly, arrogantly, she had kept within its walls, admitting none, waiting only for the ultimate triumph of Robert's return to lead her forth, envied of all eyes. . . . And Robert had come at last and had thrown a stone through the glittering structure, so that the wind of their wanton laughter blew upon her, and she was cold, homeless and cold. . . .

Yet, strangely, it was to Robert the man her heart turned when Robert the hero failed her; and, more strangely yet, to Robert's girl, who had called her mother and had kissed her cheek with gentle lips, asking for love.

Robert and Mary would never let these women taunt her, if they knew. Her house of pride lay in fragments at her feet; but love remained, and kinship, and loyalty. If she could only keep her tormentors until Robert and Mary returned, the joke would be hers, after all.

Robert and Mary lay chin-deep in the springing heather, their books unopened by their sides.

"If I only knew where I'd failed," the girl was saying rather sadly. "I've tried so hard, and I can never make you understand how disappointed I am. I *did* want her to love me!"

Robert prodded with a pencil among the heather roots.

"You've been divine to us both," he returned. "I suppose she resents your being of a different class. Her roots are deep in the soil."

"Oh, rot!" came the exasperated answer. "Just because I've got a useless handle to my name! What on earth possessed you to tell her anyhow?"

"Because I thought it might please her. She's an ambitious woman, you know; for me mostly, but through me, for herself."

"Then why resent me?"

"Because she doesn't realize her limitations," Robert answered slowly. "I think that must be what it is. A strange mixture! And I suppose she's too old to change now. I think it would perhaps be better if you went home, dearest. There's no reason why your holiday should be spoiled. I shall stay though. I owe her that at least."

"Of course you must stay," Mary agreed quietly. "Perhaps when we're married it'll come right. Well, I'm going in now, dear— No, don't you come! I'll pack before dinner and catch the six-fifteen up."

She swished and crunched her way home through the purple riot, blazing with sudden flames of gorse, and luscious with bilberries. Her broad brow was furrowed in a frown, not so much for her own disappointment, as in compassion for Robert. He loved the fierce, stiff-backed old woman, as she herself would have loved her, had she been allowed. It hurt the girl to watch his disappointment and dismay.

"It seems as though I'd spoiled everything for both of them," she thought perplexedly. "I wish to goodness I knew why!"

Never in this world or the next would the

truth have dawned on such a girl as Mary Tawlish.

At the gate of Ann's cottage she paused. It sounded as though there were visitors. Flat coarse voices and raucous laughter issued from the half-open door. Mary turned to retrace her steps. She disliked the slovenly villagers and had often given thanks for the essential difference of the woman she was to call mother. But something—perhaps it was an unusual quavering note in the old woman's answering voice—made her push open the gate and go in.

The kitchen seemed full of women, though actually there were only three. The steam from the washtub circled about their coarse grinning faces. They sat with their feet apart and their arms wrapped in dingy aprons, gazing with avid curiosity at the new-comer.

"Good morning," said Mary coolly. "Where is Mrs. Redfern?"

"Just run upstairs to fetch a letter from your young man," explained a fat woman with a disgusting handkerchief.

"Pleased ter meet you, I'm sure," put in a thin scrawny female, extending a claw in Mary's direction. "I'm Mrs. Moseley, from up the street, and I've known young Bob since he was so 'igh. Used ter run errands fer me, he did."

Mary shook the claw coldly. After all, one could not be rude to Ann's guests. . . .

At the top of the twisted staircase, old Ann stood, shaking with rage. One hand held a letter she had intended to read aloud as conclusive evidence of Mary's status. The other pressed against her thundering side. . . .

How dare that woman say such a thing! Her Robert had run errands for no one. Oh, Mary would settle them if they talked so! She would stop up here and listen, while Mary got them out of the house. . . .

She heard Mrs. Moseley's sniggering laugh.

"And o' course, us being so fond of young Bob, we was natcherally anxious to see his wife to be—especially after the way owd Ann's been talking."

" 'Ave yer lost Bob on't moor?" came the voice of Mrs. Lunn. And then Mary:

"I must ask you to excuse me now. I've got to pack before dinner."

Ann's heart stood still.

"Pack?" the women chorused. "Why—yer never going off so quick!"

"Happen you and Bob's quarreled," Mrs. Ketley queried. "That wouldn't surprise *me!* Anybody can see as yer a cut above a Redfern. Me and Mrs. Lunn was only saying to-day 'at it wouldn't last long, after you'd seen his home an' sort of realized . . ."

At the head of the stairs Ann swayed and nearly fell. Through her mind there flashed, with lightning rapidity, a series of pictures: a six-months-old baby, clutched to her breast as she drove across the bleak moors toward Cadney; a crawling blue atom, looking up and saying, "Mother"; a boy bending over his books; jumping on his bicycle for the five-mile ride to Scartop Grammar School; a young man waving good-by, as he set off for Cambridge; herself, lonely, suddenly realizing her loss. . . . Oh, Robert, Robert! . . . She loved him! He was all she had! She wanted him to be happy. . . . He *should* be happy, though it meant lowering her head to the dust of Cadney. . . .

She took one step, and faltered. No, no, she couldn't do it! After all these years. . . .

"I am leaving by the six-fifteen to-night," she heard Mary say. . . .

Old Ann prayed swiftly and vehemently. An agony of love filled her veins and swept away the last remnants of pride. Her back stiffened to its accustomed line. She descended the stairs firmly, her heart suddenly still, a dead thing in her side. . . .

She paid no attention to the gaping women. Her eyes met Mary's across the steamy kitchen, and one withered hand went out in a dramatic gesture. . . .

"Don't give him up . . . because of me . . ." she said clearly. "Take him away and ferget me. . . . *He's not my son!* . . ."

A chair shrieked on the tiled floor, Mary took a step toward her, but was waved back.

"Robert was three months old when I married his father. There's no blood o' mine in his veins. His father was a gentleman. You've no cause to be ashamed of him. . . ."

She stalked across the kitchen and held open the door. Her head jerked at the women of Cadney.

"And now you lot can get out o' my house!" she ordered.

They rose like sheep.

"Wait," Mary's voice rang out. They huddled together, eager to be away.

Mary bent down and kissed old Ann upon the lips.

"Mother dear," she said gently, "Robert has known that for years. It's one reason why I'm so proud of him, and why I love you."

The women of Cadney shuffled past them into the sunshine, while old Ann, her heart bursting with love and pride, lay in the arms of Robert's lady.

This was, at last, her day of days.

THE MISSION OF JANE *

Edith Wharton

I

LETHBURY, surveying his wife across the dinner table, found his transient glance arrested by an indefinable change in her appearance.

"How smart you look! Is that a new gown?" he asked.

Her answering look seemed to deprecate his charging her with the extravagance of wasting a new gown on him, and he now perceived that the change lay deeper than any accident of dress. At the same time, he noticed that she betrayed her consciousness of it by a delicate, almost frightened blush. It was one of the compensations of Mrs. Lethbury's protracted childishness that she still blushed as prettily as at eighteen. Her body had been privileged not to outstrip her mind, and the two, as it seemed to Lethbury, were destined to travel together through an eternity of girlishness.

* From "The Descent of Man and other Stories"; copyright, 1904, by Charles Scribner's Sons. By permission of the publishers.

"I don't know what you mean," she said.

Since she never did, he always wondered at her bringing this out as a fresh grievance against him; but his wonder was unresentful, and he said good-humoredly: "You sparkle so that I thought you had on your diamonds."

She sighed and blushed again.

"It must be," he continued, "that you've been to a dressmaker's opening. You're absolutely brimming with illicit enjoyment."

She stared again, this time at the adjective. His adjectives always embarrassed her: their unintelligibleness savoured of impropriety.

"In short," he summed up, "you've been doing something that you're thoroughly ashamed of."

To his surprise she retorted: "I don't see why I should be ashamed of it!"

Lethbury leaned back with a smile of enjoyment. When there was nothing better going he always liked to listen to her explanations.

"Well—?" he said.

She was becoming breathless and ejaculatory. "Of course you'll laugh—you laugh at everything!"

"That rather blunts the point of my derision, doesn't it?" he interjected; but she pushed on without noticing:

"It's so easy to laugh at things."

"Ah," murmured Lethbury with relish, "that's Aunt Sophronia's, isn't it?"

Most of his wife's opinions were heirlooms, and he took a quaint pleasure in tracing their descent. She was proud of their age, and saw no reason for discarding them while they were still serviceable. Some, of course, were so fine that she kept them for state occasions, like her great-grandmother's Crown Derby; but from the lady known as Aunt Sophronia she had inherited a stout set of every-day prejudices that were practically as good as new, whereas her husband's, as she noticed, were always having to be replaced. In the early days she had fancied there might be a certain satisfaction in taxing him with the fact; but she had long since been silenced by the reply: "My dear, I'm not a rich man, but I never use an opinion twice if I can help it."

She was reduced, therefore, to dwelling on his moral deficiencies; and one of the most obvious of these was his refusal to take things seriously. On this occasion, however, some ulterior purpose kept her from taking up his taunt.

"I'm not in the least ashamed!" she repeated, with the air of shaking a banner to the wind; but the domestic atmosphere being calm, the banner drooped unheroically.

"That," said Lethbury judicially, "encourages me to infer that you ought to be, and that, consequently, you've been giving yourself the unusual pleasure of doing something I shouldn't approve of."

She met this with an almost solemn directness. "No," she said. "You won't approve of it. I've allowed for that."

"Ah," he exclaimed, setting down his liqueur-glass. "You've worked out the whole problem, eh?"

"I believe so."

"That's uncommonly interesting. And what is it?"

She looked at him quietly. "A baby."

If it was seldom given her to surprise him, she had attained the distinction for once.

"A baby?"

"Yes."

"A—human baby?"

"Of course!" she cried, with the virtuous resentment of the woman who has never allowed dogs in the house.

Lethbury's puzzled stare broke into a fresh smile. "A baby I shan't approve of? Well, in the abstract I don't think much of them, I admit. Is this an abstract baby?"

Again she frowned at the adjective; but she had reached a pitch of exaltation at which such obstacles could not deter her.

"It's the loveliest baby—" she murmured.

"Ah, then it's concrete. It exists. In this harsh world it draws its breath in pain—"

"It's the healthiest child I ever saw!" she indignantly corrected.

"You've seen it, then?"

Again the accusing blush suffused her. "Yes—I've seen it."

"And to whom does the paragon belong?"

And here indeed she confounded him. "To me—I hope," she declared.

He pushed his chair back with an articulate murmur. "To *you—*"

"To *us,*" she corrected.

"Good Lord!" he said. If there had been the least hint of hallucination in her transparent gaze—but no; it was as clear, as shallow, as easily fathomable as when he had first suffered the sharp surprise of striking bottom in it.

It occurred to him that perhaps she was trying to be funny: he knew that there is nothing more cryptic than the humor of the unhumorous.

"Is it a joke?" he faltered.

"Oh, I hope not. I want it so much to be a reality—"

He paused to smile at the limitations of a world in which jokes were not realities, and continued gently: "But since it is one already—"

"To us, I mean: to you and me. I want—"

her voice wavered, and her eyes with it. "I have always wanted so dreadfully . . . it has been such a disappointment . . . not to . . ."

"I see," said Lethbury slowly.

But he had not seen before. It seemed curious now that he had never thought of her taking it in that way, had never surmised any hidden depths beneath her outspread obviousness. He felt as though he had touched a secret spring in her mind.

There was a moment's silence, moist and tremulous on her part, awkward and slightly irritated on his.

"You've been lonely, I suppose?" he began. It was odd, having suddenly to reckon with the stranger who gazed at him out of her trivial eyes.

"At times," she said.

"I'm sorry."

"It was not your fault. A man has so many occupations; and women who are clever—or very handsome—I suppose that's an occupation too. Sometimes I've felt that when dinner was ordered I had nothing to do till the next day."

"Oh," he groaned.

"It wasn't your fault," she insisted. "I never told you—but when I chose that rose-bud paper for the front room upstairs, I always thought—"

"Well—?"

'It would be such a pretty paper—for a baby—to wake up in. That was years ago, of course; but it was rather an expensive paper . . . and it hasn't faded in the least . . .'' she broke off incoherently.

"It hasn't faded?"

"No—and so I thought . . . as we don't use the room for anything . . . now that Aunt Sophronia is dead . . . I thought I might . . . you might . . . oh, Julian, if you could only have seen it just waking up in its crib!"

"Seen what—where? You haven't got a baby upstairs?"

"Oh, no—not yet," she said, with her rare laugh—the girlish bubbling of merriment that had seemed one of her chief graces in the early days. It occurred to him that he had not given her enough things to laugh about lately. But then she needed such very elementary things: she was as difficult to amuse as a savage. He concluded that he was not sufficiently simple.

"Alice," he said almost solemnly, "what *do* you mean?"

She hesitated a moment: he saw her gather her courage for a supreme effort. Then she said slowly, gravely, as though she were pronouncing a sacramental phrase:

"I'm so lonely without a little child—and I thought perhaps you'd let me adopt one. . . . It's at the hospital . . . its mother is dead

. . . and I could . . . pet it, and dress it, and do things for it . . . and it's such a good baby . . . you can ask any of the nurses . . . it would never, never bother you by crying . . ."

II

Lethbury accompanied his wife to the hospital in a mood of chastened wonder. It did not occur to him to oppose her wish. He knew, of course, that he would have to bear the brunt of the situation: the jokes at the club, the enquiries, the explanations. He saw himself in the comic rôle of the adopted father and welcomed it as an expiation. For in the rapid reconstruction of the past he found himself cutting a shabbier figure than he cared to admit. He had always been intolerant of stupid people, and it was his punishment to be convicted of stupidity. As his mind traversed the years between his marriage and this unexpected assumption of paternity, he saw, in the light of an overheated imagination, many signs of unwonted crassness. It was not that he had ceased to think his wife stupid: she *was* stupid, limited, inflexible; but there was a pathos in the struggles of her swaddled mind, in its blind reachings toward the primal emotions. He had always thought she would have been happier with a child; but he had thought it mechanically, because it had so often been thought before, because it was in the nature of things to think it of every woman, because his wife was so eminently one of a species that she fitted into all the generalizations of the sex. But he had regarded this generalization as merely typical of the triumph of tradition over experience. Maternity was no doubt the supreme function of primitive woman, the one end to which her whole organism tended; but the law of increasing complexity had operated in both sexes, and he had not seriously supposed that, outside the world of Christmas fiction and anecdotic art, such truisms had any special hold on the feminine imagination. Now he saw that the arts in question were kept alive by the vitality of the sentiments they appealed to.

Lethbury was in fact going through a rapid process of readjustment. His marriage had been a failure, but he had preserved toward his wife the exact fidelity of act that is sometimes supposed to excuse any divagation of feeling; so that, for years, the tie between them had consisted mainly in his abstaining from making love to other women. The abstention had not always been easy, for the world is surprisingly well-stocked with the kind of woman one ought to have married but did not; and Lethbury had not escaped the solicitation of such alternatives. His immunity had been purchased at the cost of taking refuge in the somewhat rarefied atmosphere of his perceptions; and his world being thus limited, he had given unusual care to its details, compensating himself for the narrowness of his horizon by the minute finish of his foreground. It was a world of fine shadings and the nicest proportions, where impulse seldom set a blundering foot, and the feast of reason was undisturbed by an intemperate flow of soul. To such a banquet his wife naturally remained uninvited. The diet would have disagreed with her, and she would probably have objected to the other guests. But Lethbury, miscalculating her needs, had hitherto supposed that he had made ample provision for them, and was consequently at liberty to enjoy his own fare without any reproach of mendicancy at his gates. Now he beheld her pressing a starved face against the windows of his life, and in his imaginative reaction he invested her with a pathos borrowed from the sense of his own shortcomings.

In the hospital the imaginative process continued with increasing force. He looked at his wife with new eyes. Formerly she had been to him a mere bundle of negations, a labyrinth of dead walls and bolted doors. There was nothing behind the walls, and the doors led no whither: he had sounded and listened often enough to be sure of that. Now he felt like a traveler who, exploring some ancient ruin, comes on an inner cell, intact amid the general dilapidation, and painted with images which reveal the forgotten uses of the building.

His wife stood by a white crib in one of the wards. In the crib lay a child, a year old, the nurse affirmed, but to Lethbury's eye a mere dateless fragment of humanity projected against a background of conjecture. Over this anonymous particle of life Mrs. Lethbury leaned, such ecstasy reflected in her face as strikes up, in Correggio's *Night-piece,* from the child's body to the mother's countenance. It was a light that irradiated and dazzled her. She looked up at an enquiry of Lethbury's, but as their glances met he perceived that she no longer saw him, that he had become as invisible to her as she had long been to him. He had to transfer his question to the nurse.

"What is the child's name?" he asked.

"We call her Jane," said the nurse.

III

Lethbury, at first, had resisted the idea of legal adoption; but when he found that his wife could not be brought to regard the child as hers till it had been made so by process of law, he promptly withdrew his objection. On one point only he remained inflexible; and that was the changing of the waif's name. Mrs. Lethbury, almost at once, had expressed a wish to re-christen it: she fluctuated between Muriel and Gladys, deferring the moment of decision like a lady wavering between two bonnets. But Lethbury was unyielding. In the general surrender of his prejudices this one alone held out.

"But Jane is so dreadful," Mrs. Lethbury protested.

"Well, we don't know that *she* won't be dreadful. She may grow up a Jane."

His wife exclaimed reproachfully, "The nurse says she's the loveliest—"

"Don't they always say that?" asked Lethbury patiently. He was prepared to be inexhaustibly patient now that he had reached a firm foothold of opposition.

"It's cruel to call her Jane," Mrs. Lethbury pleaded.

"It's ridiculous to call her Muriel."

"The nurse is *sure* she must be a lady's child."

Lethbury winced: he had tried, all along, to keep his mind off the question of antecedents.

"Well, let her prove it," he said, with a rising sense of exasperation. He wondered how he could ever have allowed himself to be drawn into such a ridiculous business; for the first time he felt the full irony of it. He had visions of coming home in the afternoon to a house smelling of linseed and paregoric, and of being greeted by a chronic howl as he went upstairs to dress for dinner. He had never been a clubman, but he saw himself becoming one now.

The worst of his anticipations were unfulfilled. The baby was surprisingly well and surprisingly quiet. Such infantile remedies as she absorbed were not potent enough to be perceived beyond the nursery; and when Lethbury could be induced to enter that sanctuary, there was nothing to jar his nerves in the mild pink presence of his adopted daughter. Jars were there, indeed: they were probably inevitable in the disturbed routine of the household; but they occurred between Mrs. Lethbury and the nurses, and Jane contributed to them only a placid stare which might have served as a rebuke to the combatants.

In the reaction from his first impulse of atonement, Lethbury noted with sharpened perceptions the effect of the change on his wife's character. He saw already the error of supposing that it could work any transformation in her. It simply magnified her existing qualities. She was like a dried sponge put in water: she expanded, but she did not change her shape. From the standpoint of scientific observation it was curious to see how her stored instincts responded to the pseudo-maternal call. She overflowed with the petty maxims of the occasion. One felt in her the epitome, the consummation, of centuries of animal maternity, so that this little woman, who screamed at a mouse and was nervous about burglars, came to typify the cave-mother rending her prey for her young.

It was less easy to regard philosophically the practical effects of her borrowed motherhood. Lethbury found with surprise that she was becoming assertive and definite. She no longer represented the negative side of his life; she showed, indeed, a tendency to inconvenient affirmations. She had gradually expanded her assumption of motherhood till it included his own share in the relation, and he suddenly found himself regarded as the father of Jane. This was a contingency he had not foreseen, and it took all his philosophy to accept it; but there were moments of compensation. For Mrs. Lethbury was undoubtedly happy for the first time in years; and the thought that he had tardily contributed to this end reconciled him to the irony of the means.

At first he was inclined to reproach himself for still viewing the situation from the outside, for remaining a spectator instead of a participant. He had been allured, for a moment, by the vision of several hands meeting over a cradle, as the whole body of domestic fiction bears witness to their doing; and the fact that no such conjunction took place he could explain only on the ground that it was a borrowed cradle. He did not dislike the little girl. She still remained to him a hypothetical presence, a query rather than a fact; but her nearness was not unpleasant, and there were moments when her tentative utterances, her groping steps, seemed to loosen the dry accretions enveloping his inner self. But even at such moments—moments which he invited and caressed—she did not bring him nearer to his wife. He now perceived that he had made a certain place in his life for Mrs. Lethbury, and that she no longer fitted into it. It was too late to enlarge the space, and so she overflowed and encroached. Lethbury struggled against the sense of submergence. He let down barrier after barrier, yielding privacy after privacy; but his wife's personality continued to dilate. She was no longer herself alone: she was herself and Jane. Gradually, in a monstrous fusion of identity, she became herself, himself, and Jane; and instead of trying to adapt her to a spare crevice of his character, he found himself carelessly squeezed into the smallest compartment of the domestic economy.

IV

He continued to tell himself that he was satisfied if his wife was happy; and it was not till the child's tenth year that he felt a doubt of her happiness.

Jane had been a preternaturally good child. During the eight years of her adoption she had caused her foster-parents no anxiety beyond those connected with the usual succession of youthful diseases. But her unknown progenitors had given her a robust constitution, and she passed unperturbed through measles, chicken-pox and whooping-cough. If there was any suffering it was endured vicariously by Mrs. Lethbury, whose temperature rose and fell with the patient's, and who could not hear Jane sneeze without visions of a marble angel weeping over a broken column. But though Jane's prompt recoveries continued to belie such premonitions, though her existence continued to move forward on an even keel of good health and good conduct, Mrs. Lethbury's satisfaction showed no corresponding advance. Lethbury, at first, was disposed to add her disappointment to the long list of feminine inconsistencies with which the sententious observer of life builds up his favorable induction; but circumstances presently led him to take a kindlier view of the case.

Hitherto his wife had regarded him as a negligible factor in Jane's evolution. Beyond providing for his adopted daughter, and effacing himself before her, he was not expected to contribute to her well-being. But as time passed he appeared to his wife in a new light. It was he who was to educate Jane. In matters of the intellect, Mrs. Lethbury was the first to declare her deficiencies—to proclaim them, even with a certain virtuous superiority. She said she did not pretend to be clever, and there was no denying the truth of the assertion. Now, however, she seemed less ready, not to own her limitations, but to glory in them. Confronted with the problem of Jane's instruction she stood in awe of the child.

"I have always been stupid, you know," she said to Lethbury with a new humility, "and I'm afraid I sha'n't know what is best for Jane. I'm sure she has a wonderfully good mind, and I should reproach myself if I didn't give her every opportunity." She looked at him helplessly. "You must tell me what ought to be done."

Lethbury was not unwilling to oblige her. Somewhere in his mental lumber-room there rusted a theory of education such as usually lingers among the impedimenta of the childless. He brought this out, refurbished it, and applied it to Jane. At first he thought his wife had not overrated the quality of the child's mind. Jane seemed extraordinarily intelligent. Her precocious definiteness of mind was encouraging to her inexperienced preceptor. She had no difficulty in fixing her attention, and he felt that every fact he imparted was being etched in metal. He helped his wife to engage the best teachers, and for a while continued to take an ex-official interest in his adopted daughter's studies. But gradually his interest waned. Jane's ideas did not increase with her acquisitions. Her young mind remained a mere receptacle for facts: a kind of cold-storage from which anything which had been put there could be taken out at a moment's notice, intact but congealed. She developed, moreover, an inordinate pride in the capacity of her mental storehouse, and a tendency to pelt her public with its contents. She was overheard to jeer at her nurse for not knowing when the Saxon Heptarchy had fallen, and she alternately dazzled and depressed Mrs. Lethbury by the wealth of her chronological allusions. She showed no interest in the significance of the facts she amassed: she simply collected dates as another child might have collected stamps or marbles. To her foster-mother she seemed a prodigy of wisdom; but Lethbury saw, with a secret movement of sympathy, how the aptitudes in which Mrs. Lethbury gloried were slowly estranging her from her child.

"She is getting too clever for me," his wife said to him after one of Jane's historical flights, "but I am so glad that she will be a companion to you."

Lethbury groaned in spirit. He did not look forward to Jane's companionship. She was still a good little girl; but there was something automatic and formal in her goodness, as though it were a kind of moral calisthenics which she went through for the sake of showing her agility. An early consciousness of virtue had moreover constituted her the natural guardian and adviser of her elders. Before she was fifteen she had set about reforming the household. She took Mrs. Lethbury in hand first; then she extended her efforts to the servants, with consequences more disastrous to the domestic harmony; and lastly she applied herself to Lethbury. She proved to him by statistics that he smoked too much, and that it was injurious to the optic nerve to read in bed. She took him to task for not going to church more regularly, and pointed out to him the evils of desultory reading. She suggested that a regular course of study encourages mental concentration, and hinted that inconsecutiveness of thought is a sign of approaching age.

To her adopted mother her suggestions were equally pertinent. She instructed Mrs. Lethbury in an improved way of making beef stock, and called her attention to the unhygienic qualities of carpets. She poured out distracting facts about bacilli and vegetable mould, and demonstrated that curtains and picture-frames are a hot-bed of animal organisms. She learned by heart the nutritive ingredients of the principal articles of diet, and revolutionized the cuisine by an attempt to establish a scientific average between starch and phosphates. Four cooks left during this experiment, and Lethbury fell into the habit of dining at his club.

Once or twice, at the outset, he had tried to check Jane's ardor; but his efforts resulted only in hurting his wife's feelings. Jane remained impervious, and Mrs. Lethbury resented any attempt to protect her from her daughter. Lethbury saw that she was consoled for the sense of her own inferiority by the thought of what Jane's intellectual companionship must be to him; and he tried to keep up the illusion by enduring with what grace he might the blighting edification of Jane's discourse.

V

As Jane grew up he sometimes avenged himself by wondering if his wife was still sorry that they had not called her Muriel. Jane was not ugly; she developed, indeed, a kind of categorical prettiness which might have been a projection of her mind. She had a creditable collection of features, but one had to take an inventory of them to find out that she was good-looking. The fusing grace had been omitted.

Mrs. Lethbury took a touching pride in her daughter's first steps in the world. She expected Jane to take by her complexion those whom she did not capture by her learning. But Jane's rosy freshness did not work any perceptible ravages. Whether the young men guessed the axioms on her lips and detected the encyclopedia in her eye, or whether they simply found no intrinsic interest in these features, certain it is, that, in spite of her mother's heroic efforts, and of incessant calls on Lethbury's purse, Jane, at the end of her first season, had dropped hopelessly out of the running. A few duller girls found her interesting, and one or two young men came to the house with the object of meeting other young women; but she was rapidly becoming one of the social supernumeraries who are asked out only because they are on people's lists.

The blow was bitter to Mrs. Lethbury; but she consoled herself with the idea that Jane had failed because she was too clever. Jane probably shared this conviction; at all events she betrayed no consciousness of failure. She had developed a pronounced taste for society, and went out, unweariedly and obstinately, winter after winter, while Mrs. Lethbury toiled in her wake, showering attentions on oblivious hostesses. To Lethbury there was something at once tragic and exasperating in the sight of their two figures, the one conciliatory, the other dogged, both pursuing with unabated zeal the elusive prize of popularity. He even began to feel a personal stake in the pursuit, not as it concerned Jane but as it affected his wife. He saw that the latter was the victim of Jane's disappointment: that Jane was not above the crude satisfaction of "taking it out" of her mother. Experience checked the impulse to come to his wife's defense; and when his resentment was at its height, Jane disarmed him by giving up the struggle.

Nothing was said to mark her capitulation; but Lethbury noticed that the visiting ceased and that the dressmaker's bills diminished. At the same time Mrs. Lethbury made it known that Jane had taken up charities; and before long Jane's conversation confirmed this announcement. At first Lethbury congratulated himself on the change; but Jane's domesticity soon began to weigh on him. During the day she was sometimes absent on errands of mercy; but in the evening she was always there. At first she and Mrs. Lethbury sat in the drawing-room together, and Lethbury smoked in the library; but presently Jane formed the habit of joining him there, and he began to suspect that he was included among the objects of her philanthropy.

Mrs. Lethbury confirmed the suspicion. "Jane has grown very serious-minded lately," she said. "She imagines that she used to neglect you and she is trying to make up for it. Don't discourage her,'' she added innocently.

Such a plea delivered Lethbury helpless to his daughter's ministrations; and he found himself measuring the hours he spent with her by the amount of relief they must be affording her mother. There were even moments when he read a furtive gratitude in Mrs. Lethbury's eye.

But Lethbury was no hero, and he had nearly reached the limit of vicarious endurance when something wonderful happened. They never quite knew afterward how it had come about, or who first perceived it; but Mrs. Lethbury one day gave tremulous voice to their discovery.

''Of course,'' she said, ''he comes here because of Elise.'' The young lady in question, a friend of Jane's, was possessed of attractions which had already been found to explain the presence of masculine visitors.

Lethbury risked a denial. ''I don't think he does,'' he declared.

''But Elise is thought very pretty,'' Mrs. Lethbury insisted.

''I can't help that,'' said Lethbury doggedly.

He saw a faint light in his wife's eyes, but she remarked carelessly: ''Mr. Budd would be a very good match for Elise.''

Lethbury could hardly repress a chuckle: he

was so exquisitely aware that she was trying to propitiate the gods.

For a few weeks neither said a word; then Mrs. Lethbury once more reverted to the subject.

"It is a month since Elise went abroad," she said.

"Is it?"

"And Mr. Budd seems to come here just as often—"

"Ah," said Lethbury with heroic indifference; and his wife hastily changed the subject.

Mr. Winstanly Budd was a young man who suffered from an excess of manner. Politeness gushed from him in the driest season. He was always performing feats of drawing-room chivalry, and the approach of the most unobtrusive female threw him into attitudes which endangered the furniture. His features, being of the cherubic order, did not lend themselves to this rôle; but there were moments when he appeared to dominate them, to force them into compliance with an aquiline ideal. The range of Mr. Budd's social benevolence made its object hard to distinguish. He spread his cloak so indiscriminately that one could not always interpret the gesture, and Jane's impassive manner had the effect of increasing his demonstrations: she threw him into paroxysms of politeness.

At first he filled the house with his amenities;

but gradually it became apparent that his most dazzling effects were directed exclusively to Jane. Lethbury and his wife held their breath and looked away from each other. They pretended not to notice the frequency of Mr. Budd's visits, they struggled against an imprudent inclination to leave the young people too much alone. Their conclusions were the result of indirect observation, for neither of them dared to be caught watching Mr. Budd; they behaved like naturalists on the trail of a rare butterfly.

In his efforts not to notice Mr. Budd, Lethbury centred his attentions on Jane; and Jane, at this crucial moment, wrung from him a reluctant admiration. While her parents went about dissembling their emotions, she seemed to have none to conceal. She betrayed neither eagerness nor surprise; so complete was her unconcern that there were moments when Lethbury feared it was obtuseness, when he could hardly help whispering to her that now was the moment to lower the net.

Meanwhile the velocity of Mr. Budd's gyrations increased with the ardor of courtship; his politeness became incandescent, and Jane found herself the centre of a pyrotechnical display culminating in the "set piece" of an offer of marriage.

Mrs. Lethbury imparted the news to her husband one evening after their daughter had gone to bed. The announcement was made and received with an air of detachment, as though both feared to be betrayed into unseemly exultation; but Lethbury, as his wife ended, could not repress the inquiry, "Have they decided on a day?"

Mrs. Lethbury's superior command of her features enabled her to look shocked. "What can you be thinking of? He only offered himself at five!"

"Of course—of course—" stammered Lethbury—"but nowadays people marry after such short engagements—"

"Engagement!" said his wife solemnly. "There is no engagement."

Lethbury dropped his cigar. "What on earth do you mean?"

"Jane is thinking it over."

"*Thinking it over?*"

"She has asked for a month before deciding."

Lethbury sank back with a gasp. Was it genius or was it madness? He felt incompetent to decide; and Mrs. Lethbury's next words showed that she shared his difficulty.

"Of course I don't want to hurry Jane—"

"Of course not," he acquiesced.

"But I pointed out to her that a young man of Mr. Budd's impulsive temperament might—might be easily discouraged—"

"Yes; and what did she say?"

"She said that if she was worth winning she was worth waiting for."

VI

The period of Mr. Budd's probation could scarcely have cost him as much mental anguish as it caused his would-be parents-in-law.

Mrs. Lethbury, by various ruses, tried to shorten the ordeal, but Jane remained inexorable; and each morning Lethbury came down to breakfast with the certainty of finding a letter of withdrawal from her discouraged suitor.

When at length the decisive day came, and Mrs. Lethbury, at its close, stole into the library with an air of chastened joy, they stood for a moment without speaking; then Mrs. Lethbury paid a fitting tribute to the proprieties by faltering out: "It will be dreadful to have to give her up—"

Lethbury could not repress a warning gesture; but even as it escaped him he realized that his wife's grief was genuine.

"Of course, of course," he said, vainly sounding his own emotional shallows for an answering regret. And yet it was his wife who had suffered most from Jane!

He had fancied that these sufferings would be effaced by the milder atmosphere of their last weeks together; but felicity did not soften Jane. Not for a moment did she relax her dominion; she simply widened it to include a new subject. Mr. Budd found himself under orders with the others; and a new fear assailed Lethbury as he saw Jane assume prenuptial control of her betrothed. Lethbury had never felt any strong personal interest in Mr. Budd; but as Jane's prospective husband the young man excited his sympathy. To his surprise he found that Mrs. Lethbury shared the feeling.

"I'm afraid he may find Jane a little exacting," she said after an evening dedicated to a stormy discussion of the wedding arrangements. "She really ought to make some concessions. If he *wants* to be married in a black frock-coat instead of a dark gray one—" She paused and looked doubtfully at Lethbury.

"What can I do about it?" he said.

"You might explain to him—tell him that Jane isn't always—"

Lethbury made an impatient gesture. "What are you afraid of? His finding her out or his not finding her out?"

Mrs. Lethbury flushed. "You put it so dreadfully!"

Her husband mused for a moment; then he said with an air of cheerful hypocrisy: "After all, Budd is old enough to take care of himself."

But the next day Mrs. Lethbury surprised

him. Late in the afternoon she entered the library, so breathless and inarticulate that he scented a catastrophe.

"I've done it!" she cried.

"Done what?"

"Told him." She nodded toward the door. "He's just gone. Jane is out, and I had a chance to talk to him alone."

Lethbury pushed a chair forward and she sank into it.

"What did you tell him? That she is *not* always—"

Mrs. Lethbury lifted a tragic eye. "No; I told him that she always *is*—"

"Always *is*—?"

"Yes."

There was a pause. Lethbury made a call on his hoarded philosophy. He saw Jane suddenly reinstated in her evening seat by the library fire; but an answering chord in him thrilled at his wife's heroism.

"Well—what did he say?"

Mrs. Lethbury's agitation deepened. It was clear that the blow had fallen.

"He . . . he said . . . that we . . . had never understood Jane . . . or appreciated her . . ." The final syllables were lost in her handkerchief, and she left him marveling at the mechanism of woman.

After that, Lethbury faced the future with an

undaunted eye. They had done their duty—at least his wife had done hers—and they were reaping the usual harvest of ingratitude with a zest seldom accorded to such reaping. There was a marked change in Mr. Budd's manner, and his increasing coldness sent a genial glow through Lethbury's system. It was easy to bear with Jane in the light of Mr. Budd's disapproval.

There was a good deal to be borne in the last days, and the brunt of it fell on Mrs. Lethbury. Jane marked her transition to the married state by a seasonable but incongruous display of nerves. She became sentimental, hysterical, and reluctant. She quarreled with her betrothed and threatened to return the ring. Mrs. Lethbury had to intervene, and Lethbury felt the hovering sword of destiny. But the blow was suspended. Mr. Budd's chivalry was proof against all his bride's caprices and his devotion throve on her cruelty. Lethbury feared that he was too faithful, too enduring, and longed to urge him to vary his tactics. Jane presently reappeared with the ring on her finger, and consented to try on the wedding-dress; but her uncertainties, her reactions, were prolonged till the final day.

When it dawned, Lethbury was still in an ecstasy of apprehension. Feeling reasonably sure of the principal actors he had centered his fears on incidental possibilities. The clergyman might have a stroke, or the church might burn down, or there might be something wrong with the license. He did all that was humanly possible to avert such contingencies, but there remained that incalculable factor known as the hand of God. Lethbury seemed to feel it groping for him.

At the altar it almost had him by the nape. Mr. Budd was late; and for five immeasurable minutes Lethbury and Jane faced a churchful of conjecture. Then the bridegroom appeared, flushed but chivalrous, and explaining to his father-in-law under cover of the ritual that he had torn his glove and had to go back for another.

"You'll be losing the ring next," muttered Lethbury, but Mr. Budd produced this article punctually, and a moment or two later was bearing its wearer captive down the aisle.

At the wedding-breakfast Lethbury caught his wife's eye fixed on him in mild disapproval, and understood that his hilarity was exceeding the bounds of fitness. He pulled himself together and tried to subdue his tone; but his jubilation bubbled over like a champagne-glass perpetually refilled. The deeper his draughts the higher it rose.

It was at the brim when, in the wake of the dispersing guests, Jane came down in her traveling-dress and fell on her mother's neck.

"I can't leave you!" she wailed, and Lethbury felt as suddenly sobered as a man under a douche. But if the bride was reluctant her captor was relentless. Never had Mr. Budd been more dominant, more aquiline. Lethbury's last fears were dissipated as the young man snatched Jane from her mother's bosom and bore her off to the brougham.

The brougham rolled away, the last milliner's girl forsook her post by the awning, the red carpet was folded up, and the house door closed. Lethbury stood alone in the hall with his wife. As he turned toward her, he noticed the look of tired heroism in her eyes, the deepened lines of her face. They reflected his own symptoms too accurately not to appeal to him. The nervous tension had been horrible. He went up to her, and an answering impulse made her lay a hand on his arm. He held it there a moment.

"Let us go off and have a jolly little dinner at a restaurant," he proposed.

There had been a time when such a suggestion would have surprised her to the verge of disapproval; but now she agreed to it at once.

"Oh, that would be so nice," she murmured with a great sigh of relief and assuagement.

Jane had fulfilled her mission after all: she had drawn them together at last.

THE MOTHER *

A Souvenir of the Siege

Alphonse Daudet

THAT morning I had gone to Mont Valérien to see our artist-friend, Monsieur B——, then a lieutenant in the mobile of the Seine. I found that fine fellow on guard. No way of getting out of it! And there he was, compelled to pace back and forth, before the postern of the fort, like a sailor on watch, while we talked of Paris, of the war, and of dear ones far away. Suddenly my lieutenant, who, in spite of his military coat, was as tremendous a dauber as ever, stopped short in the middle of his sentence, and caught my arm.

"There's a fine Daumier!" he whispered. He was looking at something out of the corner of one eye, and that small gray eye of his kindled like a hunting-dog's, as he pointed to the silhouette of two venerable figures that had just

* Reprinted from "Monday Tales" by Alphonse Daudet. By special permission of Little, Brown & Co., Publishers.

made their appearance upon the plateau of Mont Valérien.

And indeed the couple suggested some fine sketch fresh from Daumier's hand. The man wore a chestnut-colored surtout, with a collar of greenish velvet, that looked like old wood-moss; he was short and lean and ruddy, with a low forehead, round eyes, and nose like an owl's beak; his head was like a shriveled bird's head, and his air was at once silly and solemn. To complete the picture, he carried on one arm a bag, embroidered with flowers, from which protruded the neck of a bottle, and under the other arm a box of preserves, that everlasting tin box, which Parisians of those days will never see again without recalling that five months' siege of theirs. Of the woman all that one saw at first was an enormous hood-like bonnet and an old shawl whose scanty folds wrapped her from head to foot, revealing all the more plainly the poverty it attempted to conceal; now and then, however, the tip of a sharp nose peered out from the faded ruches of her bonnet, and a few spare and grizzled locks could be seen.

When they reached the plateau, the man paused to regain his breath and to wipe his forehead. They certainly could not have been too warm in that foggy, keen November air, but they had walked very quickly.

The woman never paused, not she! Advancing directly toward the postern, she looked at us a moment, with some hesitation, and as if she would speak with us; but, doubtless intimidated by an officer's uniform, she preferred to address the sentinel, and I heard her ask timidly that she might be allowed to see her son, a Paris mobile in Company Six, Third Battalion.

"Stay here," said the guard, "and I will call him."

She gave a joyous sigh of relief, and returned to her husband, and both seated themselves at a short distance, on the side of a talus.

They waited there an interminable time. Mont Valérien is so big, such a complicated affair, with its various enclosures, its bastions, glacis, barracks, and casemates! No easy task to find a mobile of the Sixth in the mazes of that town suspended between heaven and earth, hanging its huge spiral in the midst of the clouds, like Laputa's island. Moreover, at that hour from one end to the other of the fort drums and trumpets are sounding, canteens rattling. The sentry is relieved, duty-service begins, supplies are distributed; the sharpshooters are bringing in a spy, covered with blood, beating him with their gun-butts. Some peasant folk of Nanterre are come to complain to the general; an estafette comes galloping in, the man chilled, and the beast dripping with sweat. Litters arrive from the outposts with the wounded suspended upon the backs of mules, and moaning softly like sick lambs. Sailors are seen hauling a new cannon to the music of a fife, with cries of "Heave ho!" A shepherd in red trousers is driving in before him the cattle belonging to the fort, a rod in his hand, his chassepot slung across his shoulder. In the yards of the fort an incessant coming and going, men passing one another, and disappearing through the postern like figures vanishing through the low door of some caravansary of the East.

"I hope they have not forgotten my boy," the poor mother's eyes are saying all this time; and as the minutes lengthen she rises and discreetly approaches the entrance, casting a furtive glance towards the front yard, while she edges along the wall, but she dares not ask any more questions, lest she should reflect discredit upon her son. Her companion, more timid even than herself, does not budge once from the spot where he is seated; and when she returns again and again, to seat herself beside him, her heart swelling, and a look of deep discouragement visible upon her features, it is plain that he is chiding her for her impatience, and giving her no end of explanations as to the exigencies of a soldier's life, information imparted with the imbecile air of one who would have you think he knows it all.

I have always regarded with the deepest curiosity those little domestic scenes enacted amid the utmost silence, scenes of whose significance one often divines more than is actually seen, —in those pantomimes of the street, which elbow us on every side during our walks abroad, the merest gesture often revealing to us the history of a lifetime; but what specially charmed me here was the awkwardness, the naïveté of my principal characters, and it was with real emotion I witnessed all the incidents of a delightful drama of the hearth, as I followed that little dumb-show, as expressive and transparent as the pantomime of two of Seraphin's marionettes. I seemed to hear the mother remark one fine morning, "I am sick of this Monsieur Trochu, and his orders. I have not seen my boy for three months. I want to see him, to kiss him."

And the father, timorous, with an eternal air of apology for the fact of his existence, is frightened at the mere thought of what must be done in order to obtain permission to see the son, and at first attempts to dissuade her. "But, my dear, you don't stop to think! Mont Valérien—deuce take it!—is a long way off. How could you ever get there without a carriage? Besides, it is a citadel. Women are not allowed to enter."

"But—I will enter—" answers the wife; and

as he obeys all her commands, he undertakes this new errand. He goes to the *Secteur,* to the *mairie,* to the headquarters of the Army of Paris, to the commissary, clammy with fear, shivering with the cold, knocking at every door, stumbling into the wrong one again and again, waiting in line two hours before the office of one department, and that not the right one. But at last he returns towards evening with the governor's permit in his pocket. The next day they rise very early, and dress in the cold, by lamplight. The father nibbles a bit of bread, to fortify himself, but the mother is not hungry. She prefers to breakfast later with her son. And to cheer the poor mobile a little, they pile into the bag both the ordinary provisions of the siege and those reserved for special occasions, chocolate, sweetmeats, and a bottle of wine; they remember everything, even the famous box, an eight-franc box, which they had laid aside religiously for a day of need. At last they have started. When they reach the ramparts, and the gates are opened, they must show their permit. And now it is the wife's turn to be frightened. But she is reassured. The permit, it seems, is quite *en règle.*

"You may pass," says the adjutant on duty.

And not until then does she breathe freely.

"How polite that officer was to us!"

She toddles on, as agile as a young partridge.

The man can scarcely keep up with her.

"How fast you walk, my dear!"

But she is not listening to him. Above her, Mont Valérien looms against the misty horizon, and beckons to her.

"Come quickly. He is here!"

And now they have reached Mont Valérien, a fresh cause for anxiety. Suppose she should not find him! What if he is not coming, after all!

Suddenly I saw her tremble, clutch the old man's arm, and spring to her feet. In the distance footsteps were heard echoing along the vaulted passage, footsteps which she recognized. It was her son! When he appeared, the entrance to the fort was suddenly illumined for her eyes.

And indeed he was a big, splendid fellow, his bearing erect and vigorous. He came, gun in hand and knapsack on his back. His greeting was sincere, as the joyous, virile voice exclaimed,—

"Good-morning, mamma."

And suddenly knapsack, blanket, chassepot, and all disappeared from sight, and were lost in that enormous bonnet. Then the father's turn came, but it did not last so long, for the bonnet wanted everything for itself. It was insatiable.

"And how are you? Are you clad warmly enough? How are you off for linen?"

And beneath the ruches of that bonnet I could

see her eyes, and their prolonged and loving glance which embraced him from head to foot, amid a shower of tears and little laughs and kisses. For there was an arrearage of three long months due him—an arrearage which maternal tenderness was striving to pay him all at once. The father too seemed deeply moved, but he did not desire that any one should suspect the fact. He understood that we were watching him, and blinked once or twice in our direction, as if to say,—

"You must excuse her. She's a woman."

As if I could excuse her!

But the sound of a bugle interrupted all this joy unexpectedly.

"The call!" said the youth. "I must go."

"What! You will not take your breakfast with us?"

"I cannot. I am on duty for the next twenty-four hours, above, at the fort."

"Oh!" said the poor woman, and she was speechless.

And in consternation each gazed at the other for a moment. Then the father was spokesman.

"At least you will take the box," he said in a heartbroken voice, with an air of gluttony and of martyrdom which was at once touching and ludicrous. But in the agitation and emotion of leave-taking, that infernal box was nowhere to be found! It was pathetic to see those feeble and trembling hands groping for it, and to hear two voices, broken by sobs, inquiring: "The box! Where is the box?"—evidently considering this petty and homely detail not unworthy of their great sorrow. But at last the box was found, there was one long, last embrace, and then the son returned to the fort on the run.

But recall how far they had come to breakfast with him, and that it was to have been a great affair in their lives, that the mother had not slept one minute the night before, in anticipation of it, and tell me whether anything could be more pathetic than that little party which never came off, that momentary glimpse of a paradise whose door was so suddenly, so brutally, closed against them.

They lingered for some minutes, standing motionless in the spot where the boy had left them, their eyes riveted upon the postern through which he had disappeared from their sight. At length the man roused himself, and made a move towards departure. He coughed very courageously two or three times, and his voice gaining confidence, he said quite audibly and cheerfully,—

"Come, mother, let us go." Then he made us an overwhelming courtesy, and took his wife's arm. My eyes followed them as far as the turn in the road. The good man's air was furious. He brandished his bag, and his gestures were full of despair. The mother herself appeared to be calmer. She walked beside him, her head sunken upon her breast, her arms at her side. But I fancied that from time to time the shawl which covered her thin shoulders rose and fell convulsively.

(3)

THE END